Hunting in the Zoo

A Detective Pete Nazareth Novel

R.H. Johnson

Printed on acid-free paper.

Hampton, Westbrook Publishing
Princeton Junction, New Jersey
2016

First Edition

Also by R.H. Johnson

Widow-Taker
A Measure of Revenge

Hell is empty and all the devils are here.

William Shakespeare
The Tempest, Act I, Scene II

1.

Drill Sergeant Blanton Greenway hit the ground with all the grace of a 100-pound bale thrown from the hayloft of his grandpa's barn in Pawhuska, Oklahoma. Most witnesses said the punch was an uppercut. A few thought it was a right cross. Either way, the blow was a monster, and Greenway's tour of duty as a drill sergeant was in jeopardy.

His fractured jaw would no doubt be fine once doctors removed the wire in eight weeks, and his four broken teeth were deemed fixable. But the missing tip of his tongue -- he had bitten it off and swallowed it after being hit -- was problematic since the surgeon's report noted the likelihood of "moderate to severe speech articulation impairment."

"In English," the doctor said, "he's going to have a bad lisp."

"Oh, great. That's just what I need: a drill sergeant with a bad lisp," is all company commander Captain Curtis Grimes would say about Greenway's possible reinstatement. "Besides which, how does he even face the rest of us after getting his ass kicked by a raw recruit in front of everyone?"

The lopsided altercation between Drill Sergeant Greenway and Private Stone Jackson took place in late December on the 41st day of the U.S. Army Basic Combat Training course at Fort Jackson, South Carolina. Greenway was, as usual, in a trainee's face screaming insults and obscenities. A trainee -- in this case Private Jackson -- was, as usual, gamely responding, "Yes, drill sergeant," "No, drill sergeant," or "Thank you, drill sergeant" as loud as he could. Just another day in paradise.

But Greenway touched a raw nerve when he yelled, "How about I put a pretty bow in your hair?" Someone else had asked him the same question 10 years ago, when he was eight, and Jackson snapped. He got all 187 pounds of his chiseled 6-2 frame behind the punch, and the burly drill sergeant went down for the count.

After two weeks of confinement Jackson faced a special court martial, and the prosecution argued for serious prison time along with a dishonorable discharge.

"Sergeant Blanton Greenway is not just a drill instructor," proclaimed Captain Todd Henry, the attorney handling his first case as prosecutor, "he's a U.S. Army hero." Henry pointed out that in the seven years prior to becoming a drill sergeant Greenway had served five combat tours in the Middle East and had twice won a bronze star. "The unprovoked assault on Sergeant Greenway is an assault on the military chain of command and, in fact, on the nation we all proudly serve." The three officers who served as jury for the case solemnly nodded in agreement. This was, in fact, an appealing argument

But Stone Jackson's defense attorney, Major Drew Whitmore of the Army's Trial Defense Service, took immense pleasure in making a mess of the prosecution's case. Whitmore had recently been passed over for promotion to lieutenant colonel and would soon be booted from the military, so at the moment he had no particular fondness for the chain of command or anything else that might benefit the Army. He didn't know, nor did he care, what had prompted Jackson to punch his drill instructor. What he did know after nearly 20 years in uniform was how to upstage a rookie prosecutor.

"My client," Whitmore explained, "suffers from intermittent explosive disorder as described in the *Diagnostic and Statistical Manual of Mental Disorders,* which is published by the American Psychiatric Association and is accepted as the United States' official standard for classifying illnesses of this sort." The major then enlightened the jury by reading aloud relevant sections of the manual as well as half a dozen commentaries on the disorder that had been published by major U.S. hospitals and the National Institute of Mental Health. "On this basis alone we should and in fact *must* dismiss the case. Private Jackson requires treatment, not punishment."

The jury appeared unconvinced until Whitmore went on the offensive. "I regret that we must also scrutinize Sergeant Greenway's behavior, which by every reasonable measure was outside the clearly defined boundaries of acceptable conduct by a non-commissioned officer. The testimony of 15 eyewitnesses will verify that Sergeant Greenway discriminated against Private Jackson on the basis of his perceived sexual orientation."

Through his wired teeth Greenway tried hard to explain that his comment about putting a pretty bow in Jackson's hair was "a routine sarcastic motivational device" and not a reference to the trainee's sexual preferences, but all he did was dig a bigger hole for himself.

"The sergeant wants to call it *a motivational device*," said the indignant Whitmore, "but the Uniform Code of Military Justice calls it abuse. And there's no room for that in today's Army."

A week later Stone Jackson was a civilian once more, released from active duty under what the Army termed an *entry level separation*. "Basically it means you were never here," Whitmore told him when all the papers had been signed. "Now go get some help, Mr. Jackson."

Stone Jackson knew exactly what sort of help he needed.

2.

NYPD detectives Pete Nazareth and Tara Gimble were victims of their own success. After nailing two of the worst serial killers in New York City history -- one who targeted widows, another who preyed on immigrants -- they became the go-to team whenever a serious nut job hit City Hall's radar screen. As soon as one of his deep-pocketed supporters called to complain about a particular murder, the mayor was on the phone to the police commissioner demanding that "those two" be assigned the case.

Beginning in mid-January they spent several weeks taking down Vinny "The Spider" Spinelli, a mobster whose most recent victim, Aldo Guerra, had committed the unpardonable sins of not paying off a gambling debt on time and then not accepting his punishment -- usually a broken arm or leg -- like a man. So Spinelli fractured Guerra's skull with a 12-inch length of pipe filled with cement, then fed him through a wood chipper on a farm outside Morristown, New Jersey.

Had Spinelli used a newer wood chipper he might have remained a free man. But acting on a tip Nazareth and Gimble discovered bits of Guerra's pelvis at the farm, along with Spinelli's fingerprints on the chipper's controls. By the time the two detectives closed their investigation, "The Spider" was looking at five consecutive life sentences for murder and miscellaneous lesser offenses like racketeering, drug distribution, and arms trafficking.

One month after Spinelli's conviction Nazareth and Gimble were handed a case involving a series of suspicious deaths among hospital patients recovering from relatively minor surgery. Five of the deaths, the detectives discovered, stemmed from cardiac arrest triggered by intravenous delivery of suxamethonium chloride, a commonly used muscle relaxer. Another 10 deaths resulted from overdoses of either epinephrine, insulin, or digoxin.

When administered in large enough doses, of course, even the most beneficial drugs can become highly effective murder weapons, and Nurse Wilson Bodine had successfully racked up a long list of assisted suicides among people who hadn't desired to commit suicide. Nazareth and Gimble spent nearly a month pulling all the pieces together before arresting Bodine at his girlfriend's home in the Bronx. The former nurse would be eligible for parole in 2530.

Although the mayor referred to the detectives as "those two" -- something his detractors attributed to early-onset dementia -- their fellow officers had in recent months begun respectfully calling them the "Dynamic Duo," a phrase once reserved for Batman and Robin but now applied to one of the most accomplished detective teams in NYPD history. They were universally admired not only for closing the toughest cases but also for putting themselves in harm's way again and again in order to get the job done right.

Since getting engaged in December they had also become famous as "the partner partners," a description coined recently by the host of a popular morning TV show. Nazareth and Gimble were no longer just detectives. They were A-list media darlings among the New York press, in part because their professional accomplishments were outshone only by their good looks and strong personalities.

Pete Nazareth, who would soon turn 34, was the ugly duckling of the duo even though he was frequently mentioned as something of a Brad Pitt lookalike with his square jaw, boyish smile, and piercing gaze. At 5-10 and 165 pounds he still looked as though he could run a sub-4:00 mile, as he had in college, though his athletic claim to fame was now Taekwondo and a long string of major sparring championships. He had star quality, no doubt about it, but his fiancée was the real showstopper.

Tara Gimble seemed not to know how beautiful she was, but those around her definitely noticed. The 31-year-old detective wore her gleaming blonde hair fairly straight until it flipped slightly inward at her neck. Her blue eyes, high cheekbones, and strong narrow chin needed no help from makeup, which explained why she used it only when on a date with Nazareth, and then only minimally. An All-American soccer player in college, Gimble held a judo black belt, carried 120 pounds of well-toned muscle on her 5-7 frame, and was generally more than a match for any perp who doubted her toughness.

Hardly a day went by that a member of the press didn't call the NYPD's public relations office asking for time with the two detectives. But Nazareth and Gimble avoided interviews as much as they could. Being famous is not necessarily a good thing when you're on the street arresting bad guys, they explained, and they already considered each of their days to be a few hours too short. You didn't work, train, and live as hard as these two without needing 28-hour days.

Besides, their time as NYPD partners was nearing an end. Their boss, Deputy Chief Ed Crawford, was comfortable keeping them together while they were engaged. But once they got married -- something they hadn't gotten around to scheduling yet -- he would have to break up the Dynamic Duo. In the meantime, they eagerly threw themselves at whatever screwball case came along.

Hunting crazies was their specialty, and New York City had a generous supply of prime specimens.

3.

Stone Jackson was born and raised in the New Springville neighborhood of Staten Island, New York City's oft-forgotten fifth borough, in a rickety green bungalow at the edge of the woods. The home stood a few hundred feet within the boundaries of an area known as the Greenbelt, a 2,800-acre swath of protected forest filled with hiking trails, campsites, wildlife, marshes, streams, and ponds. Except for a few man-made touches the place looked much as it did in the 1500s, when it was home to the Native Americans who went by the name Lenape. If you wanted to get lost, this was the perfect spot.

When Jackson was 13 he and his friends began wearing out the Greenbelt's vast network of trails. Depending upon the weather and their moods they might head northwest to Willowbrook Park to fish for bass and bluegill, south to Latourette Golf Course to hunt for lost Titleists that they sold for 75 cents each, or east to the Pouch Boy Scout Camp to swim in 17-acre Ohrbach Lake until chased off by the ranger. All without leaving the woods.

By that time, though, Jackson was 13 going on 30 courtesy of 54-year-old Terrence Goodall, coach of the neighborhood Little League team and a prosperous self-employed insurance agent who worked out of his office in the nicest home on the block. When Jackson was only nine Coach T offered to care for him after school twice a week while Aggie, Stone's mother, took a job as a waitress following her husband's death. "This is what neighbors do," he told her compassionately. "I'm just glad I can help." Goodall's wife worked in Manhattan and his two daughters stayed obsessively busy with high school activities every day, so having young Stone in his home, he told Aggie, wouldn't be an inconvenience.

Jackson never told anyone about being molested by Coach T for two years before his mother got injured on the job and began collecting disability checks. Even after Goodall had been convicted of unrelated child pornography charges and given a three-year suspended sentence, Jackson kept his humiliation and anger to himself. He never mentioned having the pink bow braided into his then-long hair or the nausea he felt when his mother called from the diner to say she needed to work late. He just filed it all away, deep inside the meanest, blackest cavern of his mind, and promised himself he would one day settle the score.

By the time he graduated from high school Jackson had proven himself a passable student with C+ grades as well as a ferocious football player who enjoyed hurting people. And at 6-2 and a lean, rock-solid 170 pounds he did a lot of hurting. During his three years as a starting middle linebacker he set an unofficial school record for knocking opposing players out of a game, three of them with fractured legs and two with broken shoulders. He was never injured himself, largely because of his maniacal strength-training program. Prior to the start of his senior season he could bench press 350 pounds, or slightly more than twice his body weight, a feat that most fitness experts equated to running a four-minute mile. Several Division I colleges expressed interest in him, but Jackson wanted no part of that.

He had other plans.

His passion for blood-and-guts video games -- some of them secretly funded by the Department of Defense -- and his exceptional athletic ability led him to conclude that the life of a U.S. Army Ranger was right up his alley. Getting paid to kill bad guys? Hell, that was a no-brainer. Besides, he figured he already looked the part. Along with his football teammates he had taken to wearing his light brown hair in a military-style buzz cut; his intense blue eyes heightened the fearsomeness of the killer stare he had perfected during his linebacker years; and his long, hard-edged face and heavy jaw would work well under a tan beret. Yeah, he'd look seriously cool in that beret.

He was sold on Ranger training long before he visited the recruiter two days after his 18th birthday. The Army's website had done the job.

"Rangers are more than just physically strong," it read. "Rangers are smart, tough, courageous, and disciplined. Rangers are self-starters, adventurers, and hard chargers. They internalize the mentality of a *more elite Soldier*, as the Ranger Creed states and as their intense mission requirements demand."

But the Army wasn't quite ready for Jackson. He wouldn't sign the dotted line without a written guarantee of a slot at RASP -- the Ranger Assessment and Selection Program -- and the Army had no such slots available at that time. The recruiter pressed him to enlist anyway and then apply for RASP during basic training, to which Jackson responded, "I just look stupid." He knew that signing the contract without Option 40 -- the Army's RASP guarantee -- was a move only a dummy would make, and he was no dummy.

"You know and I know," Jackson told the recruiter, "that without Option 40 I'll end up as a latrine maintenance specialist, casket handler, or base mailman."

"Listen, lots of guys apply for RASP during basic and get it," Sergeant Arnold Dunce protested.

"Go into your records and show me the files on your last five recruits who did that."

"Uh, that's privileged information," Dunce said. "I can't show you personnel files."

"If you want me to sign the dotted line, that's what you'll have to do."

"I can't."

"Then I won't."

And that was that. Jackson walked out the door and wouldn't return for nearly six months, when an Option 40 slot finally came through. During that time he pumped gas at his uncle's gas station in Mariner's Harbor and stepped up his training so that he could max out any fitness test the Army might throw at him. He tacked

13

the Ranger program's recommended fitness scores to his bedroom wall and adopted them as the absolute minimum achievement.

Within two months his performance was off the chart. The recommended Ranger score for push-ups was 80 in two minutes. He could do 195 without breaking a sweat. The sit-up target was 80 in two minutes. He did 200 . . . three times every day. Two-mile run under 13:00? He was routinely under 12:00. And so it went. Physical training would be a piece of cake. He was fanatically driven.

Now and then his mother mentioned she wasn't crazy about having a soldier-son since too many young Americans were still coming home from the Middle East in body bags. For the most part, though, she was quietly out of touch. Her addiction to pain medication and one large bottle of pinot grigio per day kept her blissfully numb to most of the world's problems. She fixed his dinner -- skinless chicken and veggies five days a week -- but otherwise left him alone while he read and thought.

He read everything he could about becoming a Ranger, then a sniper, and then an American hero.

What he thought about was gutting and skinning Terrence Goodall.

4.

Haji Bakhil had waited for this day. Trained for it. Prayed for it. And finally it had come. He would have his revenge at last.

A month earlier the 27-year-old had gotten a janitor's position at the handsome East 24th Street building where Nazareth maintained his expansive 12th-floor apartment. Although Bakhil held a chemistry degree from a major U.S. university, this was the job of his dreams because it put him within easy reach of the cop who had arrested ISIS New York's top man, and Bakhil's spiritual leader, Rahman Aziz.

Aziz had been set to detonate 500 pounds of C-4 in a crowd outside One Police Plaza when Nazareth took him down in particularly brutal fashion. The terrorist had to be wheeled in and out of the courtroom for his two-week trial, during which he was convicted of the recent terrorism charge as well as the murders of several City officials, including the late Mayor Homer Bratwell, in an earlier attack. It looked as though Aziz would spend the rest of his life in prison, and for that Haji Bakhil vowed to behead the infidel Nazareth.

What Bakhil didn't know until he landed the job in the detective's apartment building was that Nazareth was no longer living alone but had been joined by his fiancée and NYPD partner, Tara Gimble. The ecstasy Bakhil felt when he learned this was something he never thought to experience outside of paradise. Killing Nazareth would be a great joy, perhaps the greatest of his life. But destroying the woman with whom the detective lived openly in sin? Sweet beyond compare!

He would kill the harlot first. Yes, he would force Nazareth to suffer the unimaginable loss of his bride-to-be before coming under Bakhil's blade himself. And the blade, God willing, would do its work slowly. He would carve off tiny pieces of the detective's flesh, one for each of the infidels who should have died in the attempted bombing at police headquarters, and do his best to make the job last not for hours but for days.

After three weeks of careful study and planning, Bakhil had the detectives' routines down almost to the minute. They were foolish creatures of habit who left the apartment together at almost precisely the same time each weekday morning and usually didn't return until late evening. But their schedule changed on weekends, and Bakhil knew he was greatly blessed to have gained this knowledge. Every Saturday morning Nazareth left the apartment by himself at 7:50 carrying a gym bag and didn't return for at least two hours.

On this particular Saturday morning Bakhil would make sure the detective returned to a special surprise. When he came home from the gym Nazareth would find Gimble's head resting comfortably on the kitchen table while her soul waited for him in hell.

"Good morning, sir," Bakhil said as Nazareth closed the apartment door behind him. Saturday morning was when the detective got his most intense Taekwondo workout of the week at Grandmaster Kim's dojang, or training hall. And today he would have the honor of sparring with a visiting South Korean master who had recently qualified for his country's Olympic team.

"Hey, good morning, Kareef." Nazareth used the name that Bakhil had put on his employment application. "How's it going today?"

"Just fine, sir, thank you. I'm glad you're wearing a warm jacket, because it is a very cold February morning out there."

"Yeah, I saw that on the Weather Channel. Barely 20 degrees. But at least it's not snowing."

"That is very good, sir. I'm not a big fan of shoveling the snow."

Bakhil busied himself polishing the elevator doors and mopping the stairwell for another half hour. When he was convinced that Nazareth was not coming back early, he quickly moved to the apartment door and removed the key he had stolen

16

from the building manager's office. He let himself into the apartment, gently pulled the door shut, and slipped the razor-edged knife from his gray janitor's coveralls. The frantic beating of his heart was the only sound he heard. Detective Gimble must be sleeping late today, he told himself. But she would not be late for her date with death.

As he passed the doorway of the first bedroom -- the one Nazareth had several years earlier transformed into an NFL-worthy fitness room -- he was shocked to find Gimble standing there in her neon-blue spandex tank top and workout shorts. She was in the midst of her deep-breathing exercises after pounding out three sets of squats with 300 pounds, and she wasn't pleased to see the knife-wielding janitor in her home.

"If you put the knife down and your hands up," she told him calmly, "I'll arrest you for first-degree burglary and leave it at that. Otherwise, I'll arrest you for burglary and assault on a police officer, and I'll make sure you're an old man before you leave prison."

"Listen to this infidel whore," he hissed, "talking bravely in her final moments."

"These are not the final moments of my workout, you asshole. I have another hour to go, not counting any time I waste on you. I've given you my best offer. Put the knife down and your hands up. You're under arrest."

Bakhil was enraged by her insolence. American women didn't know their place, and he welcomed the chance to set things right. He switched his grip on the knife so that he could deliver a downward blow to her upper body with maximum force, and he sprang into the room. Gimble had slightly less than three seconds to assess the nature of the attack -- two more than she needed.

As Bakhil's right hand drove toward her chest she took half a step to her left, blocked his forearm with both hands, and wrenched his arm behind him, forcing him to drop the knife. Though startled by the efficient defensive maneuver, he was able to regain his balance and throw a hard left punch toward Gimble's face. In one elegant, circular motion she parried the blow with her hand while using her powerful right leg to sweep his feet out from under him.

He hit the floor hard but was able to grab the fallen knife. She would not surprise him again. Now he would slice her up the middle. He got to his feet and prepared to attack, but Gimble simply stood before him grinning. Bakhir trembled with rage as he ran toward her swinging the blade furiously from side to side.

Once again she blocked his knife hand, but at the same time she turned her back into him while locking her powerful right hand onto his right ear. Using his ear as a handle she threw him up and over her shoulder onto a rack of 45-pound weight plates in the corner of the training room. The fall left him unconscious with a fractured right shoulder blade and four shattered ribs. He would also need emergency surgery to reattach his right ear, which Gimble had failed to release while tossing him through the air.

Under the terms of his plea bargain Bakhil would be sentenced to only 25 years in prison after giving up six members of a Manhattan sleeper cell. His testimony would immediately foil a massive attack on the City's subway system, and over the next few months it would lead to the conviction of a terrorist banker who had established close ties to a deputy mayor. At Gimble's urgent request the NYPD never disclosed the full circumstances of Bakhil's arrest, referring to it only as "an undercover operation that is still in progress."

Nazareth was incensed to learn that the building manager had hired a man with known terrorist links, and he was going to make sure something like that could never happen again. For the moment, though, he was just happy Gimble had been able to defend herself in grand style.

"Friends, Romans, countrymen," Nazareth said over a lunch of grilled cheese sandwiches later that day, "lend me your ears."

Gimble was moderately annoyed. "You know what, Pete?"

"I'm all ears, hon'."

"That's not funny."

"Then why are you laughing?"

"Okay, it's a little humorous, but it's not really funny. You know what I mean?"

"No, I think it's hysterical. The guy came in here to kill you, and you ripped his ear off while breaking half the bones in his back. A sweet little girl like you! That's pretty funny."

"It wouldn't be funny if I did that to someone in judo class, would it?" she asked.

"You mean you actually practice grabbing someone's ear as part of a throw?"

"No, we don't. That's the point. I got the hold all wrong."

"Seems to me you got it just right. I think the Tara Gimble Ear Throw should be something they teach at the academy. If the perp doesn't follow instructions, just rip his ear off. I think that's pretty cool."

She thought about that and smiled. "No, actually it's eerie."

He groaned as she tugged on her ear.

5.

Although Jackson's formal plans for becoming a Ranger had come unglued when he flattened his drill sergeant, he saw no reason why he couldn't follow his dreams without the Army's help. He had the right stuff and didn't need a uniform to prove it. So he would create his own training program without drill sergeants and marching and boot polishing and all the other Mickey Mouse crap that the Army called "basic." By getting rid of the time-wasting games he could devote himself fully to the task of becoming a savvy, self-reliant, ultimate weapon. He would be a force of one. He would answer only to himself. And when the time was right, he would rid America of vermin like Terrence Goodall.

For nearly a month after being released from active duty Jackson worked odd jobs and slept in a cheap motel near the fort. His plans were slowly coming together. Then in early February he found his way to one of South Carolina's largest gun shows of the year, where he roamed from booth to booth until he found exactly what he wanted. By the time he left he would have only $423 to his name, but that wasn't a problem. He'd get a steady job soon enough. First things first.

"This here is one lovely piece," the dealer assured him. Ferris Dutton smiled broadly as he handed the rifle over for closer inspection. "Mossberg MVP Patrol, bolt-action, takes 5.56 NATO ammo, and will gladly accept a 30-round magazine."

"The scope comes with it?" Jackson asked.

"Yessir. I outfit all my long guns with scopes. But if you don't want it, I can take a little something off the price."

"No, I definitely need the scope."

Jackson lovingly ran his hands over the weapon's smooth, graceful curves, raised the stock to his shoulder, and put the crosshairs on a red- white-and-blue banner that hung from the ceiling at the crowded gun show. *The right of the people to keep and bear arms shall not be infringed*, it read. A treasured line from the state's constitution.

"This is the one," Jackson nodded. Buying a gun in South Carolina is as good as it gets, he thought. See it. Buy it. Lock and load.

He set the rifle gently in the trunk of his 12-year-old Honda and drove off. *Scout-sniper Stone Jackson.* Had a nice ring to it. This was definitely going to be one hell of a happy new year.

By late the next afternoon he had found a job at a McDonald's near Clinton, S.C., along with a hellhole of a furnished apartment that would be his base of operations for his sniper training. With weekly pay of $300 and monthly rent of $325 plus utilities, he would have more than enough for necessities -- mostly food, ammunition, and gas. He figured that a spartan existence would be beneficial to his self-schooling, since it was impossible to know when his very survival depended upon being able to endure hardship. A Ranger needed to be disciplined, and Jackson was one of the most disciplined men on the planet as long as he kept his temper in check.

Hell, that business with the drill sergeant was a special case. A nothing. A zero. How likely was it that anyone else would ever taunt him again with that bow-in-the-hair line? Not likely at all. So that was behind him.

Ahead of him: the immense pleasure of planting Terrence Goodall in a well-earned grave.

6.

Most men worth $7.4 billion are reasonably satisfied. Not Archer Grande.

Yes, the 53-year-old former CEO and founder of SlashMe -- an online system for "tracking and hacking" corporate expenses -- possessed all the customary toys of the rich and famous. He divided his time among four homes -- Manhattan, Newport Beach, Aspen, and Paris -- together valued at slightly more than $280 million. He traveled the globe in a $74-million customized Gulfstream G650ER that could cover 7,500 nautical miles at mach 0.85. And he smiled on camera while hugging his 33-year-old wife, Brigitte Evianna Artois, whose mysterious dark eyes, full lips, and flawless figure helped account for the $25 million she earned each year as a model.

But, no, he was not yet president of the United States. And that, he told everyone who would listen, had to change.

At 6:00 p.m. sharp on February 20th he emerged from the cabin of his private aircraft, stood at the top of the jet's stairway, and bravely faced the howling wind and blowing snow of Buffalo, N.Y. He waved to the 1,800 boisterous fans who had come to the airport because they couldn't afford the $2,000-a-plate fundraiser being held that night at the Hyatt Regency. His frenzied supporters had begun cheering as soon as the plane touched down, and they didn't stop until he walked up to the makeshift podium on the tarmac and signaled for quiet.

"The other Republican candidates are in Florida, Southern California, and Hawaii tonight," he began, "staying warm." The crowd raucously booed Grande's opponents for the presidential nomination. "They're staying cozy. They're staying within their comfort zones. Hey, that's okay. They know their limitations. But you and I are standing here tonight in the cold and the wind and the snow because we want a president who is strong enough to go wherever he has to go and do whatever he has to do to make America great."

He waited nearly a minute for the cheering to end.

"Maybe my opponents will get here in April before New York's Republican primary," he grinned, "as long as you promise them sunshine." The audience howled derisively. "But the people of this great city don't need a fair-weather president," he told them. "You need someone who's willing to walk through fire and ice to get the job done, and that is precisely what I intend to do. I will bring jobs back to America from the sweatshops of the Third World. I will show Russia and North Korea and Iran that I can walk the walk and not just talk the talk. And I will slam the door on illegal immigrants who come here looking to live like goddamn royalty off your tax dollars."

He smiled and nodded as the throng roared its approval. The other Republican candidates had branded him a loose cannon, a warmonger, even a racist, yet he was 20 points ahead of his nearest opponent and seemed to be building momentum. On this night in frigid Buffalo, N.Y., Archer Grande was an American folk hero.

But it was time to hit the banquet and raise a few bucks for his campaign, so he slipped into the line that everyone in the crowd wanted to hear.

"My friends, for way too long we have been abused by Washington insiders who apparently love foreigners more than they love us. So it's time for America to have a leader who takes care of Americans. I am that leader. And I've got your back!"

Thunderous applause greeted Grande's final words as trophy wife Brigitte walked onto the podium, kissed her husband, and joined him in waving to the crowd. First Lady of the United States at 33. Yeah, baby. What's not to love?

The 200 people who had shelled out a total of $400,000 to dine with "The Grande" in the hotel ballroom on this wintry night were ecstatic when Buffalo's mayor introduced the candidate and stepped aside. Cameras flashed and tape rolled as he strode to the podium and gave the crowd an enthusiastic thumbs-up before launching into his pre-dinner comments.

Grande loved cameras, and cameras loved him. He stood 6-1, was lean and fit, and wore his sleek silver-gray mane swept back on both sides. Because of his rugged good looks and cleft chin he was frequently referred to by the press as a Michael Douglas look-alike, but that didn't sit especially well with him. As far as he was concerned, Michael Douglas was an Archer Grande look-alike.

The lights dimmed, and he stood alone -- and very much at home -- in the spotlight. After thanking everyone for writing their checks, he fired off a string of sharp one-liners aimed at his Republican opponents as well as the likely Democratic nominee, Alex "Sleepy Al" Boudreaux. With the crowd properly warmed up, he casually shared his thoughts on a number of relatively minor issues before rolling out the heavy artillery for his comments on foreign policy.

"Russia," he began, "is run by a thug who'll kill anyone who doesn't agree with him. Iran is run by a religious fanatic who wants the world to end. North Korea is run by a Neanderthal who gets chauffeured around in a Rolls-Royce while his people starve. And the United States of America," he bellowed, "is run by a president who thinks we should play kissy-face with these lunatics." Two minutes later the cheering finally subsided, and Grande was able to continue.

"There is one way, and only one way, to deal with the madmen who threaten America." His fans knew what was coming, and they could hardly contain themselves. "You come to the table with a big goddamn stick. And I'm here to tell you, folks, when it comes to dealing with Russia, Iran, and North Korea, yours truly has the biggest stick."

On cue all 200 guests came to their feet, clapped, and chanted, "Biggest stick, biggest stick, biggest stick." No one sat down until Grande pleaded for quiet.

"Now let's talk about terrorists," he continued. "Our president keeps telling us there are 40,000 or 50,000 terrorists hiding over there in the desert. Tell me something: how in the hell do you hide 50,000 people anywhere on this planet? Can't be done. It absolutely cannot be done. We know exactly where they are," he roared, "but our president doesn't have the guts, or any other necessary anatomical parts, to wipe these murderers off the face of the earth. You don't get rid of terrorists by wringing your hands and praying, my friends. You dust off the B-52s and incinerate the bastards."

By this time it looked as though dinner might never get served because Grande's admirers wouldn't stop cheering. But tomorrow, he knew, was another day in another city along the campaign trail, so it was time to move on.

"I have just one more thing to say before we sit down to dinner," he told them seriously, "and the top Democratic candidate wants you to believe it's a *sensitive topic*. Hey, nothing is *sensitive* unless you're too weak to talk about it. He is. I'm not." He begged for quiet before the audience once again erupted in applause.

"*Sleepy Al* Boudreaux says that once someone sneaks under a fence in Texas and has established himself illegally in the United States, we should let him stay." Boos all around. "Let me tell you what this is like. I break into your home. I steal your cash, your jewelry, your credit cards, and your two kids. And then the government says I can keep them because, well, *fair is fair*. Ladies and gentlemen," he shouted, "do you think that's fair?"

Every man and woman in the room yelled, "NO!"

"If you elect me president, we'll have a new policy for illegal immigrants," he vowed, "and I mean ALL of them. Four words, ladies and gentlemen. Twelve letters: WE STAY. THEY GO."

The room rocked with hooting, cheering, and chanting -- alternately "We stay, they go" and "Biggest stick" -- for the next 10 minutes as the candidate made his way from table to table shaking hands, slapping backs, and smiling for the cameras. He had all a man could want. Except for one thing.

He was not yet president of the United States.

7.

"Things are going great down here," Jackson told his mother when he called her a month after his Army discharge. "I'm at the top of my class."

"That's great, Stone. A few people have asked me how you're doing -- your friend Cal down the street and your cousin Jerry and a few others," she said. "I told them I hadn't really heard much because of all your training."

"Yeah, well, we don't have a whole lot of free time here on base. But if anyone asks, you can say that I've gotten a special assignment to Ranger School and sniper training. I should be home on leave in a few months, though."

"Ranger and sniper training? Wow, that sounds awfully exciting."

"It's a really elite program," he told her. "Only about one candidate in 1,000 gets selected for this program, so this is a pretty big deal."

"My son's going to be a general before long!" she gushed.

"I don't know about that, Ma, but I'm definitely on the right path."

The path he was on an hour later was the one that ran from the back door of his first-floor apartment into the 370,000-acre Sumter National Forest, where he would sharpen his Ranger skills over the next few months. After several weeks of range firing he was finally entering the South Carolina woods. But this first outing was nothing more than an orientation visit, so he planned to walk as far as he could for three hours, then turn around and hike back. He carried only a small backpack containing minimal survival gear: matches, enough food for three meals, a pair of heavy wool socks, a length of rope, and a snakebite kit. This last item seemed like a waste of money to him, but in the end he decided not to tempt fate for the sake of $10 when these woods were home to timber rattlers, coral snakes, copperheads, and a few other species that could definitely ruin his day if he were unlucky enough to step on one.

His sniper rifle was safely concealed under the mattress in his apartment because he figured he still had a lot of shooting range work ahead of him before he would carry the gun into the forest. So on today's hike his only weapon was the Buck survival knife -- a menacing black beauty with a seven-inch blade -- that he carried on a belt sheath. In the highly unlikely event someone decided to mess with a guy his size, Jackson would carve him up like a Halloween pumpkin.

He headed northeast across several branches of Duncan Creek until he reached the Enoree River, where he quietly walked banks thick with hickory, sycamore, and ash. Sharing the woods with him in the 40-degree chill were hawks, a couple of blue herons, and a few deer. The deer in particular caught his attention since they would soon become an important focus of his training. Once he mastered his rifle at the firing range, he would need live targets, and South Carolina's forests were thick with them. He had no idea when the hunting season officially began or ended, but that didn't matter. He'd shoot when he damn well felt like it.

This stretch along the Enoree River was pleasant enough but didn't offer much of a challenge for an aspiring Ranger. Although there were creeks, ponds, and marshes that might test his hiking skills, the hills in the area topped out around 400 feet, and that wouldn't cut it for the sort of survivalist training he had in mind. To get what he needed he would have to drive about an hour and a half to Sassafras Mountain in the northwest corner of the state near the North Carolina border. At 3,500 feet Sassafras could push a man to his limits, especially in winter, when ice storms heightened the danger. That's the kind of in-your-face natural meanness he had to experience in order to toughen up properly.

"Where the hell you think you're going?" someone yelled across a narrow creek not far from one of the many *No Trespassing* signs Jackson had ignored since setting out that morning.

"Me?" Jackson called back.

"No, the four people next to you, asshole." The guy was in his late fifties and might have passed for a large barrel if not for the handlebar mustache, scraggly beard, and shotgun. He spit a mouthful of tobacco juice on his right boot while keeping his eyes fixed on the trespasser.

"What's the problem, man? I'm just out walking."

"The problem, *boy*," the guy said sarcastically, "is that you're standing in the middle of 20 acres that belong to yours truly, Marlin T. Draper. And to get here you had to walk past a dozen of my *No Trespassing* signs."

"I thought the signs meant I couldn't hunt here," Jackson lied. "All I'm doing is walking."

"Where you from, moron?"

"Fort Jackson, sir. I'm on leave."

"Well, here's news, you sorry sack of U.S. Government shit from Fort Jackson. If a sign says *No Hunting*, it means you can't hunt. If it says *No Trespassing*, it means you can't walk there, crawl there, run there, or goddamn fly there. It's private property, and in South Carolina, thank the good Lord, we have a stand-your-ground law that says I can blow your ugly head off right now."

"Sir, I'm sorry I came onto your property, and I'll get off as soon as I can."

"And how exactly will you do that without walking on my property, U.S. Army boy?" Draper stood there sneering, the shotgun resting on his fat beer belly. "Don't matter if I shoot you here or over there, does it? It's all my land."

"Mister Draper, I promise never to come back on your property, and I'll be happy to drop a $20 bill on the ground here for the use of your trail on my way out."

Draper nodded thoughtfully and fingered the shotgun's trigger. He had no love of the U.S. government or anyone connected with it, and most of his brain screamed for him to shoot Jackson while he had the chance. But a tiny voice in his head reminded him that he'd probably have one hell of a hassle once the local police got involved, as they almost surely would. Even though he could claim he had fired in self-defense, he'd spend more time on this than it was worth.

"This here's your lucky day, Army boy," Draper hissed. "You empty your wallet of every damn dollar you've got, and that'll be my fee for allowing you to walk my trails today. Just put the money down and get the hell off my property as fast as you can move those two legs of yours."

"Yes, sir. Thank you, sir," Jackson answered as he emptied his wallet of $47. He put the money on the ground and began jogging in the direction of his apartment in Clinton. As he did so, Draper fired his shotgun in the air, causing Jackson to hit the ground and roll into a thicket loaded with sharp thorns. Although he could no longer see Draper, he pictured him standing there laughing his fat butt off.

No way in hell the game could end this way.

Jackson crept through the underbrush back toward the spot where he had laid his money and silently watched Draper pick up the bills and stuff them in his pocket. The guy looked around and grinned, obviously pleased with himself. Then he carefully worked his way across the stream, stepping from rock to rock, and headed toward his cabin.

For the next 15 minutes Jackson was a shadow of death as he slipped silently through the woods with his quarry in sight. He moved when Draper moved, stopped when Draper stopped, and kept the Buck knife firmly gripped in his right hand. Now this is training, he thought. No books. No drill sergeants. Just me and the enemy deep in the woods.

After another 10 minutes Draper grew tired, sat down on a fallen log, and gently laid his shotgun on the ground beside him. He pulled a tin of Timber Wolf chewing tobacco from his jacket and stuffed a wad in his right cheek. A younger, nimbler man might have been able to pick the gun up in time, but in the three seconds it took Jackson to cover the distance between them Draper had absolutely no chance.

With his powerful left hand Jackson grabbed Draper's hair and yanked his head back. With his right he jammed the blade of his survival knife against the guy's fleshy, exposed throat.

"Well, now, Mr. Pigshit," Jackson whispered in Draper's ear, "ain't life funny."

"Hey, now, I didn't do you no harm, boy," the guy whined. "I was just havin' a little fun with you."

"Robbing a man at gunpoint is what you call having fun in South Carolina, you redneck son of a bitch? Then maybe you'd like to see how we have fun with people like you back in New York City."

"Now listen, mister, you take your money back, no problem. And we'll just forget the whole damn thing. Hell, you can even come back here and hike around whenever you'd like. How's that?"

"Give me your wallet while I think about that," Jackson told him. Draper slowly removed his wallet and handed it over. "Well, well. My $47 plus, oh, let's see, another $60 of yours. I just hit the lottery, didn't I?"

"Yes, sir, you sure did. No problem. Keep it all. I shouldn't have been pestering you like that, you being a soldier and all."

"Oh, you've got that right, lard ass. Now stand up and take one big step forward." While Draper did as he was told, Jackson picked up the shotgun. "Okay, now let's go back to the stream where you had a little fun with me."

"Aw, come on, now. There's no reason to keep at this, son. I apologized and gave you my money. Keep the shotgun if you want it," he said. "I'll just go on home, and this will be over."

"It's over when I say it's over, Marlin T. Draper. Start waddling."

They retraced their steps to the stream, where Jackson ordered Draper to sit with his back against a river birch and tied his arms behind the tree's slender trunk.

"That too tight, *boy*?" Jackson asked him.

"No, it's fine."

"Good. I'm glad to hear that," Jackson said. And he was serious. He didn't want any marks on Draper's wrists when this was all over. "Now you sit here and don't move. Are we clear, boy?"

"Yes, sir. We're clear. Hey, listen. Why don't you just leave me here tied up," Draper pleaded, "and go on your way. We'll both forget this ever happened, okay?"

"It's stupid to forget important lessons, boy. You have to remember everything you learn in combat if you plan to stay alive. So I'll remember today for a long, long time." He waded into the stream, hoisted a 20-pound rock, and came back to Draper.

"Is that your stream?" Jackson asked.

"Yes, sir, it is."

"Then this must be your rock."

"Not if you want it," Draper said nervously. "Hell, you want it, it's yours."

"That would be robbery," Jackson said. "It belongs to you, and I think you should have it." With both hands he swung the rock at Draper, knocking him unconscious with a fierce blow to the left temple. He calmly walked back into the stream and replaced the rock exactly where he had found it.

He untied Draper, hauled him up into a fireman's carry, and walked him to the stream, where he placed him face down in the water next to the large rock. Then he walked ashore and waited. One minute. Two. Three. Draper never moved. Jackson checked the guy's neck for a pulse and found none. So he dropped the shotgun in the stream. Poor Marlin T. Draper. Out hiking in his own woods, slips on a rock in the stream, and ends up very dead. Yep, highly believable story.

First confirmed kill for scout sniper Stone Jackson.

Man, it felt good.

8.

Nazareth and Gimble spent part of the second week of March staying warm in their down sleeping bags at night and sweating in full combat gear throughout the day. Such was life at the Urban Warfare Training Center in Israel's Negev Desert. The training center -- a seven-square-mile mock Arab city built in 2005 by the U.S. Army Corps of Engineers for the Israeli Defense Forces, or IDF -- was created to offer state-of-the-art training in the strategies, tactics, and weaponry of urban combat.

Although the program had been designed with Middle East operations in mind, the NYPD's top brass believed that much of the curriculum could be readily applied to the streets of New York City. So when Israel's Minister of Public Security formally requested that Nazareth and Gimble visit Jerusalem to share their investigative techniques with the *Mishteret Yisra'el* -- the national civilian police force -- the police commissioner struck a bargain. The detectives would spend three days sharing what they knew with their Israeli counterparts, after which Nazareth and Gimble would receive three days of intensive field training at Base Tze'elim.

"Seriously?" Gimble said to liaison officer Alam, or Colonel, Ariel Meir at 6:30 a.m. on the second day of training. "It's 40 every night and near 80 every day?"

"If you want to be warmer at night, Detective Gimble," he laughed, "you really must come here in early August sometime. You definitely won't need a sleeping bag. Of course, at that time of year it's 100 during the daytime."

"Come alone if you want to do that, Tara," Nazareth added, "because I have zero interest in running through the desert in August."

"Okay, okay," she said. "Message received. But it's really difficult to dress for the occasion when we have a 40-degree temperature swing every day."

"This is actually a good thing for training purposes," Meir explained, "because it reflects one more element that is beyond your control in battle. And this is why we have you sleeping outdoors instead of in cozy officers' quarters. If the enemy has taken control of important buildings in a town or city, you and your police colleagues could very easily find yourselves sleeping outside in rain or snow if you hope to secure the perimeter."

"It does make sense," Gimble said, "and I suppose I'll survive. So what's on the agenda for today?"

"We're going to spend the next 12 hours on what we formally call *parameters of the urban terrain* -- or more simply the special problems that come with fighting in a city. And I believe this will prove to be extremely valuable to both of you. Today you will fight an enemy who knows how to use the unique geography of a city to his great advantage."

Meir was right on target, of course. Throughout the day and early evening the two detectives had to overcome the sorts of challenges they might easily face in any of New York City's five boroughs, though especially in Manhattan. They faced a highly mobile street-smart enemy who used tall buildings and narrow alleys as sniper posts, who wormed his way into sewage tunnels in order to move unseen from one street to the next, and who knew the best places -- abandoned cars, trash bins, and the like -- to set booby traps.

"The thing you must always remember," Meir told them at the end of the long day, "is that the urban combatant has a seven-to-one advantage over you when he is inside the buildings he knows best. He knows the basements, the rooftops, the tunnels, the fire exits -- absolutely everything. And you cannot compete with that level of knowledge. What you must do, therefore, is draw him out of that comfortable nest, no matter how long it takes. If you go in after him, you stand a very good chance of dying."

"I'm feeling a little dead already after all this heat today," Nazareth confessed. "Smarter, for sure, but just a little dead."

Meir smiled. "I'm glad to hear that, Detective Nazareth, because I know that you and Detective Gimble are very fine athletes. So if we have succeeded in wearing you both out, our program must be tough enough."

"Oh, you've got that right," Nazareth said. "So what does tomorrow hold for us?"

"I believe you'll both enjoy tomorrow a great deal," Meir told them. "We'll be simulating very intense close-quarters combat, both armed and unarmed. You'll be laser-shooting against some of our best marksmen, and you'll be going hand-to-hand with some of our country's best martial artists."

"Now that sounds like fun," said Gimble, eager to test her judo skills against some major competition.

"Well, I must confess that we'll be tilting the playing field just a bit," Meir said. "Detective Nazareth will face one of our top judo people, while you will go up against a very serious Krav Maga expert." Nazareth perked up at the mention of Krav Maga, a highly efficient and sometimes brutal unarmed combat system developed especially for the Israeli Defense Forces.

"I'd really like to do some Krav Maga training myself," Nazareth said excitedly, "especially since I'm here in its birthplace."

"You will probably need to do that when you return home, Detective Nazareth," Meir grinned. "Tomorrow you will most likely be worn out when you finish battling David Penzik."

"Wait, didn't he win a judo gold medal at the last Olympics?" Gimble asked.

"Absolutely, Detective Gimble. He is quite proficient."

"Better get a really good night's sleep, Pete," she taunted. "And make sure you have plenty of Motrin for tomorrow."

"Back at you, Tara. I hope you enjoy your first Krav Maga lesson."

Early the next morning Gimble was killed by a sniper firing from the roof of the eight-story building to her left. She had unwisely focused on the adversary in building A while the sharpshooter in building B lined up his head shot and squeezed the trigger.

It was worse for Nazareth, who was killed twice within the first 15 minutes of laser-shooting. In two simulated assaults on a terrorist position he had taken a round to the heart and one to the gut. The computer sensors determined that both hits would have been fatal.

"What I want you to remember," Meir told them gravely when the session had ended, "is that you would have died here today if this had been actual combat instead of laser practice. You're excellent marksmen, but you made the mistake of assuming your enemy was less skilled. A thug with a handgun may not be able to do what our IDF snipers did to you. But who says the thug you are chasing doesn't have highly expert back-up? If you are overconfident, as is often the case, your enemy can lure you into the kinds of traps we set for you today."

"No question we were outmatched," Nazareth said, "and I do believe that overconfidence played a major role. It certainly did for me. I assumed that I was the baddest guy in town when I should have recognized my opponents had a clear advantage. Same thing could easily have happened in New York City. Only difference is I wouldn't be here analyzing what went wrong."

"If it is any consolation, Detective Nazareth, I can tell you that in New York City you will not likely face anyone with the skills of today's opponents," Meir assured him. "But you should always plan for the worst. Remember what happened here when you find yourself facing this same kind of situation at home."

"So now that we've gotten our butts handed to us in shooting," Gimble said, "I assume we get pounded by your martial-arts experts."

"I can't predict what will happen, Detective Gimble," Meir said amiably. "The sand pit is a highly unpredictable place."

"Sand pit?"

"Yes. You and Detective Nazareth will work on your hand-to-hand techniques in the sand pit while wearing full gear. That includes your boots," he added, "since we want to simulate real-world combat rather than the sort of thing you might see in a martial-arts school."

They were met at the pit by two IDF soldiers who looked as though they had been sculpted from blocks of granite. David Penzik was the reigning Olympic judo champion in the men's heavyweight division and looked like someone who could pull a tank uphill without breaking a sweat. His female colleague, meanwhile, was one of the IDF's top-rated Krav Maga instructors. Though Shira Zingel was only 5-10 and 150 pounds, she looked to be 100% muscle and 120% serious.

Nazareth and Gimble had a bad feeling about this.

After the four had been introduced and had tested each other's powerful handshakes, Meir laid out his rules for the pit -- a forbidding, sunbaked arena that measured 10 feet by 10 feet and was filled with three feet of sand.

"You will all wear protective gear: full head cover with face shield, chest and groin pads, and martial arts gloves. You may not throw sand -- even though in actual combat that could certainly be a valuable tactic -- and you may not bite. If you find yourself in a choke hold or other position from which you cannot escape, you must signal your surrender either by speaking or by tapping your opponent. Is everyone clear?"

Nazareth and Gimble realized immediately that the rules governing combat in the sand pit were quite unlike those they followed in their martial-arts training halls. There were no guidelines on the amount of contact they could make or on the techniques they could employ. This was destined to be a winner-take-all simulation of battlefield combat.

First up in the pit were Gimble and the Krav Maga expert, Shira Zingel.

"Here is what you must know, Detective Gimble," said Meir. "Krav Maga incorporates techniques from every self-defense system on the planet, and it is deadly in the extreme. You may attack absolutely any body part that is available, including the eyes, which is why you are wearing face shields. I'll be the judge. If I believe that you have successfully attacked your opponent's eyes, the contest will be over. Otherwise, you fight until one of you yields."

"Understood," Gimble replied.

"Then you may begin."

Gimble bowed to her opponent as she would normally do back home in the dojo, or training hall. In return she took a convincing front kick to the midsection and quickly found herself sitting in the sand with Zingel's forearm pulled tightly against her throat. Game over. She tapped out, and Zingel politely helped her to her feet.

"Rule number one," Meir smiled, "is there are no rules in combat. Krav Maga is meant to tear your opponent to pieces. You do whatever it takes to preserve your life. That is all. It is the most vicious kind of street fight you will ever encounter."

"So I don't think I'll bow this time," Gimble joked.

"That would be wise," Meir offered. "Ready, and fight!"

Zingel immediately lunged toward Gimble and attempted to claw at her face mask, but the detective successfully converted her opponent's forward motion into a brilliantly executed *ippon seoi nage*, or one-arm shoulder throw. As soon as Zingel's back hit the sand, Gimble delivered a powerful elbow strike to the face shield. End of fight.

"Well done," said Meir as Gimble helped Zingel to her feet. "You used your judo knowledge but strengthened it by attacking with your elbow. I give you a B. If you want an A," he added, "next time attack the eyes when they are available to you. Then the fight is truly over. Okay, ready, and fight!"

The two women fought three more times, each of them growing increasingly determined to win. Their fifth and final session went nearly four minutes -- a brutally long time in the afternoon heat -- with Zingel the victor after clawing at Gimble's face mask with her powerful right hand. Meir judged that the attack would have disabled Gimble had she not been wearing the protective gear, and that was that.

"And now, gentlemen, it's your turn," Meir said as he waved Nazareth and Penzik into the pit. At 210 pounds the Israeli judo champion had the detective by more than 40 pounds, none of it fat. "I expect this to be an eye-opening experience for you, Detective Nazareth," Meir told him, "but we can discuss that later."

"One request," Nazareth said.

"By all means."

"Don't let him kill me."

"David has never killed anyone in training," Meir answered. "Maimed, yes. Killed, no."

"Now I feel much better."

"Okay, gentlemen. Same rules as the women. When you can take no more, either yell or tap out. Ready, and fight!"

Nazareth had seen what happened to Gimble when she bowed, so he skipped that part and instead launched one of his strongest Taekwondo moves, a spinning back kick with his right foot. That is, he tried. Before he was halfway through the kick his left boot drilled deep into the sand, he lost his balance, and then crumbled face down under Penzik's attack. The detective tried but failed to fight off the choke hold and had to yield before he passed out.

"Well that was certainly instructive," Nazareth laughed. "I now know that spinning kicks aren't meant for sand pits."

"That is absolutely true," said Meir. "You will also find that almost *any* kick is difficult because of the sand and the weight of your boots. This is nothing at all like working barefoot on a mat."

"You've got that right."

"And this is why we practice under these conditions. You must train far outside your comfort zone if you want to live a long life, Detective Nazareth. Now try not to let David kill you again. Ready, and fight!"

Penzik charged immediately, reaching for his opponent's neck. Instead of retreating, Nazareth stepped into the attack, grabbed hold of Penzik's shirt, neatly rolled the much larger man over his hip, and immediately drove his open palm into the guy's face mask.

Penzik was impressed. "Excellent move," he said as Nazareth helped him up. "It's what we call *tsurikomi goshi*, one of the 40 original throws of judo. The pulling hip throw is an extremely effective technique against a larger opponent."

Nazareth brushed sand off his uniform. "Basically I was just trying to stay alive," he laughed. "You've now seen 50% of my throwing techniques."

"All right, you each have one kill," Meir shouted. "Ready, and fight!"

They had only one more battle, but it was epic. They fought each other nonstop for nearly 12 minutes before Nazareth once again had to tap out of a choke hold. He flopped back in the sand and tried to catch his breath.

"Dead again," he said. "This is getting to be a habit."

"But as you can see," Meir smiled, "David is near death himself. Aren't you, David?" Penzik simply patted his chest and nodded. "To fight in the sand pit for nearly 12 minutes with David is quite an accomplishment, I can tell you. You gave away a lot of weight, and the sand pit is much better suited to grappling than to kicking. So he had real advantages over you. And yet he had trouble killing you."

"Yeah, I'm really glad I was hard to kill."

"You should be, Detective Nazareth. David's opponents -- whether here in the sand pit or in actual combat -- generally die within the first minute. You may have set a record. But now, ladies and gentlemen, I believe it's time for some Dancing Camels."

The detectives were naturally confused. "Dancing camels?" said Gimble.

"Yes, exceptionally fine beer brewed in Tel Aviv by the Dancing Camel Brewing Company."

"Oh, I'm with you 100% on that," Nazareth said eagerly.

At the end of the long day the four martial artists sat with Meir in the shade and enjoyed their cold beer. But the colonel didn't let the conversation stray too far afield of the training mission. In fact, he gave Nazareth and Gimble some homework for when they got back to New York.

"First, I recommend that you cross-train in each other's martial arts. As you saw today," he said, "what wins in genuine hand-to-hand combat is a mixture of everything. Judo alone or Taekwondo alone may not get the job done when your lives are on the line. Second, even though you are both expert marksmen with handguns, I strongly urge you to master the rifle as well. Knowing how to handle a sniper rifle could be invaluable one day. At the very least this training will help you better understand your enemy."

"Check and check," Nazareth said. "I agree totally. Tara and I have died enough here in Israel. I'd like for us not to die in Manhattan."

"Let us all drink to that," said Meir. The five of them clinked glasses and traded war stories late into the evening.

9.

Campaign manager Vincent Chandler didn't enjoy being screamed at poolside by Archer Grande at the billionaire's Upper East Side mansion. But the candidate's 20-point lead in the Republican race had slipped to 16 points between the end of February and mid-March, and Chandler thought it best to keep his mouth shut during the tirade. Talking back might get him fired, which meant his dream of becoming White House chief of staff would go down in flames. Besides, for $30,000 a month he was basically prepared to take whatever Grande dished out.

"Let's make sure we're on the same page," Grande fumed as he toweled off after swimming his customary 30 minutes in the $375,000 heated lap pool. "I'm paying you to increase my lead, not shrink it. Do I have that right, Vince?"

Keep the answers short and gutless, Chandler warned himself. "Yes."

"Good. So I didn't get that part wrong. Now, if I had a 20-point lead last month and have a 16-point lead this month, does that mean I'm doing better?"

"No, it doesn't."

"Then I must be doing worse. Am I right?"

"Yes, you are."

"And I'm paying you so I can do better, not worse?"

"Yes." Chandler fought like a champion to keep his eyes on Grande's face even as the boss's wife left the $40,000 tanning bed next to the fake waterfall and ambled topless toward the pool. Allowing his gaze to linger on Brigitte's magnificent form wouldn't just get him fired. It might get him held underwater for, well, for as long as it took him to drown. Archer Grande was possessive about most of his toys, lovely Brigitte chief among them.

"So that must mean you're deliberately ripping me off, Vince," Grande bellowed. "You're cashing your paychecks while doing the exact opposite of what I'm paying you for. Am I right?"

"I'm not trying to rip you off," Chandler said carefully, "but I certainly need to do better." He bit the inside of his cheek so hard that he momentarily saw stars. It was either that or watch Brigitte glide slowly and seductively into the warm water at the far end of the pool. The taste of blood helped him focus on keeping his job.

"On that we agree, Vince. You need to do better." Grande tossed his wet towel on a lounge chair and grabbed a cold bottle of Veen water. He called over to Brigitte. "Would you like one?" Grande had lately become hooked on Veen, an elegant spring water bottled in Finnish Lapland and priced alongside decent California wines. His wife shook her head gently from the pool. She had only gotten as far as her hips, and from a distance she appeared to be bathing nude. Chandler looked away quickly as Grande turned back to him.

The cold water, and perhaps the sight of his young bride in the pool, seemed to have quenched the boss's anger, and Chandler took a deep breath. He had survived yet another eruption. How many more of them, he wondered, could his 44-year-old heart take? Being hired by Archer Grande had solidified his reputation as one of the nation's most gifted campaign managers, but if he was honest with himself he knew the job might eventually kill him.

"Let's have a seat, Vince, while you tell me how you're going to widen the gap between Pinocchio and me." Grande didn't much like any of his Republican opponents, but he absolutely loathed Lander Enfield, a shrewd old-school backroom politician with a colossal nose.

"Arch, one of these days you're going to slip and call him Pinocchio on camera," Chandler said gently, "and the vultures will be after you for appearance discrimination."

Grande was dumbfounded. "Please don't tell me there's actually something called *appearance discrimination.* You're making that up, right?"

"No, I'm not. In fact, it's one of the hottest new specialties among legal professionals."

"See, now I know you're just screwing with me. You said *legal professionals* instead of *ambulance-chasers.* And we've had that discussion before, haven't we?" he grinned.

"Yes," said Chandler, a graduate of NYU Law School, "we've had that discussion many times. But seriously, if you call him Pinocchio during an interview, we'll all wish to hell you hadn't."

"Got it. I'll work on that. So tell me how you get my points back."

"Here's what happened. In the last debate the moderator . . ."

Grande interrupted. "That guy's a serious asshole, and I want him off the air." Chandler put his hands up, hoping to calm the coming storm. "No, listen," Grande yelled, "he needs to go, even if I have to buy the damn network just so I can fire him. I want that guy gone."

"May I continue?"

"Yeah, go ahead."

In the most recent Republican debate, Chandler explained, the moderator had suckered Grande into wasting the night on the kinds of egghead issues that his opponents loved -- trade imbalance, infrastructure renewal, alternative energy sources, and other interesting but monumentally boring stuff.

"It was all bullshit," Grande ranted, "and that guy's days are numbered. I guarantee you he'll be selling pencils on a street corner by the time I'm finished with him."

"Right, it was all bullshit. Your opponents have more bullshit than Old MacDonald's farm. What they do *not* have," Chandler reminded him, "is passion. Passion trumps bullshit every time, and passion is what wins you this election. You've got to forget about discussing America's foreign policy toward East

Dingleberry and stick to stuff that makes people's hearts beat faster."

"Okay, Russia, illegal immigrants, terrorists, and all that. Understood. But I need something fresh. You're right. We need to inject more passion into this thing."

"And I have an idea that will grab you 10 more points." He had been waiting to lay this idea on the candidate, and finally the moment seemed right.

"I'm listening," Grande said as he sucked down the last of his Veen.

"Mr. and Mrs. Grande are expecting their first child."

"This is news to me, Vince. And you better be kidding."

"About the idea? I'm not kidding at all," he said seriously. "Right now Mr. and Mrs. Main Street see you and your wife as gods on Mount Olympus. They have trouble relating to you as real people. But that changes when you announce there's a baby on the way. Trust me, all my research shows there's nothing like parenthood to help you connect with the man in the street."

Grande shook his head, struggling to believe what his ears told him he had just heard. "So my wife should get pregnant? That's your great idea?" He waved to Brigitte, who had by now swum underwater to the near end of the lap pool. "Hey, Bree, come on over here for a second. You've got to hear this."

"No, listen," Chandler protested furiously.

But Brigitte had already raised herself onto the pool's ledge, pushed her wet hair back with both hands, and walked toward them in all her nearly naked glory. Chandler's gut begged him to study every square inch of her centerfold body while his brain pleaded with him to keep his job. His brain won. He glued his eyes to her face as she approached the table.

"Vince has an idea for winning the election," Grande told her. "He thinks you need to get pregnant."

"Really?" she laughed. "I work out three hours a day to look good in front of a camera, and you think I should get pregnant and gain 50 pounds?" She put her hands on the table, leaned toward him, and looked him in the eye. "Three words, Vince. Will. Not. Happen. Comprenez?"

"Yes, I understand," he sputtered. "Arch didn't give me a chance to explain what I have in mind."

"Oh, I think I know what you have in mind," she smiled, "if I end up pregnant."

He hoped his face wasn't as red as it felt. "All I meant," he said slowly, "is that **we say** you're pregnant. If we do that now, we have three months before anyone expects you to look pregnant. And we will absolutely pick up at least 10 points along the way."

Grande's face brightened. "Wait a second," he said. "Finish the story. I think I'm getting this."

Chandler nodded and gave his boss a knowing glance. "And then just before the convention we learn that, tragically, Mrs. Grande has suffered a miscarriage."

"And yet," Grande added, "three days later my wife is there at my side, bravely campaigning for the good of our nation."

"Arch, that story will bump up the sympathy vote all the way through November. You will destroy everyone, no question."

"I will not wear maternity clothes," Brigitte announced. "No chance."

"You don't have to wear anything . . . I mean anything special," Chandler said as he began to sweat. "Three months into the pregnancy you don't need maternity clothes."

"Okay, fine," she said. "But what happens when the world finds out I wasn't actually pregnant?"

"Only three people know," Grande replied. "And the three of us will take that secret to our graves."

"Amen," said Vincent.

"Fine, then," Brigitte said sweetly. She kissed her husband on the top of his head. "Just let me know when I'm pregnant."

Both men watched her sway gently toward the pool.

10.

Vincent Chandler's math was way off. He had predicted a 10-point jump in the polls when Brigitte Grande announced her pregnancy. What they had gotten instead was a 17-point leap, and now at the end of March the boss enjoyed a 33-point margin over Lander "Pinocchio" Enfield. Two more Republican candidates had dropped out of the race, aware that the longer they stayed, the dumber they looked.

Riding the crest of this latest wave, Grande stepped to the podium at The Plaza Hotel in Manhattan with Brigitte by his side. They still looked like a god and goddess, but campaign manager Chandler had been right on target. Mr. & Mrs. Main Street were now connecting with Grande in a way they hadn't before. Apple pie, motherhood, and lots of spin. The happy couple stood in the spotlight and waved.

Among the 500 guests seated comfortably in the Grand Ballroom for the pre-cocktail address were Detectives Pete Nazareth and Tara Gimble, who had been handed tickets earlier that day by their boss, Chief Crawford. The tickets, he told them, had arrived by messenger from Mayor Elliott Dortmund's office along with orders for the two detectives to attend. No reason why. Just be there. End of story.

"Any idea how much these tickets cost?" Gimble asked as she and Nazareth settled into their chairs.

"If you mean our two," he said, "I'd say zero. I assume the mayor gets a free ride for events like this, especially from his buddy Archer Grande. But if you mean everyone else's tickets, a thousand each."

"So Grande's campaign picks up $500,000, give or take, for a couple of hours of his time?"

"Ain't life grand?"

"It is for them, I guess. How pregnant is the wife supposed to be?"

"One hundred percent," he deadpanned.

"Wiseass. Let me rephrase: how many months pregnant is she?"

"Just a couple of weeks," Nazareth told her, "according to the press release."

"Since when does a young supermodel take time off to have kids?"

"I'm with you. I really can't imagine her having kids at this point in her life. But from what I hear Grande got a huge bump in the polls after the announcement."

"If I were a cynic . . ."

"Which of course you're not . . ."

"I'd say maybe she got pregnant just to pick up a few votes."

"If so, it worked. On the other hand, maybe they just figured it was time."

"Yeah, maybe. But the timing is flawless, isn't it?"

"No doubt about it."

The crowd cheered wildly as glowing mother-to-be Brigitte left the stage so that her husband could do his thing. And this evening he would do it in spades.

"Ladies and gentlemen, my research team is the best in the business," he bragged, "and I'm going to share with you something I read in the report they gave me this morning. Russia's president, Iran's top ayatollah, and the imbecile god-king who runs North Korea all hope a Democrat wins in November."

The ballroom shook as though a small nuclear device had been detonated. Grande's admirers roared, stomped, and whistled for two minutes before he could finish his thought. This was why they were here.

"And I understand where they're coming from," he told them. "A Democratic president will continue the current administration's policy of . . ." He paused and looked out over the audience. "May I speak frankly?" he asked innocently. More cheering and hooting. "The current administration's policy of kissing our enemies' asses," he shouted.

A minute later Grande was finally able to quiet the crowd, but not for long.

"Well, let me explain my policy. It's simple: our enemies play ball according to our rules, or they get hit over the head with a big goddamn bat." As his fans howled in delight, Grande stretched his arms out to his sides and mimicked his favorite aircraft, the B-52. "Kaboom!" he yelled.

When the cheering finally ended he added, "We've got problems right here at home. In fact, our problems crawl under the fences or jump off the boats every day. And you know who I'm talking about." Yes, the crowd knew . . . and couldn't wait to hear what was coming.

"The Democrats insist we should let all these poor, hard-working illegal immigrants," he said sarcastically, "stay here and live off your tax dollars for the rest of your life . . . and your children's lives . . . and your grandchildren's lives. And the Democrats don't want me saying bad things about what they call *the immigration issue*. Hey, here's news. It's not an *issue*. It's a *cancer*. So this is my simple proposal. It's called GTHB. As in *go the hell back*."

Nazareth and Gimble eyed each other in the midst of all the well-heeled fanatics who together had shelled out half a million dollars to hear Grande's venomous rant this evening. The people around them looked normal, but obviously something was way, way off here.

"Okay, listen," Grande said as he motioned for calm. "We have some bartenders over there who are waiting to fill our glasses. Well, not all of our glasses," he grinned. "Brigitte can't have alcohol for a few months." Much cheering and clapping for his wife, who stood in the front row and waved regally.

"One last comment, and then we drink. Terrorism," he said gravely. "The current occupant of the White House tells us we're doing everything we can. He says we can't do more because the CIA and the DIA and the NSA and all the king's horses and all the king's men don't know where the 50,000 terrorists are hiding over there in the desert. But take a look at this." An image appeared on the huge screen behind him. It was a high-resolution satellite photo taken somewhere above the Middle East.

"You can't see it yet, but keep watching." He clicked the remote, and the image grew larger. He clicked again, then again, then again. By the time he stopped, everyone in the ballroom could clearly see what appeared to be thousands of people milling about the streets of an ancient city.

"I'm not permitted to tell you where this is, but I can tell you who," he nodded. "You have here roughly 7,000 terrorists who live openly and safely in a city located about 13 miles from what my research team has identified as an ISIS training camp." The crowd gasped. "This photo was taken three days ago by *my* research team using *my* satellite. So now you and I know what the president and the joint chiefs and all the spy agencies say they don't know."

The audience finally stopped jeering, and it was time for Grande's finale.

"My friends and fellow Americans," he said, "I've told you before and I'll tell you again, I've got your back. That's my campaign theme, right? So let me translate what that means for terrorists. On my first day in the Oval Office," he roared as he thrust his finger toward the satellite photo behind him, "those 7,000 terrorists will find themselves in a big smoking hole in the sand."

Brigitte rejoined her man onstage as the adoring crowd chanted, whooped, and yelled for more. But it was time for martinis and champagne. Archer Grande had worked enough magic for one night.

Gimble took Nazareth's arm as they walked toward the parking garage after their evening with the rich and crazy.

"I think the guy's off his rocker, Pete. He scares the hell out of me."

"That's because he reminds you of some of the psychos we've put behind bars. Richer and more talented maybe, but definitely unhinged. I'd heard that about him, of course, but you can't fully appreciate it," he said, "until you see the guy work a crowd like that."

"This may sound a little far-fetched," she offered, "but watching him in front of that audience reminded me of the old clips you see on the History Channel about Hitler hypnotizing the Germans before World War II."

"It's not far-fetched at all, Tara. I think he's dangerous. He's a living, breathing monument to hate, and he's not afraid to say things that normal people would keep to themselves. This tells me he's missing a few cards in his deck. And think about it. Tonight he didn't even talk about his idea of having all American Muslims carry special identity cards."

"Adolph Hitler once again," she said. "He doesn't talk like a president, Pete. He talks like a dictator. I'm actually surprised someone hasn't taken a shot at him."

Nazareth looked at her closely and nodded. "I think you've just explained why the mayor sent us there tonight."

"Because someone's planning to take a shot at him?" she asked.

"Maybe, maybe not. But I wouldn't be surprised if we end up babysitting this guy whenever he's in town, which is a lot."

"But he's already got Secret Service protection, and surely he must have his own security people."

"And thank God for that. But if anything happens to him in New York City," Nazareth explained, "the mayor would never hear the end of it. So I'm betting my last dime you and I are going to be attending a lot of Grande's rallies. I hope I'm wrong."

"But you doubt it."

"I do."

"God help us all if this guy gets elected."

"I hear they need experienced detectives in Iceland."

She thought about that. "Too close. Maybe Australia."

He gave her a sympathetic smile. "Even better."

11.

Stone Jackson was hands down the best burger-flipper Elmont Wiggins had ever seen in his 15 years as the restaurant's manager. The guy had great reflexes, excellent eye-hand coordination, and predatory focus. Absolutely nothing distracted Jackson when he was grilling up beef.

So Wiggins was willing to overlook the fact that the young man he called "the Grillin' Fool" ate at least a dozen burgers -- no bun, no cheese, no ketchup -- every day he was on the job. Hell, they threw out a lot more than that anyway, so why mess up a good thing? Besides, this way he wouldn't have to give Jackson a raise. Letting him eat a dozen free burgers was a hell of a lot cheaper than paying him a higher hourly wage.

What Wiggins never noticed was that Jackson routinely switched hands precisely every 10 minutes. He'd flip burgers with his right for 10 minutes, then switch to his left, then go back and forth like that throughout his entire shift. It wasn't the sort of thing most people would pick up unless they had been told to look for it, and no one would have cared anyway. Well, no one except Jackson. He was in training.

The ability to use either hand for complex tasks was something Jackson viewed as essential to his success as a Ranger. Lose the use of one hand in battle, he reasoned, and you'll die unless your other hand is equally adept at handling a knife, gun, or radio. So for the past two months he had begun using both hands for virtually every daily task. He could now flip burgers, brush his teeth, comb his hair, and use his phone equally well with either his right or left hand.

He could also load and fire his rifle lefty if necessary. This was a bit awkward since his bolt-action rifle was configured for a right-handed shooter, but he learned how to make do. In a pinch, he would be able to shoot nearly as well with his left hand as he could with his right. And he had gotten exceptionally good with his right.

Jackson spent almost as much time at the firing range near his apartment as he did flipping burgers, and by late March he was deadly from 200 yards in. At 200 yards he could group 10 shots in a four-inch circle. At 50 yards he generally grouped the shots in a circle the size of a silver dollar. And 50 yards, he figured, would be just about the right distance for his work on Staten Island, since Terrence Goodall's home backed up to the woods. The sex abuser didn't stand a chance.

In addition to firing his rifle every day Jackson continually stepped up his fitness program at the cheapest, grungiest place in town. At Hoke's Gym there were no pretty girls in lavender spandex, no laundered towels folded neatly for the guests, and no fancy machines to do most of the work for you. What you got instead was the smell of sweat, weight racks loaded with massive iron plates, and an all-male clientele that looked like a prison riot waiting to happen.

The regulars had been royally unimpressed when Jackson first walked in. They figured a tall, lean guy like him should be swatting tennis balls at the country club or maybe shooting hoops at the playground. But after watching him bench press 400 pounds and squat 600, they all nodded to him respectfully and stayed out of his way. No one knew the guy in the brown military T-shirt, but everyone knew not to screw with him.

One element of Jackson's training had been a failure, however. After disposing of Marlin Draper in Sumter National Forest he had wisely steered clear of the local woods. The police were still operating on the theory that Draper had slipped on a rock, struck his head, and drowned. These things do happen, they said. But if Jackson got caught trespassing on someone else's land, perhaps the police would begin connecting the dots in a whole new direction. And he didn't need that, especially since his time in South Carolina was winding down. He was nearly ready to go home. All he needed was a bit of serious field training.

Before setting out for Sassafras Mountain, where he would test his hunting and survival skills in snow, ice, and sub-freezing temperatures, he called home to check in with his mother. He was surprised when Mrs. Carmody, the next-door neighbor, answered the phone. The old woman was sorry to tell him that his mother had died a week earlier.

"I tried getting hold of you, Stone," she cried softly, "but all I could find was an old phone number your Mom had, and that was just a pay phone at some Army base. The person I spoke with there said he didn't know you."

"Yeah, Mom knew that I've been away on a special assignment," he told her, "and couldn't give her a phone number. So I've been calling her once a week. I had no idea she was sick." In fact he was sorry, but not especially surprised, to learn that she had died a week earlier. You can only drink so many alcohol-and-barbiturate cocktails before your body decides it's had enough.

"Well, it was a heart attack, Stone. She was buried last week next to your father. I'm awfully sorry you didn't know," she told him. "I'm at the house right now cleaning out the fridge."

"I really appreciate that, Mrs. Carmody," he said. "And I appreciate your trying to get hold of me. But my duty location is classified, and there's no way you could have tracked me down."

"I never liked the Army because of things like that. Your family should always be able to reach you if there's an emergency. I remember the same thing happened about 20 years ago with my cousin Bessie's son," she continued, "and the whole family was a mess about it."

He was now getting more information than he needed, so he cut the conversation short. "The lieutenant is calling for me, Mrs. Carmody. The operation I'm involved in right now should be over in a few weeks, and I'll be able to get home right after that. In the meantime, can I call you to check on things now and then, just in case you need me?"

"Of course, Stone. You call anytime you want. And when you get here you'll find a brown envelope on the kitchen table," she said. "A few years ago your Mom gave me a copy of her will, and last week I called the attorney who wrote it for her. She left everything to you, of course, and the attorney is working on all the necessary papers."

"You're terrific, Mrs. Carmody." He wrote down her number and hung up. So now he was officially alone in the world. Odd feeling. But he figured as long as he had his rifle and a little money, he'd be okay. So he continued packing for what he viewed as his "mountain ranger" test.

Early the next morning he drove an hour and a half northwest to Table Rock State Park near the town of Rocky Bottom on the North Carolina border. He left his car in an empty parking lot, strapped on his backpack, and began the 10-mile hike to Sassafras Mountain, at 3,500 feet the highest point in South Carolina. The morning was a touch chillier than he had expected: 22 degrees and windy. But since he carried 55 pounds on his back, and since one grueling stretch of the trail rose more than 2,000 feet in the space of three miles, he knew that staying warm would not be a problem.

His problem was the snow that had collected in the area throughout the winter. Sassafras Mountain's wilderness offered spectacular scenery in all directions: distant peaks, massive rocky outcroppings, and even an impressive waterfall whose spray had coated nearby trees with thick layers of ice. But one wrong step could easily send him plunging 50 feet into the middle of nowhere.

Aside from the slippery conditions Jackson was very much in control. His winter combat boots would keep his feet dry and warm despite the snow cover, and he wore multiple layers of expedition-grade winter clothing from head to toe. Finally, in his backpack he carried all the shelter he would need: a sturdy one-man tent, a down sleeping bag rated to 30 below, and an inflatable down-filled sleeping pad with a built-in pump. The three items accounted for only seven pounds in his backpack, leaving plenty of room for food, clothing, and necessary hardware.

He carried the rifle -- loaded, naturally -- in a waterproof case slung over his shoulder. The case would keep the rifle safe and dry no matter how bad the weather. Unfortunately, it would also prevent him from firing as quickly as he might want. There was really no way around this trade-off. If he needed instant weaponry, he would have to reach for the Buck knife on his belt.

After three hours of rugged hiking, much of it off-trail so that he could test his abilities with the Army-surplus compass, he was sitting on a rock seven miles from the starting point enjoying a snack of beef jerky, peanuts, and a few pieces of dark chocolate. Since he was making good time he decided to boil some snow for drinking. This would allow him to save the bottled water in case he really needed it. He unpacked the small camping stove, attached it to one of the three 16-ounce propane cylinders he carried, and was about to click the matchless ignition when he heard an ugly commotion somewhere off to his right.

The rifle was out of its case and ready in Jackson's hands within 30 seconds. He rose slowly and moved stealthily through the thick woods toward the sound. After traveling 40 yards through glistening snow that in some places was more than a foot deep he looked out over a clearing, in the middle of which were three wild turkeys whose raspy, metallic calls were eerily unnatural in the otherwise quiet forest.

No point in beating himself up for not having recognized the sound. After all, he had never been a hunter as a kid on Staten Island, and he had never fired his rifle at anything other than a paper target. But here was his first opportunity. The turkeys were so busy making their awful noise they failed to notice the intruder with the rifle.

Leaning hard against an oak trunk to help steady his aim, Jackson put the crosshairs on the middle of the largest bird, held his breath to minimize his body's movement, and gently squeezed the trigger. The 5.56 mm military round exited the Mossberg's 20-inch barrel at 2,800 feet per second and hit the turkey with more than four times the force of a Smith & Wesson .38-caliber revolver. Two of the turkeys squawked into the woods. The third disappeared in a red mist.

Jackson had just gotten his first valuable real-world lesson in something known as *terminal ballistics*, the science of how a bullet works its deadly magic on a flesh-and-blood target. He had heard the process likened to a rock being placed in a bucket of water. If you lower the rock gently, the water barely moves. But if you throw the rock as hard as you can, the water moves violently outward. In the turkey's case the force generated by the well-placed round created an internal shock wave that caused the bird to explode.

While this might not be the ideal outcome for most hunters, it was highly pleasing to Jackson, who smiled to think of Terrence Goodall's head vanishing from his shoulders. That's what all this training was about in the first place: eliminating the pedophile who had turned a young boy's life upside down. Had the guy preyed upon other neighborhood kids? Jackson assumed so, but it wasn't the sort of thing he and his friends ever talked about. Either way, the world would be vastly better without Goodall in it.

Two hours later Jackson stood alone at the summit in a cruel north wind and admired the Blue Ridge Mountains of North Carolina in the distance. He also admired his own effort. Sweat poured off his forehead, and his thighs were on fire from the fast climb, but he had mastered Sassafras Mountain under miserable conditions. This had been a man's test, and he gave himself an A+. For most of the hike he had stayed off the marked trail and taken whatever looked to be the most isolated and most treacherous route to the top. When your life is in your own hands like this, you grow tough or die. And he didn't plan to die.

He looked at his watch and set a new goal for himself. For exactly one hour and 15 minutes he would hike off-trail down the mountain, and wherever he was at that point is where he would make camp for the night. This seemed to him a challenge worthy of a Ranger. It was the sort of dangerously arbitrary situation that combat could throw at you and that a well-trained man could take in stride. So he set his course and took off through the woods.

He traveled in a straight line the whole way. When he encountered a fallen tree, he went over or under it, never around. He waded through icy streams, pushed his way through frozen thickets, and slid down perilous rock walls. And he studied the snow, alert for signs of other hikers. But all he saw were animal tracks. The survivalist books he had been reading over the past two months helped him identify the most common prints in the snow: lots of deer, a few rabbits, and a raccoon or two. Since he was eager to test his marksmanship on live targets, he carried the rifle out of its case now, pointed toward the ground but ready for action.

An hour and fifteen minutes later he half walked, half slid down an especially steep snow-covered slope that led to a small clearing that was growing dark in the late afternoon. This was it. Home for the night. As he began pushing the tent stakes deep into the snow he noticed the large tracks off to his left. From 10 feet away they appeared to be boot prints, and he was hugely surprised to think that other hikers had recently been in this remote section of the woods. Then he walked closer.

Animal tracks. He carefully placed his right foot over the largest of the depressions, and his stomach jumped when he saw that the print overlapped his boot in every direction. From the obvious claw marks at the print's front edge he could tell it had been made by a large black bear, and judging from the number of prints in the clearing he assumed this was a spot the animal visited frequently. Common sense immediately told him to find another campsite, and fast. But running in fear wasn't something a Ranger could do. On the contrary, the very word *fear* needed to be ripped from his vocabulary if he was going to make his mark in this world.

He finished prepping his camp.

Night had fallen by the time he set up the tent, inflated his insulating mat, and laid out the down sleeping bag. The process had taken too long, and he knew it. He needed to work on this. But at the moment what he needed most was a fire, so he cleared the snow from a three-foot circle, ringed it with rocks, and laid some logs on a bed of twigs and branches. Within a few minutes the campfire's glow lit up the snowy woods in every direction, a signal that scout sniper Stone Jackson controlled the area.

After a reasonably filling meal of beef stroganoff and cheesecake -- both made by adding boiled snow to packets of freeze-dried mix -- he sat by the campfire and read. His well-worn *Ranger Handbook* wasn't on the list tonight. What he studied instead was *Stalking North American Wildlife,* a paperback he had bought for less than a buck online but that had become a permanent part of his field gear. Written by J.B. "Grizzly" Watts and based largely on the author's own experiences in the American wilderness, the book offered startlingly graphic insights into how the stalker often becomes the stalked. Example: in February of 2009 inside Yellowstone National Park an ambitious but unarmed wildlife photographer tracked a 165-pound male cougar to its den, where the man's gnawed bones were found two months later.

The section on black bears most definitely held Jackson's attention because much of what he had heard about the creatures was all wrong. For instance, curling up in a ball and lying still if attacked works only with a bear whose behavior is defensive, as it might be with a mother bear protecting her cubs. If the bear thinks you're food and goes on the offensive, however, lying still on the ground just gets you eaten faster. What you need to do is fight back and pray hard.

Running, Jackson also learned, doesn't help if you're trying to elude a black bear, since it has a top speed of about 30 miles per hour despite its bulk, which can be as much as 600 pounds. And climbing a tree is a seriously dumb idea, since black bears enjoy climbing trees and frequently hang out in them to relax. What you need to do, Watts advised, is avoid all contact with black bears, and the best way to do that is to prevent them from smelling any food you might have with you. Black bears have an incredible sense of smell, and a hungry bear will sniff out dinner every time.

Jackson found the information about the bear's sense of smell rather unsettling, since he had just finished eating his freeze-dried beef stroganoff. Was the meaty odor still wafting through the forest, luring the bear toward the campsite? Was there anything else in the backpack that might attract the animal? How far from the tent should he hang his food sack before turning in tonight?

Above all, was the rifle's safety off? Answer: yes, absolutely.

By 10:30 Jackson had read all he needed for one night, and the sleeping bag called to him. After throwing a few more logs on the fire, he slipped into the tent and fell asleep with the rifle at his side. He had proven his worth today. What's more, he had done it on his own. No drill sergeants, no Mickey Mouse, no wasted effort. He had learned by doing.

When he jolted awake shortly after 1:00 a.m. he couldn't identify the muffled sound outside his tent. But something was most certainly out there, and it seemed to be messing with his gear. He locked his powerful right hand on the rifle stock and with his left quietly drew aside the door flap. The campfire was now nothing more than a pit of glowing embers, so his eyes adjusted quickly to the darkness. As he slipped his finger over the trigger and steadied the barrel with his left hand, he saw the man cutting the food sack from the tree branch.

"If you move," Jackson told him, "I'll spray your guts all over that tree."

"Hey, man, don't shoot," the guy said while raising both hands high in the air. "I thought you were my friend, Barton. I was just messin' around."

"The only mess here will be you if you do anything I don't like."

"Hey, man, it's okay. I was just having some fun. I thought you were someone else is all."

Jackson quickly worked the gun in all directions, fearful the guy had accomplices. But, no, it was just the two of them, and only one held a rifle.

"Keep your hands up high and come toward me very slowly," he said. The guy eyed the rifle and did as he was told. He heard the ice in Jackson's voice.

"Everything's cool. I'm sorry I startled you. I thought you were someone else. Hey, my name's Jethro."

When the guy was about 10 feet away Jackson ordered him to his knees near the fire pit.

"Pick up a couple of those logs, Jethro, and throw them on the fire."

"Sure, no problem." The wood hissed as a bit of snow hit the fire, and in a few seconds the logs burst into flame. "Yeah, that feels great."

Jackson pointed the rifle at the center of Jethro's chest. "What won't feel great is a 5.56 NATO round ripping through you. So I'm going to ask you a very simple question, and if I think you're lying, you die. Do you understand?"

The guy swallowed hard and nodded. "Yeah, sure. I understand."

"Why did you come here? And if you tell me you were just messing with one of your friends, it'll be the last thing you ever say."

Jethro quickly considered his options, then decided he had nothing to lose by telling the truth. "I come up here sometimes to rip off campers."

"How did you know I was here?" Jackson asked.

"I saw a car in the base parking lot, and I drove up the main road to check things out. I saw you heading off the summit in this direction."

"How did you find my camp?"

"Your tent is almost right on top of a trail that runs across the mountain," he said. "I drove back up here around midnight and saw your fire. So I waited and then followed the trail here."

"You do this often?"

"Not so much in the winter," he said, "but a lot in the spring and summer."

"And what kinds of things do you rip off?"

"Anything I can find. Mostly cameras, cell phones, camping gear. Sometimes wallets."

"And you thought I might leave all my gear outside the tent for some asshole like you to steal?" Jackson asked with a nasty edge to his voice.

"Hey, man, I'm just trying to make a buck, you know? It's nothing personal."

"But you were going to steal my food, right? That's not personal?"

Jethro knew there was no right answer to this last question, so he kept his mouth shut.

"Crawl over there and get the food sack." Jackson ordered, "Then bring it back here and toss it to me." Jethro did so as quickly as he could.

Jackson rummaged through the food sack until he found what he was after. "Now lie flat on your stomach with your hands at your sides," he said. He walked over and put the muzzle of his rifle against Jethro's head and told him not to move. Using his left hand and his teeth, Jackson tore open a packet of peanut butter and spread it all over the back of the guy's ski jacket. Then he did the same with a packet of strawberry jelly.

"You wanted my food, and now you've got my food all over your nice ski jacket. How's that, Jethro?"

"That's fine, man. I deserved it. No problem."

"Good. I'm glad to hear that. Now get up and start walking."

Jethro stood and turned in the direction of the main access road, where his car waited.

"Not that way," Jackson said. He pointed the barrel of his gun in the opposite direction.

"Man, it'll take me all night to get out of here if I go that way," the guy complained.

"You think I care?"

"No, I guess not."

"Then here's the deal," Jackson told him. "I'm going to follow you down the trail for a while to make sure you're on your way. If you say anything, I shoot you. If you stop walking, I shoot you. If you look back, I shoot you. Nod once if you understand what I just said."

Jethro nodded and began trudging through the heavy snow. In the low light he didn't notice the bear tracks beneath his feet as he left the clearing and entered the dense night woods. Jackson followed for 30 yards, then stopped and watched the guy disappear in the dark. When he was convinced Jethro had kept walking, he returned to the campsite and warmed himself by the fire.

Twenty minutes later he heard agonized screams in the distance. Black bears generally forage at night, and the hungry 400-pounder that had detected the sweet smell of Jethro's ski jacket wasted no time in tracking down dinner. Jackson smiled and crawled back into his sleeping bag for the night. According to *Stalking North American Wildlife*, he had nothing to fear from a well-fed bear.

The next morning he rose at dawn, ate a hot breakfast, then hiked down the mountain to his car. His time in South Carolina had come to a successful end, and in a few days he would resume his field training inside the Staten Island Greenbelt.

Scout sniper Stone Jackson was on his way home.

12.

"How in the hell does an ultra-liberal, cop-hating mayor become best buddies with an arch-conservative, racist, gun-crazy Republican presidential candidate?"

"The real answer is it doesn't matter, Pete," Chief Crawford told Nazareth, who had just learned he and partner Tara Gimble were going to help oversee security for Archer Grande. "The mayor called me personally -- something he has never done before -- and said this belongs to you and Tara. But since you're interested, I'll tell you that Mr. Mayor and Mr. Lunatic Fringe went through prep school together and are business partners on a couple of land deals. That's as much as I know."

"Grande has Secret Service protection, for crying out loud."

"Right. But he also now has credible death threats from unnamed loonies who swear they'll kill him if he campaigns in New York City," Crawford said, "and Mayor Dortmund doesn't want that to happen."

"Because maybe he's hoping for some cushy, useless job in Washington if Grande gets elected," Nazareth sneered.

"Maybe. But he already has a cushy, useless job. I think he just wants to avoid the huge black eye of having a presidential candidate shot on his watch. That would look bad on TV."

"Well, gee, we don't want him looking bad on TV, do we?"

"Hey, Pete, you know I don't care how he looks," the chief said as he poured himself another coffee from the old pot behind his desk. "I just don't want him calling me anymore."

A few minutes later Nazareth broke the news to his partner, who wasn't pleased that an otherwise pleasant April morning had been spoiled by the taint of politics.

"So we're supposed to assess credible death threats against Grande?" she said, clearly annoyed. "That's the assignment the mayor has just dumped on us?"

"Right you are."

"He knows we work homicides, right? So he decides we should be intelligence experts instead?" She didn't want to be guilty of shooting the messenger, especially since she loved him, but she needed to let off some steam. "Maybe he'd like the Jets quarterback to pitch for the Yankees this season."

"Might not be a bad idea, actually," he grinned. "But look at the bright side, Tara. It could've been much worse. He could have assigned us to Grande's security detail, which he didn't do,"

"And thank God for that. I couldn't be around that self-satisfied hatemonger every day." She shook her head. "I'd probably shoot him myself."

They spent the next two hours slogging through a mind-numbing list of allegedly credible death threats that an aide to some useless paper-pusher had compiled and faxed to Chief Crawford.

"Whoever put this together is either really stupid," Gimble said in disgust, "or high on something. Those are your two choices, Pete."

"I pick stupid. Listen to this one. *Woman in deli heard man say Archer Grande should be fitted for cement shoes.*"

"And?"

"And nothing. That's the whole thing," Nazareth laughed. "Some nitwit in City Hall thinks we should visit every deli in the City and find a woman who thinks Grande is a jerk."

"Which he is."

"Of course."

Not all of the items on the list were laughers, however. At the other end of the spectrum were threats like the one that had been phoned to Grande's campaign headquarters early in the week on a recorded line: *Next time Archer Grande addresses a rally in New York City will be the last. He wears a bullseye on his forehead.* Nazareth and Gimble couldn't begin to imagine how long it might take to track down just one threat of this sort. Yes, they had a clear recording of someone's voice. But had the caller been dumb enough not to use a disposable cell phone? Unlikely. So that meant they had eight and a half million suspects if the caller lived in New York City. If, on the other hand, the caller lived outside the City, they had several hundred million suspects.

Nevertheless, Mayor Dortmund demanded what he termed "a crystal-clear plan of attack" by the end of the day.

"You want to hear my plan, Pete?" Gimble asked.

"We're not going to shoot the mayor, Tara. Absolutely out of the question," he joked, "even if we'd be doing the City a favor."

"No, that wasn't my idea, though it has some appeal. Dortmund is a mindless bureaucrat, so we give him a mindlessly bureaucratic written summary of what we intend to do," she explained. "We *delineate tactics, prioritize actionable threats, coordinate the deployment of available resources,* and generally mutilate the language until no one has any idea what we've said."

"Tell him a lot of nothing . . . but in terms that will satisfy him."

"That's the plan. We follow up on the few legitimate leads we've got while burying him with daily written updates," she said. "After two days he'll forget all about us and go back to doing whatever it is he does all day."

"You mean nothing?" Nazareth grinned.

"Working on his reelection isn't nothing, Peter Nazareth. Please show some respect."

"I do apologize, Tara Gimble. How about if I go over this list again and pick off a few *actionable* death threats while you *address, assess,* and *digress* in our first report to Dortmund?"

"Sounds like a plan," she smiled. "But I expect to get paid by the word."

By the end of the day Nazareth had zeroed in on eight reported death threats he believed could actually be investigated, while Gimble had crafted a seven-page, single-spaced analysis of their "plan of attack." Chief Crawford was delighted.

"I have no idea what this says, Tara, but it's great. Sounds like something the mayor might have written, actually."

"We'll make sure he gets an update just like it every day," she told him. "I'll change a few words ending in *ize* or *eze* and add a few new high-sounding, incomprehensible terms, and we should be good. Won't take more than 15 minutes a day, I'd guess."

"Great. And what about actual threats? Do you see anything real in that pile of crap he sent over?"

"I think so," Nazareth nodded. "The most vicious stuff has been posted online by a group calling itself American Vigil, so that's where we'll begin. I don't know anything about the group, but the language is scary. Tara and I will pay them a visit in Brooklyn tomorrow morning."

"If you need back-up, take it," Crawford told him.

"We'll check things out first. No sense in calling in the cavalry before we know more about the organization."

"Okay, Pete. But as usual you've got whatever resources you need."

"Thanks for that. We'll keep you posted."

At 9:30 the next morning the two detectives sat in their unmarked car outside the long-abandoned Red Hook Grain Terminal in Brooklyn and felt extremely fortunate to have gotten the recent Israeli urban warfare training under their belts. The air was rich with the odor of rot, oil, and dead fish from the Gowanus Canal, one of the most polluted bodies of water on the planet, and the terminal itself was even worse. Twelve stories high and more than 400 feet long, the building was an outrageous monument to decay, a breeding ground for rats, black mold, and menace. The place definitely looked like a war zone.

"We've got the right address?" Nazareth asked.

"This is absolutely the address that's been posted by American Vigil," she said, "but it's hard to imagine anyone actually living or working in there."

"On the other hand, this is the sort of place where an outfit like American Vigil belongs, isn't it?"

According to its online rants American Vigil aimed to "cleanse America of those whose preaching serves to undermine personal freedoms." And at the top of the organization's list of evildoers was Archer Grande, the man American Vigil had tagged as "the country's #1 threat to democracy." This sort of criticism was protected, to a certain point, by the Constitution. American Vigil stepped over the line when its reputed leader, Commandant Lincoln Harper, wrote that Archer Grande would be dead before June.

The detectives scanned the massive building and thought back on the lessons learned in Israel. Snipers on rooftops. Lookouts in windows. Booby-trapped doorways. The grain terminal offered unlimited potential for ambush. But before they could decide whether to enter alone or call for back-up, someone yelled from behind them.

"Hey, you two. This is private property." A 68-year-old heavyset guy in a gray security guard's uniform walked up to them with his hand resting on the grip of his revolver.

"NYPD," Nazareth told him as he and Gimble showed their shields.

"Ah, good guys," the man smiled. "We never get good guys down here. I'm Ray Watkins, NYPD retired. Fifteen years now."

Nazareth and Gimble introduced themselves and told Watkins why they had come.

"I pass by here maybe 10 times a day," Watkins said, "and I've never seen anyone but the usual characters -- graffiti artists, vandals, crack addicts, and such. If someone is actually living in there, I've never seen him."

"But it wouldn't take much for someone to stay out of sight," Gimble said. "If you don't actually go through the building, it's possible someone has set up camp in there."

"Yeah, for sure. And there's no way in hell I ever go in there, believe me. I took this job to pay for trips that my wife and I take, not to cover funeral expenses."

"Do you work night shifts here?" Nazareth asked.

"Not many, but some. If I have to cover for one of the other guys I'll do a night shift now and then."

"And you've never seen a light on inside at night?"

"Nope, never. But I only see this side of the building at night," Watkins told him. "Please don't repeat that, detective. I'm supposed to walk the entire perimeter. But I'm not doing that at night by myself, even when I'm carrying. Life's short enough."

"I'm with you," Nazareth nodded. "So if someone is hiding out in there, he's keeping the light low and stays on the other side of the building."

"Around here anything is possible, detective, but I really can't imagine anyone living in that wreck." The words were barely out of Watkins' mouth when Gimble saw someone at a window on the building's third floor.

"Behind the car," she yelled. "Possible shooter." All three of them saw the figure at the grain terminal's broken window. Whoever it was saw the commotion outside and promptly disappeared.

"All right," Nazareth told the others, "enough of this. I'm going to get some back-up here. We have no idea how many people are in there or whether they're armed." He was about to make the call when someone reappeared at the building's window waving a sheet of white paper back and forth.

"What the hell's that supposed to mean?" Watkins asked.

"Could mean anything," Nazareth answered, "but I'm guessing it's supposed to be a white flag." He thought for a moment then said, "You two stay behind the car while I drive up closer to the building."

"Not a good idea, Pete," Gimble argued. "If he's got a rifle up there, you're finished."

"I think I'm okay. But you two keep your weapons handy in case I'm wrong."

"Let's just get some help, Pete. We don't need to do this alone," she pleaded.

"I don't want a dozen cops here for no reason, Tara. Just be ready to shoot if this goes wrong." She shook her head and drew her gun.

Nazareth slipped into the driver's seat and slowly pulled within 50 feet of the building while Gimble and Watkins crouched behind the vehicle. As they got closer the young guy at the window began calling to them. "We're coming out. Don't shoot."

Two minutes later 19-year-old Benny Liotta and his 20-year-old girlfriend Mirabel Ciccone walked out of a side door with their hands held high. In Liotta's right hand was a thin laptop computer that Nazareth ordered him to place on the ground before moving forward. Gimble, meanwhile, scanned the windows above, worried they were all being set up for the kind of attack they had experienced in the Israeli desert. But the attack never came.

Benny "Commandant Harper" Liotta and Mirabel Ciccone were C-minus community college students who had decided to dabble in revolutionary politics by creating American Vigil, of which they were the only members. A smattering of online posts indicated the organization's blog might have a few sympathetic readers, but that's where it ended. As for the "commandant" and his girlfriend, they both cried hysterically when Nazareth told them they were being arrested for making terroristic threats, a class D felony punishable by up to seven years in prison.

Gimble caught her partner's eye and motioned for a side discussion.

"Can you watch these two for a moment?" Nazareth asked Watkins.

"You bet, detective." He kept his hand near his gun, but Liotta and Ciccone weren't thinking about moving.

"Real terrorists don't cry this hard, Pete," she said softly.

"Meaning you'd like to cut them some slack?"

"Trespassing is a misdemeanor, but it has real consequences. It's on their records, right? But they don't face prison time."

"How do we know just by looking at them that they don't really want to kill Archer Grande?" he asked. "What do we say two months from now if one of them puts a bullet in the guy's head?"

"Do you think that's likely?"

"Not really."

"Do you think it's even possible?"

"Judging from the volume of tears I'd say no."

"So then?"

"Fine. Trespassing it is."

A few minutes later Liotta and Ciccone were in the custody of officers from the 76th Precinct, and the detectives were on their way back to Manhattan.

"You know," Nazareth said, "somewhere in New York City someone has probably just been murdered while you and I were out here playing hide-and-seek with two rebellious adolescents who are threats only to themselves. When did we sign up for this?"

"We didn't. We just got lucky," she laughed. "We're the Dynamic Duo, Pete. We can do anything."

"Well, right now we're wasting our time. Today American Vigil, tomorrow more of the same, I bet."

"The pay's the same as it was yesterday, Pete," she said calmly.

"But the job satisfaction has dropped to zero. You and I have better things to do with our time." He sat quietly for a few minutes. "Since you're the bleeding heart who wanted to cut the bad guys some slack today, pizza's on you tonight."

"You're right. It's the least I can do after going soft on those two hardened criminals."

"And make sure you write this up big for the mayor's report, will you?"

"We were superheroes, Pete. Archer Grande can sleep soundly tonight."

13.

Terrence Goodall sat out back on the raised cedar deck and drained his first Bud of the day. Something about the warm April morning made the brew taste especially good, but he counseled himself to wait another 22 minutes before sucking down another. His long-standing rule was only one beer before noon.

Aw, what the hell. A day like this and a man can't relax in his own home and enjoy a couple of cold ones before noon? The cardinals called to each other deep in the woods, clusters of golden daffodils bloomed along the rock garden, and the spring air was so exhilarating that for just a moment he was mildly dizzy. He reached into the cooler and pulled out an ice-cold can.

The years had taken a toll on him. He carried far too much weight on his 5-9 frame, and his bloated, jowly face and scraggly beard made him look older than his 64 years. His hair was still more brown than gray but desperately needed to be washed and cut. Goodall could easily have passed for homeless had he not lived in what was still one of the nicest homes on the block.

But moments like this one invariably carried him back to the good times, when everyone in the neighborhood, kids and parents alike, called hello to Coach T at the beginning of a new baseball season. All the parents, Aggie Jackson among them, wanted to get their kids on his team because he always had a fine won-lost record and genuinely liked his players. Of course they didn't know, though some later suspected, that Coach T did more than like a few of his players.

He was deeply gratified that none of the boys he'd molested over the years had ever accused him, much less testified against him. Twenty-eight kids and not one squealer! Surely that counted for something. He had chosen wisely among his flock, preying upon either the weakest ones who could be easily intimidated or the sad ones -- especially the fatherless, like Stone Jackson -- who seemed starved for affection. If he could do it all over again the only thing he would change about that period of his life was the online child-porn group that had led to his arrest. Why the hell had he hooked up with those losers anyway when he had the real thing? Why had he gone for the pictures and videos on top of everything else?

No good answer for that. Just one of those crazy things. Yes, given the chance to start fresh he would forget about the pictures, but he would most definitely continue with the young neighborhood boys. He could have kept that good thing going for the rest of his life, he figured. And now he was out of business except when he traveled abroad, which he did as often as his bank account would allow.

Those damned pictures!

His wife had filed for divorce within a week of his plea bargain. The D.A. might have been satisfied that Goodall's testimony would lead to the convictions of a dozen other kiddie-porn dirtbags, but Roselyn Goodall wasn't. She didn't want to spend another day under the same roof much less a lifetime. Had she suspected something was a bit off about him? Maybe, maybe not. There were little things now and then -- a word, a look, a gesture -- but nothing that had prepared her for his arrest. Her husband and the father of her two daughters was on page one, guilty of possessing child pornography! How in the hell does that happen?

She would never know how much worse it had actually been because her daughters never said a word about Daddy's excessive interest in them. One lived in Costa Rica now, the other in Spokane. Neither would ever be returning to Staten Island. They had minimal contact with their mother, whom they blamed for not seeing what was going on, and none at all with each other or dear old Dad. With enough therapy they might at some distant point put the terrible nightmares behind them.

And of course Roselyn never knew what her husband had been up to with the neighborhood boys. No one did. Well, Coach T and his chosen few did, but they weren't talking. People on the block had shunned both Terrence and Roselyn once news of the arrest hit the *Staten Island Advance,* and that was more than she could take since she had done nothing wrong. So one day she packed three large suitcases and drove off, leaving her attorney to work out a one-time cash payment for her share of the house.

For several weeks following Goodall's arrest and conviction many, though not all, of the parents whose boys had played for Coach T asked their kids whether they had been molested. All the kids denied it, whether out of embarrassment or fear. Only one parent, Patty Underwood, kept hammering away at the issue even after her son Robbie had insisted Coach T was a great guy. For a time she was viewed as the local champion of children's rights and the go-to person whenever the press needed a powerful quote relating to the abuse of children.

She had done her homework meticulously and always kept the key facts on the tip of her tongue. In a brief series of well-attended community meetings she explained that in 89% of child sex-abuse cases the molester is someone known to the children, often a caregiver, family acquaintance, or family member. She told them that the average pedophile molests an astonishing 260 victims during his lifetime. And she stunned them with the news that 90% of convicted pedophiles get arrested for the same crime once out of prison.

But in time even her friends grew weary of the drumbeat of dreary facts and urged her to move on. The neighborhood kids were getting older, they told her, and didn't want to talk about Coach T anymore. Besides, Coach T was no longer coaching. He was just the oddball recluse who lived alone down the street and apparently continued to muddle along with his insurance business. So Patty Underwood finally dropped the subject. Even she had to agree that everyone had forgotten all about Terrence Goodall.

The sun warmed his face and his sagging bare chest as he leaned back against the cushioned lounge chair and looked across the deck toward the woods. Those woods are what had drawn him here in the first place. He remembered how he and Roselyn had first walked the empty lot after a January snowfall and fantasized about the home they would build for their future family. The oaks and pines were heavy with snow that day, and what surrounded them was, as Robert Frost had once said, lovely, dark, and deep. In time they would have neighbors on both sides -- not too close, though -- but the Greenbelt forest behind them would forever be protected.

His pleasant daydream was interrupted by the snapping of a branch somewhere in the underbrush, and he immediately felt goosebumps rise on his arms. He walked to the railing and studied the trees. Nothing moved except leaves in the breeze. But he had heard it. It was there. Part of him wanted to walk to the woods and investigate while the rest of him, most of him, wanted to go into the house and lock the door.

A moment later he jumped back and nearly fell over the lounge chair as two large deer bolted from the thicket and ran toward the house. "Son of a bitch," he screamed as his heart began racing. He exhaled deeply. "Scared the piss out of me."

The reaction surprised and embarrassed him. Since when was he afraid of a sound in the woods? He studied his hands, which shook uncontrollably.

"Pull it together, man," he told himself as the deer ran off. At 11:57 he opened the cooler for his third Bud of the day.

14.

On April 14th at precisely 5:00 a.m. Stone Jackson commenced phase two of his training. After downing a glass of milk with three raw eggs stirred into it, he strapped on his Buck knife, slung a day pack over his shoulders, and walked out the back door and into the Staten Island Greenbelt. He was a happy man, but one day soon he would be even happier. His date with Terrence Goodall was approaching.

A week ago after a long drive up from South Carolina he had entered the family home for the first time in months. It was his now. Tattered, silent, but his. He thought about his mother when he dumped all her clothes, knickknacks, and prescription bottles into black lawn bags and put them to the curb. She had been a good person, sure, but he still wondered how she couldn't have known about what Coach T was doing. Had she or hadn't she? Either way he remained bitter. She had put him in the care of a monster and never thought to ask whether everything was okay. Was it ignorance or acceptance? Had she worried more about that damn job than her own son?

Once the last of her belongings had been set out for the trash pick-up he washed the floors. Mrs. Carmody had cleaned out the fridge and straightened up the kitchen, but the entire house needed some serious attention before he could feel comfortable. He spent a long day getting the place inspection-ready, and it looked as good as it was going to until he got around to painting. Now and then he was interrupted by old neighborhood friends who stopped by when they saw his car in the driveway. He told them Army life had been amazing but that he had been forced to leave when they discovered a problem with one of his heart valves. Everyone was sorry for that and wished him well.

He, on the other hand, was sorry for nothing. Three days earlier he had landed a part-time job as a bank teller -- 20 hours a week, $17 an hour. His mother had left slightly more than $9,000 in her bank account. And the house was all his. A Ranger could be gloriously happy with a hell of a lot less.

So his spirits were high as he set out on a Saturday morning for a hike he figured would cover about nine miles through the Greenbelt. The route he had mapped out would take him first through Blood Root Valley, named for the small bloodroot plant whose delicate white flowers blossomed there each spring. After that he would go east to High Rock Park, then north into Pouch Scout Camp, and finally up to Deere Park where the Greenbelt met the Staten Island Expressway, an ugly parking lot of a highway anchored by the Goethals Bridge on one end and the Verrazano-Narrows Bridge on the other. His primary goal was to reconnect with the terrain because it had been years since he and his friends had roamed these woods. But he also wanted to practice being invisible, since stealth would be a critical component of his upcoming live-fire missions. He would steer well clear of homes and businesses and do his best to avoid other hikers.

Despite the early hour Blood Root Valley was wide awake by the time Jackson arrived. Squirrels, rabbits, and snakes skittered through the woods, marshes, and meadows while a red-shouldered hawk glided elegantly overhead, scanning the ground for a warm meal. He heard cars in the distance but saw no one on the trails. So far so good.

As he approached Manor Road, a well-used thoroughfare that ran north-south through the Greenbelt, he prepared for his first important brush with civilization. He crouched low as he entered a thicket alongside the road and hid there, utterly motionless, while he studied the landscape in all directions. Nothing but an occasional car. After a few minutes of watching he was able to gauge when a vehicle traveling at the typical rate of speed was about to enter his field of vision. He waited, listened, and finally sprang from the bushes and ran across the road back into the forest. Again he crouched low and listened. Nothing. He was safe.

Today was merely a field exercise, a game. In time, though, his very survival could depend upon remaining hidden in the wilderness, so he was deadly serious about the challenge. His mission was to spend half a day in the woods without being spotted, and he didn't intend to fail the test.

Things got riskier as he entered the 143-acre Pouch Scout Camp at the heart of the Greenbelt since the place was in use throughout the year. He had no way of knowing whether any scouts were camping there this weekend, so he moved gently among the trees and shrubs, listening for unnatural sounds. Nothing. When he walked the shoreline of Ohrbach Lake he heard fish breaking the surface of the water but saw no one. He was alone.

But as he began walking up a steep incline at the northern edge of the lake he was jolted by voices from somewhere over the hill ahead of him. Loud but muffled. He slipped into a stand of tall shrubs and waited. Less than 15 seconds later three young guys, teenagers he thought, flew down the hill on their mountain bikes, bouncing wildly over the tree roots that covered the trail and jumping over a pair of tree trunks that had fallen during the hard winter.

Were they Boy Scouts or just local kids who had snuck in for some fun? No way of knowing. Yet the answer was important to him. If they were scouts, then others probably roamed these woods. And on this day they were an enemy to be avoided. But if they were locals, their antics could easily attract the attention of the resident park ranger, and that was someone Jackson didn't want to meet. Avoiding the kids was a game, but not coming face to face with the ranger was serious business. The last thing he needed was a witness who could identify him once his operation went live.

Since it was time for a snack anyway, he settled in amongst the shrubs and relaxed. After 10 or 15 minutes he'd have a better idea of what he was up against and proceed accordingly. He was in no particular hurry.

The bikers didn't return, and the ranger never appeared. Jackson was free to continue his trek, and he spent the remainder of the day hiking up to a spot near the S.I. Expressway, then back home via a completely different route. He was extremely pleased with the way things had gone. No one had seen him even though he had crossed a couple of busy roads and come within 30 yards of some homes along the way. More importantly, he had found a number of choice locations from which he could safely fire when the time came -- places that offered a clear line of sight as well as ready access to well-concealed escape routes.

His next outing, he already knew, would be longer and more intense. For that trip he would set out in early evening, camp in the woods overnight, and scout the locations of specific targets. It would be a vitally important intelligence-gathering mission whose success or failure would determine his readiness for actual combat. Although he was desperately eager to engage the enemy, he was smart enough to realize that being fully prepared for battle was essential.

He was determined to do this right.

His discipline crumbled nevertheless when he got within 200 yards of his back door and passed Terrence Goodall's house. He couldn't see the place because of the heavy undergrowth at the edge of the woods, but he knew it was there. If he lived another hundred years this was a place he could never forget. Goodall's home was literally a stone's throw away, and Jackson found it impossible to pass by without taking a closer look.

He carefully scanned the woods in all directions to make sure he was alone, got low to the ground, and moved silently into the bushes. He crept on all fours toward the back yard and with his fingertip gently moved aside a single leaf so that he had a partial view of the grounds.

And there was Goodall, sitting on his deck looking out over the woods. Jackson's eyes widened and his jaw tightened when he saw Goodall lounging in the late-morning sunshine without a care in the world. The man who had ruined an untold number of lives sat there naked from the waist up, looking like a bear that had layered on fat before hibernation, and contentedly sipped his beer.

A powerful voice deep inside a primitive part of his brain screamed for Jackson to do it. Don't think about it. Don't put it off. Do it now! Race across the yard, run up the stairs, and slit his throat. The fat man can't move fast enough. He'll never escape. Kill him. Kill him while you have the chance!

Jackson grabbed the Buck knife's handle and prepared to leap from the bushes when all those weeks of hard training kicked in. His temper had gotten him booted from the Army, true enough. But something like that wasn't going to happen again. He was a new man, a scout sniper, and his actions would be governed by knowledge, logic, and military discipline. Killing the enemy wasn't personal. It was simply a professional duty.

Killing Terrence Goodall would be all business.

As Jackson backed out of the bushes, pleased that reason had conquered emotion, he put the full weight of his right knee on a fallen branch. The branch snapped loudly enough to frighten two deer that had been grazing alongside the thicket. Both deer bolted toward Goodall's yard as Jackson crept softly into the woods and vanished.

He'd reappear another day.

15.

By the time March morphed into April Archer Grande held an astonishing lead over all other presidential candidates, both Republican and Democratic, in the number of death threats received each day. The average daily figure was 897, or 613 more than his closest rival. That, however, was before one of the nation's leading conservative magazines branded him "a repellent thug whose most lasting legacy if elected would almost certainly be World War III."

At that point the number of daily death threats aimed at Archer Grande spiked to 1,384.

Nazareth and Gimble had pleaded for administrative help and gotten it from Chief Crawford, who assigned four college students from the NYPD's cadet program to assist the detectives in assessing each of the threats. Following the magazine article they added two more cadets, but it was still almost impossible to keep up with the workload generated each day by phone calls, emails, Facebook, Twitter, websites, blogs, snail mail, and tips from concerned citizens.

The death threats fell into two main categories: those that urged others to kill Grande, and those in which someone claimed he or she was going to kill him. Most threats were swiftly dropped from further consideration once they were labeled "not credible." The credible messages were marked either orange or red according to their assigned threat level. Orange threats were those that urged others to kill Archer Grande, and these were passed along to the FBI and Secret Service. Red threats, on the other hand, went first to Nazareth and Gimble. These were threats from someone who claimed he or she would assassinate the candidate. While these would also soon be turned over to the feds, the detectives wanted to determine whether they needed to take immediate action on their own.

The hottest case in the red category involved Vernon Pitcher, a smart but unhinged malcontent from somewhere in Manhattan. Gimble had picked up the file from one of the cadets, and she was alarmed by what she saw. Pitcher, or whatever his real name was, had emailed Grande's campaign headquarters a set of eight photos. Seven of the photos, all of very high quality, showed the candidate standing at a variety of podiums addressing audiences during his most recent New York City rallies. Whoever had taken them had stood dangerously close to Grande. Close enough, in fact, to kill him.

The eighth photo was an anomaly. It was an amateurish shot with poor definition and showed an array of assault weapons spread out on what appeared to be someone's living room floor. Whatever nut had sent the email apparently had a major-league arsenal at his disposal.

The message accompanying the photos was brief and direct: "I can't miss. Either Grande drops out, or I drop Grande."

Since Archer Grande was scheduled to speak at a Midtown luncheon the next day, Gimble wasted no time pulling the team together. The resident computer whiz, Martha Newall, was assigned the task of tracking down the email's origin. So far all she knew -- or at least thought she knew -- was that the message had come from a device somewhere in Manhattan. Given enough time, she told Gimble, she should be able to get the location down to a single building. Worst case, maybe a city block.

One of the forensics experts, Fernando Gutierrez, analyzed the eight photographs to check whether, in fact, the photographer had been close to Grande when they were taken. Answer: yes, without a doubt. Photos shot from a greater distance with a telephoto lens would have shown some blurring around the edges of Grande's image, and that simply wasn't the case. Best guess: the photographer stood no more than 50 feet from the podium at each rally.

Finally, Gimble sat together with Nazareth and Chief Crawford to assess whether they should pull the Emergency

Services Unit in for this one. Two detectives weren't going to be able to lock down the would-be assassin's building, much less an entire block.

"I'm having trouble seeing this as a credible threat, Tara," the chief said as he shook his head. "If you're going to murder someone, you don't send out photos documenting where you were and when."

"I hear what you're saying," she said, "but he's given us clear proof that he can make good on the threat. I don't think we can gamble."

"Well, if I planned to kill someone, I'd just kill him and not leave any clues," the chief replied, "but I suppose we've got to run with this. Whoever took the pictures certainly has access to the rallies for some reason and has no trouble getting close to Grande."

"Tara and I have kicked this around," Nazareth said, "and believe the guy we're looking for -- supposedly Vernon Pitcher, although we haven't been able to find anyone local with that name -- is a professional photographer with press credentials. No way someone takes photos as good as these seven with a cell phone. And press credentials would explain how he gets so close to the podium."

"The only puzzling element," Gimble added, "is that the photo showing the weapons is pretty crude. We don't understand why the same person would take seven pro-quality shots and one that looks as though it came from a kiddie camera."

Crawford nodded. "That sort of inconsistency is a red flag as far as I'm concerned. Something's off about this, but I'll support whatever decision you guys make. If you need ESU for this, I'll make it happen."

A short time later Gimble got a visit from Gutierrez, whose analysis of the photos had turned up two key facts. First, the picture of the assault weapons was a fake -- nothing more than a photo of a photo in a gun magazine. Second, Gutierrez believed he had identified the photographer who had taken the seven shots at Grande's rallies.

"I thought the style looked familiar," he explained, "and I went back through a bunch of news reports of Grande's recent speaking engagements. One of the *Times* photos is virtually identical to one of the pictures this guy sent. If it's not the same photographer, I'd be very surprised."

"Do you have a name?" Nazareth asked.

"Yeah, Boyd Dowling. Excellent freelance photographer whose work is routinely in a whole bunch of major newspapers and magazines. The guy's a real artist, and his work is very much in demand."

"Does he live in Manhattan?" said Gimble.

"Village," he nodded. "Here's the address."

Boyd Dowling was, as Gutierrez had told them, a famous and famously talented photographer, and the detectives couldn't begin to imagine him as a would-be assassin. But facts don't usually lie. Since they knew where the guy lived and didn't need ESU to storm a building for them, they drove to Greenwich Village and parked outside the building where Dowling occupied a huge loft. Before exiting the vehicle they trained a pair of binoculars on the top-floor windows to see whether anyone seemed to be watching. No movement, no one looking back at them.

They slipped into the building behind a resident who had just returned from grocery shopping. The young guy had started to protest when Nazareth flashed his shield and put his finger to his lips.

"NYPD official business," he told the guy. "What floor do you live on?"

"First. Hey, what's going on?"

"No time to talk about it right now. Please go to your apartment, and stay there until you hear from us again. And in the meantime," he added, "do not call anyone else in the building. Understood?"

"Yeah, sure," the guy answered. He was obviously rattled. "Should I leave the building?"

"No need for that," Nazareth said. "Just stay in your apartment, and we'll stop by when it's okay for you to come out."

That issue settled, the detectives took a rickety but generally cooperative birdcage-style elevator to the top floor, drew their weapons, and knocked on the door. From deep inside the unit they heard someone call, "Be right there." Dowling was appropriately surprised when he opened the door and found himself facing two armed detectives.

"Whoa! What the hell is this?" he blurted as he raised his hands. No one had told him to do that, but it seemed like a decent idea. The detectives relaxed and lowered their weapons when they saw the guy was unarmed. Nazareth told Dowling who they were and said they needed to speak with him either in his home or at One Police Plaza. He invited them in.

The immense loft had windows on all four sides, one of which overlooked Washington Square Park. The walls were hung with framed examples of Dowling's work throughout the world: Beijing, Tuscany, the Himalayas, Antarctica, and a host of other exotic places. Scattered here and there among the rest were striking images of famous people in action: presidents, CEOs, athletes, and princes. One of the photos showed an angry Archer Grande roaring at an audience in Manhattan. Nazareth and Gimble looked at each other knowingly.

As the three of them sat down at the long dining room table, Gimble placed the eight photos in front of their reluctant host.

"Please tell us about these," she said with steel in her voice.

Dowling was immediately shocked by what he saw. "Where did you get these?" he asked as he flipped through the first several shots of Archer Grande.

"Where do you think we got them?" said Gimble.

"I have no clue. These are my photos, but I haven't sold them to anyone. So no one should have them but me." He paused when he reached the eighth photo showing the assault weapons. "This one isn't mine, obviously. I don't know what I'm supposed to say about it."

"You sent all eight photos to Archer Grande's campaign headquarters along with your death threat," Nazareth said as he watched the guy's eyes.

"What? Are you out of your mind? I'd never send a death threat to anyone," he protested, "least of all Arch. He's my number-one collector. He's the only reason I can live in a place like this."

"You agree that these are your photos?" Nazareth asked.

"All but this one, yeah. None of them sold, though. I sold a few from the same assignments, but not these," he explained. "These are file images. No one else has them."

"We have them," Gimble said.

"Yeah, well, I can't explain that. No one should have these." Nazareth studied Dowling's face and thought the guy was either telling the truth or deserved an Academy Award. Instinct guided him to the only question that seemed to make sense.

"Where do you store photos that don't get sold?" he asked.

"Same place I store the photos that *do* get sold. In the cloud." Nazareth wasn't the most high-tech guy on the planet, but he knew that the cloud was a massive global network of data-storage centers. Gone were the days of saving paper files or even your own digital files when everything could be stored safely in, well, thin air. The cloud.

"You don't need hard copies?" Nazareth asked.

"Not unless someone plans to hang a print. The work is all digital. I use digital cameras, I edit with digital tools, and I store my work digitally in the cloud. I keep back-up files on a DVD, but I never need them."

"Did you send these seven photos to anyone?"

"Sure, but these weren't used. In each case there were better photos from the same shoot."

"How much do you know about the cloud, Tara?" Nazareth asked.

"If you're asking whether cloud data storage can be hacked," she nodded, "the answer is yes, definitely. It's not easy, though. Most of the security issues come on the user's end. If Mr. Dowling has been emailing his images to newspapers and magazines, that's most likely where they got stolen."

"All of the publications I work with have secure systems," Dowling insisted, "or I wouldn't send my images that way."

"Any system can be hacked," she said casually, "but my guess is the problem's on your end. Do you ever look up restaurant menus online?"

"Yeah, sure."

"A significant percentage of online menus have been infected with code that allows the hacker to slip into the user's system. It's known as a *watering hole* attack, and you'll probably never know you've been hit. Do you have your own website?"

"Sure. That's how most people find my work."

"Can they buy your photos through your website?"

"Except for my corporate clients," he said, "that's how everyone pays."

"Then there's a very good chance your website has been hacked by someone using what's known as an *SQL injection attack,* which basically injects hidden commands into your system and unlocks the database. It's very simple to do," she said, "and anyone can download the hacking software for free."

"How do we find out who breached Mr. Dowling's systems?" Nazareth asked. He had heard enough to convince him that the photographer wasn't the person behind the death threats. "The guy we're after is still out there."

"Agreed," Gimble said. "Whoever sent the death threat to Grande's campaign office was either trying to implicate Mr. Dowling for some reason or -- and I think this is more likely -- just needed to rip off a set of photos and assumed we'd never track down the actual photographer."

"So how do we find him?"

"Fernando Gutierrez, no question," she said. "If Mr. Dowling gives us some access to his systems, I'm sure Detective Gutierrez can track this guy down in a hurry."

"You can have all the access you want," Dowling said. He smiled for the first time since seeing the two guns at his door. "In the meantime, I'll be looking for someone who can put a padlock on all my files."

Eighteen hours later Nazareth rang a doorbell in Midtown not far from Central Park. When Parker Simpson, aka Vernon Pitcher, finally opened the door he was shocked to find two detectives and two uniformed officers, all with guns drawn. Gimble handed him the search warrant and began reading the guy his Miranda rights while the others stormed into the elegant apartment with its high-priced view.

Simpson slumped back in his wheelchair and considered what life would be like during his years in prison. His computer would shortly disgorge all of the detailed information he had assembled on Archer Grande's travel schedule as well as the death threat he had emailed to the campaign office. The police also confiscated printed copies of the eight photos along with a 10-page manifesto he had planned to release prior to the assassination attempt. At the top of the evidence list, naturally, was the Remington M24 sniper rifle that Gimble had found at the back of a utility closet off the master bath.

Parker Simpson didn't care much for Archer Grande's politics, but that wasn't what had prompted the death threat. This was personal. Three months earlier two members of Grande's security team had escorted Simpson, drunk and disorderly, out of a rally in Brooklyn. When he reached the sidewalk he looked over his shoulder and began screaming vulgar insults. A moment later he was screaming in pain after walking into the path of a speeding VW Beetle. Had the vehicle been an SUV, Simpson would have been DOA. Instead, he suffered a badly fractured femur that had required surgery, a full-leg cast, and several weeks in a wheelchair.

If all had gone according to plan he would have been out of the wheelchair and far enough along with physical therapy to put a bullet in Grande at an upcoming New York City rally. And he most likely could have pulled it off. Simpson had, after all, been a nationally ranked member of his university's rifle team, and after graduating had become highly proficient with a number of advanced weapons. His pride and joy, though, was the Remington with its Leupold Mark 6 scope capable of 18x magnification.

His hands would never touch it again.

16.

April 21. Commence operation 6:45 p.m. Sunset 7:37 p.m. Greenbelt overnight. Improvised shelter. Primary objective: reconnaissance.

Jackson put the pen back in his camouflaged parka and tucked the mission log in a side pocket of the waterproof military-grade knapsack. His first night operation in the Greenbelt was going to be somewhat more challenging than he had anticipated. Staten Island's average low temperature in April is 42 degrees, with a record low of 19 set in 1982. Tonight's forecast: 29. Cold would be an issue. But in a few months he'd have the opposite problem: hot, humid weather and clouds of mosquitoes.

No one said life as a scout sniper would be easy.

He locked the kitchen door behind him and stepped off into the evening with 40 pounds of gear on his back. Much of the weight represented food, because he chose not to use the freeze-dried provisions he had sampled back in South Carolina. Sausages, three eggs, a hunk of raw beef, and two potatoes would provide a real dinner tonight and a man's breakfast in the morning. The extra clothing was rolled neatly inside plastic bags to make sure it stayed dry, even though there was no rain or snow in the forecast. And the serious equipment -- propane camp stove, LED lantern, sleeping bag, insulating mat, and such -- was meticulously stowed so he could set up camp as quickly as possible.

The rest of the weight in his backpack came from the rifle and ammo. His Mossberg MVP Patrol had a nifty feature that allowed him to remove and replace the gun's stock without tools. This meant he could break the rifle down to fit inside his knapsack yet be able to have the weapon ready for firing in less than a minute. He didn't plan to use the gun this time around, but if he needed it for some reason it would be there.

One of the mission's key objectives was once again to avoid all contact with other hikers, so he took his time winding through the lonely woods and reached the southern boundary of the Pouch Scout Camp about 20 minutes before sunset. This gave him plenty of time to build a stack of long, straight branches for constructing a basic lean-to shelter. First he created a simple frame from two vertical support branches and one long horizontal branch as a crossbar, similar to a football goal post. Next he rested several layers of branches against the crossbar at a forty-five-degree angle, creating a cozy triangular space large enough to sit or lie down in. Finally he covered the sloped roof with brush and leaves to help keep out the wind.

The lean-to wouldn't win a beauty contest, but it was an ideal and potentially life-saving shelter for someone who might one day need to live off the land. Hope for the best, he thought, but prepare for the worst. Less than an hour after arriving at the campsite he sat inside his improvised shelter, rifle at his side, and cooked dinner on the propane stove while his campfire provided ample warmth for one man. Another segment of his training had gone extremely well.

He spent the next hour studying an aerial photograph. At precisely 4:00 o'clock the next morning he would rise, fix breakfast, and break camp. By 5:00 sharp he would move out and make his way to the northeastern boundary of the Greenbelt just above the Richmond County Country Club golf course. There he would map and photograph the woods adjacent to the back yard of Francis Mayfield, age 56, who according to an online sex-offender database had been convicted of molesting an 11-year-old girl.

Jackson was incensed that Mayfield had been released after serving only 10 years of a 25-year sentence. The guy's wife still insisted her husband was innocent despite unmistakably clear evidence to the contrary, so she welcomed him home like a hero. Together they lived quite comfortably in one of Staten Island's finest neighborhoods and wanted for nothing thanks to the money, loads of it, that Mayfield's late father had left him several years prior to the molestation conviction.

It got worse. Following his release Mayfield had filed suit against the City of New York for abuse he claimed to have suffered in prison. Newspaper accounts of the lawsuit didn't specify what sort of abuse the guy had alleged, and Jackson didn't care. As far as he was concerned, molesting an 11-year-old was a crime punishable by death, and that sentence would be carried out in less than two weeks.

Jackson had wisely concluded that he should sandwich his primary target, Terrence Goodall, between other deserving but lesser targets. Since he wouldn't know any of the other convicted child molesters, he would never hit the NYPD radar screen after their executions. Even if the police somehow connected him to Goodall's past, they would have no reason to suspect him of being a serial killer. Yes, getting rid of two or three other child molesters was a sound way of disguising his true target while also making the world a better place.

After planning his route for the next morning Jackson fired up his cell phone and checked the day's news online. The top story concerned a Manhattan man who had been arrested for threatening the life of Republican presidential candidate Archer Grande. Same old, same old, thought Jackson. Lots of screwballs out there, guys willing to kill for no good reason. He was about to click off the story when he noticed an interesting reference to an organization calling itself American Vigil and was able to track down copies of the group's most recent Internet posts.

"Archer Grande is the next Adolph Hitler," one of the rants began, "and what the world needs is someone brave enough to put a bullet in his head before he establishes America's own version of the Fourth Reich." Jackson found several of the commentaries fascinating, but the link to a short book by philosopher Claus Berggren grabbed hold of his soul and refused to let go.

In 1952 Berggren had published a now-forgotten work, *The Man Who Should Have Killed Hitler,* a carefully researched bit of non-fiction examining the actions of *SS-Gruppenführer* Gerhard Schuler, one of Hitler's most trusted generals and onetime head of Hitler's elite bodyguards. According to Berggren, Schuler had grave concerns about *der Führer's* methods and motives and had confided in his wife, Margarethe, that someone needed to rid the world of this *narren aus der Hölle,* or "fool from hell."

Whether out of fear or, worse, out of a desire to continue enjoying the good life as one of Hitler's top henchmen, Schuler never did more than talk. He enjoyed his lofty rank, did the madman's bidding, and was ultimately sentenced to death at Nuremberg for crimes against humanity.

Throughout the book philosopher Berggren posed the question that now haunted Jackson: "Who shall we say was the more despicable criminal: Adolph Hitler or the man who easily could have assassinated him before he slaughtered millions? What is quite clear is that Schuler understood perfectly well what Hitler intended to do. Yet even though he had daily access to this monster, Schuler chose not to act, thereby dooming countless others to extermination. When challenged with the greatest moral decision of the past 2,000 years he considered his own life worth more than all others combined."

Many Germans, Berggren noted, had indeed tried to kill Hitler, but each was found out and executed. The one man who could have succeeded in ridding the world of Hitler's menace was also the one who chose not to act on behalf of humanity. "When good men stand idly by and watch evil at work," Berggren concluded, "civilization is doomed."

Stone Jackson vowed not to stand by and do nothing.

When he awoke at 3:58 a.m. the next morning he felt more alive than ever. He now embraced two missions: to rid the world of Terrence Goodall, a pedophile who had escaped justice for far too long, and to eliminate the very real threat of a second Adolph Hitler in Archer Grande. After those two, who knew? Jackson intended to become America's living, breathing conscience, the one man who could be counted on to right great wrongs and eradicate evil wherever he found it. He would be the hero of all those video games he used to play, only this time on a real battlefield with a real weapon and a real cause. Greatness surely awaited him.

Frost covered the ground outside his lean-to, but he remedied the chilly morning with a small campfire. After a hot breakfast of scrambled eggs and sausage he broke camp and used his phone's GPS device and his knowledge of the woods to approach within 25 yards of Francis Mayfield's back patio. It had taken him precisely 34 minutes to reach the morning's key destination, find a suitable thicket from which he could observe the house, and settle in to wait for sunrise at 6:37. He had wanted to be in place long before daylight in order to reduce the risk of being seen by anyone, and once again his forward thinking paid large dividends. At 6:20 one of Mayfield's neighbors walked into the woods with his aging Golden Retriever and passed within five feet of the sniper position. Fortunately for everyone the dog didn't react to Jackson's scent. Eight minutes later the man and his dog returned home.

As soon as the kitchen light flickered on at Mayfield's, Jackson put the rifle to his shoulder and watched the child molester move under the scope's crosshairs. How easy it would be to squeeze off a round. In less than a second Mayfield would be plastered all over the far kitchen wall, a disgusting wretch on his way to hell. But this was not the right morning. Not enough research had been done. Not enough planning had gone into the mission. So Jackson set about photographing the landscape and sketching a detailed map that he would study carefully over the next week.

After 45 minutes of successful reconnaissance Jackson crept out of his lair and hiked toward home. Even though the overnight mission had gone as planned, he was troubled. The neighbor with the dog had triggered a concern. What if the police used tracking dogs when they investigated Mayfield's shooting? Simple answer: the combination of a keen sense of smell and dumb luck could easily bring the dogs to his back door. Sure, these woods contained lots of distracting smells -- other dogs, deer, Boy Scouts, and such -- but he wasn't going to bet his life on the possibility that tracking dogs might not be able to follow his scent.

A few minutes later he had settled on a revised plan of attack. Instead of hiking all the way to Mayfield's house he would drive his car to a secluded spot, enter the Greenbelt to complete his mission, and drive home when he was finished. As long as he parked in a different place each time, he could operate this way indefinitely. At the same time, though, he realized he needed to change the way he managed his reconnaissance hikes, since any one of those could produce a trail the dogs might be able to follow. From now on he would insist upon one week AND rain between scouting and killing. This, he believed, would take the tracking dogs out of play.

The only acceptable level of risk from this point forward was zero.

17.

"Zero, as in none, nada!" Archer Grande bellowed. "Do you understand me?" Nazareth and Gimble nodded in unison. "There is zero chance I'll drop or change one of my New York City campaign dates because wackos are crawling out of the woodwork. I'll run for president, and you'll keep the crazies away."

The detectives had reluctantly called on Grande at the mayor's insistence. Given the recent spike in death threats, the mayor wanted the candidate to trim his campaign schedule for the City. But he made it clear that the detectives were to present the idea as their own, not his. They knew, of course, that Grande would go ballistic when they suggested he run and hide, and they hadn't looked forward to this session. On the other hand, a direct order from the mayor was something they didn't have the option of ignoring.

"I understand your reluctance, Mr. Grande," Nazareth said as calmly as possible, "but..."

"There's no *but* here, detective. And what I'm feeling isn't *reluctance*. It's rage. I'm mad as hell that you came here to ask me to stop campaigning because you can't do your job."

"Adjusting your schedule isn't the same as not campaigning," Gimble replied gently. "All we're suggesting is a few changes that would make it more difficult for someone to plan an attack."

"Suggestion noted," he said sarcastically. "Now here's my suggestion to you. Practice protecting the next president of the United States, because in a few months that's who I'm going to be. And if you don't know how to do the job, turn it over to someone who does." He barreled out of the conference room and on to the next photo op.

By the time the detectives had left the campaign headquarters Nazareth was ready to put his fist through the nearest brick wall. He hated stupid ideas. He hated even more having to take credit for someone else's stupid idea. And he was pretty sure he hated Archer Grande.

"Tara, if I shoot that self-satisfied son of a bitch myself, will you turn me in?"

"Reluctantly, yes, Pete. But if you shoot the mayor? Well . . ."

"How about a twofer? Both of them together aren't worth spit. And yet one is mayor of the world's greatest city, and the other has a good chance of being elected president. How in the hell can that happen?"

"Unfortunately, Pete, we'll never get to vote for the best people America has to offer," she said. "We're always stuck with politicians who know how to game the system. Even a so-called outsider like Grande is a politician first and foremost. He's an expert manipulator who has enough money to pull the right strings. He's as much a conniving politician as the conniving politicians."

"Boy, do I hate having to grin and bear it like that."

"We had no choice. It was dumb, but we did it, and it's over. End of story."

"Not quite," he said. "We still have a few thousand screwballs who want to kill Archer Grande."

"And will not succeed, Pete," she told him. "No way it's going to happen on our watch."

Back at his headquarters, meanwhile, Grande was once again using campaign manager Vincent Chandler as his personal punching bag.

"What in the hell were you thinking?" Grande screamed from behind a desk the size of a small aircraft carrier. Chandler was wise enough to let the storm pass without comment. "Those two asshole detectives were wasting their time by wasting my time, and where I come from that's a lose-lose. Are we now in the lose-lose business, Vince?"

"We're definitely not in the lose-lose business," he said meekly.

"Then why did you put them on my schedule, Vince? Is it okay for me to ask that question? Please tell me if I'm talking out of turn here."

"No, Arch, you're not talking out of turn. It was my bad. I thought that since the mayor appointed them to assist with security, you might want to meet them."

"Tell you what. Anyone else wants to meet me, have him come to one of my rallies, and I'll sign his cocktail napkin. Otherwise, you waste *your* time on crap like this, not mine. Understood, Vincie Boy?"

Chandler hated being called Vincie. Worse, Grande knew it. Chandler briefly fantasized about killing the boss himself but let the thought go since so much of his future -- okay, his entire future -- was riding on the election. If Grande won, as most experts predicted, Vincent Chandler would be one of the top guns in the White House, therefore Washington, therefore the world.

"Understood, Arch. Won't happen again."

"Good. Now tell me why my numbers are down again in the latest polls."

Chandler wanted to tell him that watching poll numbers from one day to the next is a fool's game since the numbers bounce around meaninglessly according to the whims of voters and the alleged experts who conduct the polls. But suggesting that Archer Grande was in some way a fool could result in termination, perhaps even life-ending termination. Grande insisted on being the smartest guy in every room.

"It's just a blip, Arch. The two polls you're referring to are strictly Amateur Hour, and we shouldn't react to them."

Grande's stare was a frightening mix of fire and ice. "Whenever a poll is up," he said slowly, lingering on the word *up*, "you always take credit. But whenever a poll is down, you tell me it's a mistake or a blip or an outlier. Are you trying to play heads you win, tails I lose with me, Vince?"

"I don't really think I do that, Arch."

"But I really think you do. In fact, I *know* you do. So cut the crap and tell me how we get a nice big bounce in the numbers," he said. "I want a big damn jump in the numbers, and the ball's in your court."

"Well, actually, I do have an idea," Chandler smiled. "But I think we should hold off a bit on this one."

"Let me guess. My wife is having twins."

"Not a bad idea, but no, that's not it. I'm thinking assassination attempt."

"Now that's a stroke of genius, Vincie Boy," Grande mocked. "We have someone try to kill me. Absolute genius. And by the way, the reason those two do-nothing cops were here is that people already want to kill me."

"If I guaranteed you'd get at least a 10-point jump in the polls heading into the Republican convention, would you still think it's a dumb idea?" Chandler asked calmly. "I've done a lot of research on this one, Arch. A failed assassination attempt would unite voters, both Republicans and Democrats, like nothing else could. Assassination attempts always create coast-to-coast sympathy, and you would ride into the election with an absolutely insurmountable lead."

"You're serious? You have research to back this up?"

"Reams of it, yes. The numbers are as clear as can be. Historically America's response to an assassination or assassination attempt has been a gigantic patriotic coming together."

"You just said *assassination or assassination attempt.* Do you realize what you said?"

"Arch, I was simply giving you the historical facts. What I have in mind would be a well-staged, completely safe assassination *attempt.* The initial bounce in the polls might be 20 or 25 points, at least 10 of which will stick going into November."

Grande was suddenly interested. An extra 10 points going into November was something he could get his head around.

"Sit down, Vince. Let's talk about this."

18.

Judith Mosely, city editor of the *Staten Island Advance*, stared at the letter on her desk and debated whether she should show it to the boss. Merrill Trotter had been with the newspaper for more than 30 years, first as a summer intern and now as managing editor, and he was no stranger to crackpot letters. He was also well known in the newsroom for not spending his finite supply of energy on time-wasting topics. As far as he was concerned his staff always had more serious stories than they could handle, thus approaching him with a time-waster was best done infrequently if at all.

Still, she thought, what if this thing turns out to be real? What would she tell Trotter when the story took off without the *Advance* covering it? Well, duh. She'd never tell him. That would be career suicide. But secrets do get out, don't they? Yes, eventually Trotter might find out she had passed on the biggest local story in recent years, and she'd be clearing out her desk. No choice here. She had to tell him.

"Yes, Judith," Trotter said as he removed the pipe from his mouth. The pipe, unlit these days, was a vestige of an earlier time when newsrooms and smoke were nearly synonymous. New York City law prevented him from lighting up until he was in the car on his way home, but a man could still carry an unlit pipe filled with tobacco and not risk prison time.

"I wanted you to see this. It's a little off the wall," she said, "but it's well enough written that I'm not sure it's the work of a complete screwball."

Trotter adjusted his bifocals and read the neatly typed sheet she handed him.

> And the Lord said to Gabriel: "Proceed against the bastards and the reprobates, and against the children of fornication, and destroy the children of fornication."
> 1 Enoch, 10:9

So says the Bible, and so it shall be. I will rid this land of its reprobates, fornicators, molesters, and rapists. I know who they are, and they cannot hide. They are the spoilers of children, and the first will die on the first of May.
Gabriel

"This isn't a complete screwball? He thinks he's the angel Gabriel, but he's not nuts? And, for the record, Judith," he said, "there's no Book of Enoch in the Bible."

"The Book of Enoch never made it into the Bible," she replied, "but it's real. It dates back to 300 B.C. and was supposedly written by Noah's great grandfather. And Gabriel is usually portrayed as an archangel who serves as God's special messenger. Put the two together in a message like this, and I think it's worth looking into."

"Aside from killing someone on May 1st -- which is three days from today -- what do you suppose this loose screw has in mind?"

"Well, I'm not sure, of course, but I assume he's talking about child molesters," she told him, "of which we have hundreds here on Staten Island."

Trotter's patronizing grin indicated he wasn't buying any of this. "And Gabriel, or whoever he is, knows who all the child molesters are. Is that right?"

"Anyone who wants to know can find out online," she said. "It's very much in the public domain. Several websites show you exactly where known sex offenders live and provide full details on their convictions. I can show you if you'd like."

"Fine, show me."

She did. In less than a minute she had called up a map pinpointing the location of nearly 200 sex offenders whose crimes ranged from indecent exposure to rape. The site showed the name, address, age, photo, and physical description of each offender along with the crime he or she had committed. In addition, each point on the map was color coded to mark offenders who had assaulted children.

"This is public information?" Trotter was incredulous.

"You bet. And if I want additional information on any sex offender I can pull up a full conviction report in about 30 seconds."

"Hard to believe," he said shaking his head, "but there it is. I wonder how often this information is used to target sex offenders. Not that I care a whole lot."

"Fairly often, as it turns out. A high percentage of the people shown on these sorts of websites claim to have been harassed or attacked as a result of the information," she told him, "but it's impossible to verify. And nobody really gives a damn except for the sex offenders."

"Okay, look, I'm interested enough to have someone dig around a little on this. Find out whether a nut calling himself Gabriel has sent these kinds of threats before -- either to us or to other newspapers -- and look back through our files for the past couple of months to see if any child-molestation reports pop up. It's possible," he nodded, "that a recent incident has prompted a vendetta."

"Okay. I'll have one of the interns run with it."

"That's fine. But if you don't come up with anything credible, I don't want a story. We're not in business to run hate letters from screwballs."

"Got it."

Trotter shook his head and couldn't help but smile as Mosely walked out of his office. The Archangel Gabriel, he thought, right here on Staten Island. What next?

19.

On his way to and from his bank teller's job three days each week Jackson looked for places where he would be able to park his car near the woods without attracting attention. He searched primarily within developments whose homes backed up to the Greenbelt but weren't packed too closely together. This way he could park between homes, and people in the neighborhood wouldn't know exactly which house he was visiting. Finding a relatively new development was extremely important, though. In Staten Island's older neighborhoods everyone knew everyone else and kept an eye on things. But in the newer neighborhoods most residents were happy to remain as anonymous as they had been in Manhattan, Queens, or wherever else they had migrated from.

He eventually found exactly what he was looking for off Rockland Avenue near the southern end of High Rock Park. It was a new development of boxy, look-alike homes with plenty of fashionable, gas-guzzling SUVs parked on the wide, looping street. Here he could park his car close to the main road alongside a wooded lot, grab his knapsack from the trunk, and step into the woods. Simple. The hike to Francis Mayfield's home would be no more than three miles round-trip.

The chief sticking point with this plan was the time of day he should choose for the kill shot. If he camped overnight in the Greenbelt and nailed Mayfield in early morning, he would be returning to his car in broad daylight with a knapsack on his back. Would someone notice? Highly likely. Scratch that idea.

What about shooting Mayfield at night? That would certainly be safer, but how do you shoot someone who's inside his home? Jackson had no intention of breaking down the guy's door to get at him. No, this had to be a sniper shot from 25 or 30 yards. Would he be able to draw the guy out of his house at night?

He smiled when the idea hit him. It was an old idea, one that took him back many years when he and a few of his friends had raised some hell with their slingshots. Several times one summer they had wandered through the woods far from their own neighborhood and fired marbles through people's windows. Once they had even shot out the windshield of a new Caddy that a proud owner had parked, safely he thought, behind his house. Great fun. Harmless stuff, really, compared to some of the vicious things kids did nowadays. Yeah, this would work. If he put a marble through Mayfield's kitchen window the guy would most likely turn on the back patio lights and run out to investigate. Problem solved.

At 8:33 p.m. on May 1st Jackson reached his chosen parking spot alongside the woods and turned off the headlights. He had already disabled the interior lights and trunk light, so from this point forward he would operate in the dark. He carefully scanned the neighborhood with his field glasses. When he saw no one on the street ahead he moved quickly to the trunk, removed the knapsack, and disappeared into the Greenbelt. His first real mission had begun.

For 15 minutes he cleared his own path, struggling in the dark with thorny shrubs, sharp branches, and fallen trees. Eventually, though, he intercepted the trail he had used two weeks earlier and was comfortably on his way slightly ahead of schedule. Between the bright moon and the soft LED light on his compass he had no trouble finding his way to Mayfield's place, and at 9:07 he was settled quietly inside the same bushes he had used as a sniper hide on his first visit. The plan called for sitting absolutely still for 15 minutes while he watched and listened for intruders.

No signs of people or dogs this time. But, yes, there were subtle shadows moving against the blinds on Mayfield's bright kitchen window. 9:22 p.m. Game on.

He lovingly assembled the rifle, inserted the 10-round clip, and loaded the only round he would need. Once the rifle was ready he set it on top of his knapsack and picked up the slingshot. Tonight there would be no homemade slingshot and marbles. No, for this mission he used a sleek, pro-grade slingshot paid for with cash at a New Jersey sporting goods store along with .30-caliber steel shot for ammo. With a bit of practice he could use an outfit of this quality to take down small game, but at the moment the only target he cared about was the large kitchen window.

Timing was critical, so he practiced the moves a few times. Fire the slingshot. Place it on the knapsack. Pick up the rifle. Aim. Fire. Remove the rifle stock. Pack everything. Walk away. No need to run. Twenty-three seconds start to finish, not including the time it would take Mayfield to leave his house and investigate the broken window.

He took a long, deep breath to help slow his heart rate. He checked his right hand and smiled. Rock steady. This was why he had been born.

He placed the steel ball in the leather pouch, aimed the slingshot, and fired. The sharp crack was barely audible from 30 yards, but whoever had been in the kitchen at that moment certainly noticed. Jackson heard muffled shouts from the house as the kitchen overhead light flashed on. He locked himself in a stable cross-legged sitting position, raised the barrel of his Mossberg, and waited.

Less than a minute later Francis Mayfield emerged from the shadows at the back of his house and stood in front of a bright security spotlight, Louisville Slugger in hand. He was perfectly backlit -- a wide, black target framed by brilliant white.

"You little sons of bitches," Mayfield shouted at the woods. "I catch you I'll break your goddamn necks." Interesting, Jackson thought. Maybe someone else has been using slingshots here. But tonight it gets even better.

One gentle squeeze of the trigger was all it took. The round ripped into Mayfield's chest, savaging his heart and upper lungs. He hit the ground with a dull thud.

Jackson was already out of the bushes and walking back toward his car before Mayfield's wife left the house and discovered the body. Her screaming in the distance struck him as pleasantly musical in some strange way.

A man could get used to this.

20.

Managing editor Merrill Trotter and city editor Judith Mosely had to make a quick decision if the story about Francis Mayfield was going to make the front page of the morning's edition. It was after midnight, and headline writer Bud Weissman had offered two choices: **TODT HILL MAN SLAIN IN BACK YARD** or the somewhat less sympathetic **CONVICTED CHILD MOLESTER SLAIN**.

"I worry that labeling him a child molester in the headline is sort of like trying him twice for the same crime," Mosely told her boss. "But it does work well with the story about Gabriel's threat."

"It calls him a convicted child molester," Trotter said brusquely, "and that's what he was. If you don't want to be called a child molester on page one, don't molest children. Use the headline that tells the full story. I'm going home."

The *Advance* had run a short article about the threat from "Gabriel" a few days earlier despite Trotter's assumption that this was just another garden-variety crackpot letter. Now he was awfully glad he had gone out on a limb. Staten Islanders had been told about the threat, and now the newspaper's reporters were able to reference that item in today's lead news article. This was hot stuff.

Detectives from the one-two-two -- or 122nd precinct headquartered on Hylan Boulevard -- had been unable to provide much meat for the story because of the late hour. Yes, a guy had been shot. Yes, he was a convicted child molester. Yes, he was dead. Yes, the round was probably fired from a rifle. No, they had no suspects. No, they hadn't been able to track the killer through the woods at night. And, no, they couldn't comment on "Gabriel," because they had not seen the letter published a few days earlier in the *Advance*.

The police would be on the case at sunrise the next day and would attempt to follow any trail the killer might have left in the

Greenbelt -- if, in fact, that's how he, or possibly she, had approached the victim's home. But the lead detective, Steve Troiano, wasn't overly optimistic about tracking someone through the vast expanse of protected woodlands. Sure, they could bring in sniffer dogs, but the dogs would be working on *a* trail, not necessarily *the* trail.

"See, the problem is we don't have something for the dogs to smell before they begin tracking," Troiano told the reporter. "If we can have them sniff an article of clothing or something the perp handled, then the dogs know who they're after. But this way they'll pick up the scent of anyone who has been in the woods lately, and that's potentially dozens of people from the neighborhood."

"So you don't expect a quick arrest?" the reporter asked.

"I don't expect an arrest until we actually begin investigating," Troiano answered a bit sarcastically. "That's how we normally do it: investigate, then arrest."

The *Advance's* May 2nd edition didn't make good reading for two key audiences. First was the Island's population of registered sex offenders, in particular those who had been convicted of molesting children. At least 20 of them called the precinct that morning to demand special police protection from the self-proclaimed vigilante "Gabriel." Desk Sergeant Dan O'Malley, whose niece had been molested seven years earlier, gave them all the same answer: "We do our best to protect all citizens, not just those who have been convicted of molesting children."

The second unhappy audience consisted of Mayor Elliott Dortmund and everyone who was within shouting distance of him that morning. This was a man who had built a career on keeping bad news under wraps, so he was furious that New York City's ugly underbelly had once again made headlines.

"Where the hell do you find a detective who tells a reporter he doesn't expect to make an arrest?" he screamed at the police commissioner, who had been rousted out of bed at 5:37 a.m. and told to be in the mayor's office by 7:00.

"I'm not sure that's exactly what he said, Mr. Mayor."

"I can read, can't I?"

"Yes, sir, you can." Just barely, he thought.

"Then I guess I know what I'm talking about, don't I?"

"Yes, sir." It would be the first time, though.

"Then lose Detective Big Mouth and put those other two on this case."

"Which other two are we talking about?"

"The two who specialize in the serious nut jobs. Your two superheroes."

"You mean Nazareth and Gimble?"

"Are they your two superheroes?"

"I guess so."

"Then that's who I mean."

"Mr. Mayor, they're both in Manhattan, and the crime is on Staten Island. I think we need to give the one-two-two precinct at least a few days to go after this."

"If I want you to think," Dortmund snapped, "I'll let you know. This is a direct order. Tell those two you've got another crazy for them!"

Chief Crawford apologized for once again being the bearer of ill tidings, but his two star detectives were actually pleased about the assignment. The mayor had agreed to pull Nazareth and Gimble from their Archer Grande duty, at least until they arrested this Gabriel character. They were back to solving homicides and out of the babysitting business.

"So how many hours do we have to solve the crime, chief?" Nazareth grinned. "I'm sure the mayor knows precisely how long this should take us."

"We all know he doesn't care whether you ever arrest the guy as long as the story disappears from the newspapers. With Dortmund," the chief sneered, "it's all a p.r. game. It's always about cosmetics. He's like a damned ostrich with his head stuck in the sand. If he doesn't see it, all's well."

"Have you spoken yet with the Staten Island precinct?" Gimble asked.

"Yeah, no problem on their end. Everyone knows what Dortmund is like. Besides, the heat's off them now."

"And on us," said Nazareth.

"Yep, on us. Some things never change, right?"

"Driving to Staten Island from Manhattan every day is going to get old, though," Gimble said.

"Well, actually the commissioner solved that problem for you. He doesn't intend to take any flak over a long-distance investigation," the chief told them, "so he's authorizing temporary quarters for both of you on Staten Island. Find what you want, and I'll take care of the bills."

"We probably don't need to be there all day every day," Nazareth said.

"That's up to you. As long as we can say you're temporarily located on Staten Island, we remove one more potential p.r. problem for Mr. Mayor. And my life is dedicated to pleasing Mr. Mayor."

"Understood. So Tara and I will head over today and see what we've got."

"Don't forget your hiking boots," the chief laughed. "The Staten Island Greenbelt is a little bit different from Manhattan."

The difference became agonizingly clear three hours later as the detectives walked into the woods from the victim's back yard. An overcast sky and steady westerly wind made the Greenbelt an uninviting place in which to launch what had the potential to become a high-profile homicide investigation. The forest floor, soggy from rain earlier in the week, had been churned to ankle-deep mud by police who had unsuccessfully searched the area for clues. Street clothes wouldn't work here.

On this first visit to the crime scene they were accompanied by Detective Steve Troiano, who had incurred the mayor's wrath by speaking honestly with a reporter. He was glad to be rid of the case since he was set to retire in less than six months and really didn't need City Hall looking over his shoulder. But he offered his support to Nazareth and Gimble just the same.

"What we've got so far, as you can pretty much see, is a mess," Troiano said. "We know the shooter was set up in these bushes here, and we're pretty sure he hiked south after killing Mayfield -- whose death, by the way, is no loss to society whatsoever. We had the dogs here early this morning, and they followed a trail to a development a couple of miles away. If the dogs had the right trail, the perp must have had a car waiting there."

"But there's really no way of knowing whether the dogs were following the right scent," Gimble offered.

"Correct. But keep that a secret," he whispered, "or the mayor will have your butt."

"Right," she grinned. "That's just between us incompetents."

He gave Gimble a thumbs-up. "I've heard you're no stranger to the battlefield, Pete," Troiano said. During his time as a Marine officer Nazareth had earned a silver star for heroism in the Middle East.

"True, but it didn't look anything like this," Nazareth told him. "Over there it was all sand or rock caves, not acres of mud. Plus anyone you saw was the enemy. In these woods everyone we'll see is a friendly, with one exception. That makes it tougher."

"Agreed. This is like being in the Maine woods or maybe out in Oregon someplace. If you want to get lost," he nodded, "this is a great place to do it."

Earlier in the year Nazareth and Gimble had hunted a serial killer who had taken refuge amid Central Park's 843 acres, where the odds of finding the guy had been impossibly low. Now they looked out on nearly 3,000 acres of raw wilderness and wondered where to begin. At least in Central Park there had been paved walks or roads to speed their way. Here they faced nature in all its rugged, unvarnished glory.

"I looked online when we drove over today," Gimble said, "and I saw that there are formal trails in the Greenbelt."

"True, but this guy doesn't seem to like them much," Troiano explained. "If, in fact, we were tracking the right person, he went wherever he wanted to go. Sometimes he stuck to the trail, but just as often he picked his way through the trees and the bushes. The dogs also spent a hell of a lot of time running along a couple of streams. Looks as though the guy walked through the water as much as possible to throw us off, which he did."

"What did you find at the exit point?" Nazareth asked.

"Boot prints. That's it. Whoever we tracked just walked out of the woods onto the street. Judging from the muddy boot marks on the pavement we figure he got in a car and drove off. But, as I said, we don't know whether this was the right guy."

"So at this point we've got nothing," Nazareth shrugged.

"But at least you've got plenty of it," Troiano laughed.

Gimble poked at the edge of the thicket where the shooter had hidden, reached into her pocket for a pen, then inserted it into the spent shell casing she had found in the mud. She held it up for the others to see.

"I'll be damned," Troiano said. "Guess we had too many feet stomping around here this morning."

"My guess is whatever prints or scent might have been on it are long gone," Gimble said, "but we'll check. Recognize it, Pete?"

"Unfortunately, yes," he said. "What you've got there is a 5.56 NATO round that most self-respecting snipers would use. Assuming that casing belongs to our perp, we don't need to wonder why one shot did the trick."

"Isn't it odd that he'd leave this behind?" she asked.

"It's probably not something he planned to do. But if he's using a bolt-action rifle he probably chambered a second round immediately after the first shot, and this thing just jumped out of the rifle. Didn't have time to look for it in the dark, I assume. On the other hand, if he wore latex gloves while loading, which a pro would, no problem. We wouldn't get his prints or scent even if the casing hadn't been stomped into the mud."

"You're thinking he's a pro?" Troiano asked.

"He's no rookie, that's for sure. He found excellent cover, took his target down with a single shot at 30 yards, give or take, and most likely used a sniper rifle. So whether he's a professional hit-man or just a serious beginner," Nazareth told them, "he's not going to make this easy for us."

"Wouldn't it be nice to track someone stupid for a change?" Gimble asked.

"Yeah, definitely. But, trust me, this isn't him.

21.

Grande was seriously interested. "Okay, so someone tries to assassinate me. First tell me how this affects the polls. Then explain in excruciating detail what sort of assassination attempt you have in mind."

Campaign manager Vincent Chandler was riding tall in the saddle once again. After coming up with the successful idea about getting Grande's wife pregnant -- well, sort of -- he had struggled to find the next great idea. And here it was. He knew this one would put his boss's lead out of reach.

"I've got tons of data on how assassination attempts affect popularity," he explained. "I've looked at both the U.S. and other developed countries, and I've compared assassination attempts on elected officials as well as candidates. Bottom line: on average you get a minimum 15-25% jump in favorable ratings across the board -- that means not just within your own party," he added enthusiastically, "but from all parties."

"That's a pretty wide gap, 15-25%," Grande noted.

"You'd be at the high end. The bigger the elected official or candidate, the bigger the impact. You'd go into November with a lead no one could touch. The election would be over before it began."

"Okay, I like that part a lot. Now tell me about the assassination attempt, and don't tell me I get shot."

Chandler knew he was about to wade into troubled waters, but he had hard data to support his position. "The research is pretty clear, Arch. No wound, no change in the polls."

Grande's nasty scowl said it all. "You're kidding, right? You actually think I'm going to take a bullet? Are you on drugs?"

"Listen, Arch, I'm talking about a wound that simply draws blood, not something that actually does serious damage. All we need is a damned scratch. The rest is all spin. By the time I'm finished with this, you'll be a hero."

"And what doctor is going to agree with you that a scratch is actually a near-fatal wound?"

"Your new personal physician who'll happen to be at the scene when you get shot. I have a guy all lined up, Arch. Top-notch surgeon with a great reputation in Manhattan. And it just so happens he'd love to be our next secretary of health and human services."

"Why? Is that a good job?"

"Secretary of anything is a good job. All you need is a scratch on your arm, and this guy will swear you're fighting for your life."

Grande pursed his lips and looked off into the distance as he usually did when giving serious thought to a subject. Chandler knew the boss was hooked.

"How do you know I'll get nicked," Grande asked, "and not blown away?"

"You get the best talent money can buy."

"And who might that be?"

"You want his name?"

"Hell, no. I don't want to know anything except whether he's good."

"Arch, this guy could shoot a toothpick out of your mouth at 500 yards. Retired SEAL with 137 confirmed kills, so many medals he can't wear them all at the same time without risking back damage, and a burning desire to have a home in Nantucket."

"Which he can't afford."

"Which he will most certainly be able to afford once he puts a little scratch on you. I can easily channel the money through the campaign."

"How far away would he actually be?" Grande asked.

"Maybe 200 yards, which is nothing for this guy. My idea," Chandler said, "is to do this on Staten Island on July 6th. You have a huge outdoor rally that afternoon at the big shopping mall, then a brief outdoor speech at the country club before you sit down for dinner with some of your top contributors. The outdoor speech at the country club is where you get shot."

"And I get taken away by ambulance?"

"A private ambulance, yes, with your personal physician in the back trying to save your life."

"Which he does."

"Which he does. You'll be in a private hospital, and no one other than us will know the extent of your injuries."

"Except for the public," Grande smiled.

"Oh, yes. The public will learn how Archer Grande bravely faced death, made a full recovery, and marched forward to save America."

"Love it. Except for the getting shot part. Have you spoken with this sniper about that?"

"Yeah, Hunter says . . ."

"No names!" Grande screamed.

"Sorry, Arch. The sniper thinks a flesh wound to the upper arm would look great for the crowd."

"No way in hell I'm getting shot in the arm, Vince. No way. This guy misses a little and I get a bullet in the heart. Let him nick my ass instead. The margin for error is greater."

Chandler was outraged. "Whose side are you on? Great headline: ARCHER GRANDE SHOT IN THE ASS. Then we rush you away to a private hospital for emergency treatment of your butt. Can you imagine the field day the press and your opponents would have with that? How many shot-in-the-ass jokes do you think they'd come up with in, oh, five seconds?"

"Okay, fine. Not the ass. Upper thigh then. I want a lot of meat on the target in case your sharpshooter isn't as good as you think he is."

"This guy is just about the best on the planet, Arch. And he'll know -- because we'll tell him -- precisely when you're going to stop moving and give him a perfect target. In less than one second you're up 20 points."

Grande mulled everything over for a moment. Something was obviously gnawing at him.

"What's wrong, Arch?"

"I'm just wondering what happens a year from now . . . or maybe four years from now when I'm running for reelection," Grande said cautiously, "and this guy comes crawling out of the woodwork and decides that extortion is a great retirement plan."

"He'll never rat us out."

"How can you be sure?"

Chandler grinned. "You really want to know?"

22.

Nazareth and Gimble lucked out. Through department contacts they were quickly able to rent a large detached home off Richmond Road less than a quarter of a mile from High Rock Park in the Greenbelt. The place belonged to a retired NYPD assistant chief who was touring the country with his wife in their $200,000 motor coach and wouldn't be back until late-summer. For $1,900 a month the detectives got a gorgeous home in a fine neighborhood as well as ready access to both the Greenbelt and the 122nd precinct on Hylan Boulevard. They hoped they wouldn't be working the Gabriel case for more than a week or two, but they were happy to be set up in something far better, and cheaper, than $180-a-night hotel rooms.

Now that they had a temporary roof over their heads they were able to focus entirely on the Gabriel case, and their first move was to study the file on the late Francis Mayfield's young female victim. Although Mayfield had spent 10 years in prison, the detectives figured someone in the victim's family might have decided that time served wasn't nearly enough to compensate for damage done.

But they also wanted to study cases of girls who had recently been sexually assaulted by unidentified attackers. Child molesters, they knew, generally have dozens of victims as well as a high rate of repeat offenses once released from prison. This suggested that a victim other than the one whose testimony had put Mayfield behind bars might well be responsible for the payback killing. In certain neighborhoods on Staten Island the police and the courts were not the preferred method of righting wrongs. A father with a baseball bat was sometimes viewed as a much more reliable judge and jury. Perhaps Mayfield had touched the wrong girl since leaving prison.

"I hope you have a lot of time on your hands, Detective Gimble," said Nadia Zelesky, who managed case files for the local precinct. "Let's see here. Sexual assaults against girls under 18 for the past three months. That's 132 files."

"You can't be serious," Gimble replied. "In three months?"

"Yes, ma'am. Some of the research I've looked at says one in every three girls is sexually assaulted before adulthood. If that's true," she shook her head, "then these 132 reports don't even scratch the surface of what's actually happening out there."

Gimble was shocked. When she and Nazareth had decided to expand their investigation by looking beyond Francis Mayfield's accuser they had no idea how far the net would need to be thrown.

"Is there any way to break those 132 files down into manageable parts?" Gimble asked. "There's no way we can look at all of them."

"I can eliminate the ones in which the girl was assaulted by a family member," Zelesky nodded. "That would get you down to 41 files."

"The rest were attacked by a family member? I find that hard to believe."

"Believe it, detective. No one knows for sure what the right figure is, but the experts believe 50-70% of sexual assaults against girls are committed by family members." She shook her head sadly. "Home is where the jungle is."

Gimble figured she could wade through 41 files and select the ones that seemed likeliest to have triggered a revenge killing. Nazareth, meanwhile, wondered how to go about determining whether the family of an abused girl might be involved in her attacker's killing. How do you even begin to ask something like that without hurting a family that's been hurt enough? He had no good answer for that.

After an hour of examining case files in one of the precinct's private interview rooms they had the sinking feeling that this investigation might last forever.

"In at least three of the cases I've looked at so far," Gimble said, "it's almost impossible to believe the victim didn't recognize her attacker. These were daytime assaults that happened near home or school, and in each case the investigating officer says the victim and her family were generally uncooperative."

"Then why would the family have gone to the police in the first place?"

"They didn't. In two cases a neighbor called the police after finding the victim, and in the third case a school teacher called it in. As soon as the parents got involved, the victims said they couldn't remember a thing about their attackers."

"Which tells us that maybe the kids knew their attackers," he reasoned, "and the family decided to handle this on their own."

"Always a possibility," Gimble nodded.

"So if Mayfield happened to assault one of these girls and the parents knew who he was . . ."

"Then one of the parents could have decided to blow him away," she said.

"Which means," he concluded, "no one is going to admit to knowing him."

"Correct."

"In that case," Nazareth said, "let's begin by visiting the girl, actually a young woman now, whose testimony put Mayfield away. She and her family won't be happy for the visit, but we've really got no choice. If we get nowhere, we'll double back and take a look at some of the other girls."

Early that evening the detectives showed up unannounced at the expansive Great Kills home of Simon and Darlene Frye, parents of 23-year-old Michelle Frye, who had been molested by Francis Mayfield a bit more than 11 years earlier. The parents weren't pleased by the visit, but they weren't entirely surprised either. They invited the detectives into the living room where a 100-pound Doberman sat motionless by the coffee table, waiting for instructions. A slight wave of Darlene Frye's hand sent the dog on its way.

"I assumed someone would stop by here to see if one of us had decided to put that worthless piece of trash out of his misery," Simon Frye told them plainly. "And I can't say I hadn't thought about how wonderful that would feel after what he did to our daughter."

At first glance the guy looked like someone who could easily take care of business. He stood 6-3 and was obviously fit, but he walked with a pronounced limp. Frye saw that the detectives had noticed.

"Right leg is gone below the knee," he said. "Iraq. So I'm not big on running through the woods shooting child rapists."

"You read the newspaper article," Nazareth said.

"Sure. Several times, in fact. I was hoping to find something about Mayfield being skinned alive before he was shot," Frye told him, "but it wasn't there. That guy deserves to be dead, but being shot isn't my idea of justice. He deserved a lot worse."

Darlene Frye took a sip of her martini and set the glass on an end table alongside the couch. She wore a slight, somewhat ironic smile. "Do you know anything about our daughter, detectives?"

"Nothing more than we found in the original police report," Gimble said.

"That report was about a bright, healthy young girl who didn't have a care in the world," the mother said. "The young woman who now lives here is quite different. Our daughter suffers from RTS -- rape trauma syndrome -- and is in pain almost all the time. Physical pain as well as emotional pain. She's afraid of crowds, afraid of men, afraid of woods -- which is where she was assaulted -- and afraid to leave her room if there's a stranger in the house. All the therapy in the world hasn't gotten her over this. She'll never be over this."

"I'm truly sorry for her and for you, Mrs. Frye," Gimble said gently. "And my partner and I are sorry to intrude like this. But we can't not investigate."

"I understand, detective," the woman smiled. "You have a job to do." She picked up the martini and took two large swallows.

"Mr. Frye, I need to ask where you were on the night Mayfield was shot," Nazareth said.

"Finishing dinner with an Australian client at Per Se in Manhattan," he said. "I run my own investment firm right here on the Island, but for certain out-of-town clients I generally go into the City for either lunch or dinner. I can show you the dinner receipt if you'd like."

"That's not necessary, Mr. Frye. I can check if I need to. Mrs. Frye?"

"Right here, detective. Always right here. If Simon isn't here, I am. If I'm not here, Simon is. Our daughter can't be alone yet," she said somberly, "so one of us is always here. And Mars, of course."

"Mars?" Gimble said.

"The Doberman," she said. "Also the Roman god of war. Anyone who tries to break into our home won't live to tell about it."

"Understood."

"And detectives," Simon Frye told them, "I can also assure you that I didn't hire someone to kill Mayfield. I once thought about that, actually, but in the end I decided that one life destroyed in this family was enough. I wasn't going to risk ruining my own as well. So I'm ecstatic that he was finally punished, but no one in this family did anything to make it happen."

"Unless prayers do get answered," his wife added as she finished her drink.

By the time they got back in their car following the interview Gimble felt almost ill.

"I don't hate much about this job, Pete," she began, "but persecuting the innocent on behalf of the guilty absolutely disgusts me. We shouldn't have been here tonight."

"That's Tara my fiancée talking," he smiled. "But Tara the detective understands we had no choice. We're on the case, and the Fryes needed to be visited. And, for the record, the next interviews may be a great deal tougher."

"You mean the girls who either couldn't or wouldn't identify their attackers?"

"You bet. It's possible Gabriel is a very unhappy father who decided to do the world a favor. If we assume Mayfield assaulted other girls," he said, "which is a pretty safe bet given what we know about these types, there's a good chance one of them pointed him out to Daddy."

"Certainly could happen."

"Yep. Does anyone stand out in the cases you looked at today?" he asked.

"A few of the cases look a little off to me, as though the families know more than they told the police," she nodded, "but one in particular caught my attention. Maybe we start out there in the morning."

"Morning it is. In the meantime, I'm hungry."

"Then let's hit that Denino's place everyone keeps telling us has the best pizza on the planet," she said. "Can't possibly be as good as Garlic."

Two hours later, after their visit to Denino's in Port Richmond, Nazareth and Gimble came up with a split decision. He voted Denino's sausage pizza number one in New York City, but she had it number two behind Garlic in their Manhattan neighborhood. "You better be nice to me," she grinned, "or I'll rat you out to your buddies at Garlic. No more instant delivery during snowstorms."

"You can't testify against your future husband, Tara. That just isn't done."

She shrugged. "Sometimes the court of public opinion is harsher than a court of law, so just mind your manners. I've now got something on Perfect Pete, the Boy Scout."

"Hey, I kinda like *Perfect Pete*."

"God help us all."

They could have used a bit of help from God the next morning when they visited the home of Vito Passaretti on a narrow street three blocks off Father Capodanno Boulevard in Midland Beach. Passaretti, wife Adriana, and 14-year-old daughter Lisa lived in a ramshackle 600-square-foot beach bungalow that might have been a beauty when it was built in 1917. But after nearly 100 years of service the one-story home looked about ready for retirement. The roof was a bit wavy, and the right exterior wall bulged like a kiddie pool with too much water in it. Five large trash cans, all filled with scraps of building materials, lined the front of the house -- three on one side of the door, two on the other. A scroungy black-and-white mutt tied to a mimosa tree yapped as the detectives left their unmarked car.

The front door opened as they approached the house, and Vito Passaretti leaned out with both arms hugging a stack of flooring scraps that he tossed onto the already full garbage can nearest him. A few pieces managed to balance atop the heap, but most clattered to the ground. He eyed Nazareth and Gimble suspiciously.

"You lost?" he growled at them. Passaretti stood 5-9 and had a bulging gut that stretched his soiled wife-beater to the limit, but his shoulders and arms were broad and powerful. This was a man who could do some damage in a bar brawl.

"NYPD," Nazareth said, "Detectives Pete Nazareth and Tara Gimble." They both showed their ID and shields.

Passaretti nodded. "Okay. And?"

"And," Nazareth told him, "we're here to talk about your daughter. We can talk out here, or in the house, or at the precinct. Your choice."

"We'll go inside," he said. "Place is a total wreck right now, but it's better than the front yard."

The detectives were surprised to find that the inside wasn't a wreck at all, except for some scraps of molding, laminate flooring, and broken tiles that had been swept into neat piles. Passaretti was working on the final room of a DIY remodel, and the entire place glistened.

"Your house looks great," Gimble said, much impressed with the interior. "Did you do all this yourself?"

Passaretti allowed himself a bit of a smile. "Yeah, ripped everything out and put it back together. I've been at this for a month solid," he said. "All my vacation time plus four days unpaid, but I'm almost finished. Anyway, I needed a break."

"You call this taking a break?" Gimble laughed.

"Yeah, I work road construction. Jackhammer. Sixty grand a year plus all the concrete dust I can breathe," he nodded. "I shoulda been a cop like my old man told me."

"Was he a cop?" Nazareth asked.

"Nah, but he spent a lot of time in patrol cars. So what do you want to know about my daughter?"

"We're hoping that your daughter might have remembered something about her attacker that would help us find him," Gimble said. "Sometimes it's a few weeks before victims can recall everything that happened."

The guy shook his head. "Nope. She remembers nothing about him."

"Is she here?" Gimble asked.

"Nope. She's at school, and my wife's at work."

"And you're absolutely positive," Nazareth asked pointedly, "your daughter has no information that might help us catch this guy? You've asked her recently?"

"Yeah, I asked her this morning before she went to school. She said she'd let me know if she remembered anything so I could call the police right away."

Nazareth and Passaretti stared each other down.

"Why do I get the feeling you don't want to cooperate, Mr. Passaretti?" Nazareth asked.

"Let me put it this way, detective. You saw this neighborhood when you drove in, right? Ain't much to look at. But this is an old-school kind of place. Always lots of eyes looking out the windows, watching for stuff that doesn't belong here. Know what I mean?" he asked.

"Yeah, I think so," Nazareth answered.

"So most of the time we stop trouble before it starts, and that's that. But with my daughter, this didn't happen. We found out after the trouble," he nodded, "not before, you know? But it's okay. The guy, whoever he was, just scared her. She wasn't raped. The guy touched her, she screamed, he ran. End of story. For murder maybe we call the police. But not for something like this."

"Let me ask you a hypothetical question, Mr. Passaretti," Gimble said. "In this neighborhood if you knew who did something wrong -- something like what happened to your daughter -- how would you handle it if you didn't call the police?"

He smiled. "Just hypothetical, right?"

"Yes, just hypothetical."

"In that hypothetical case I guess the girl's father would visit the man who did this thing," he shrugged, "and break both of his legs so bad he'd limp like a broken rocking horse for the rest of his life."

"But if that happened," Gimble said, "then, hypothetically, the man who attacked the one little girl could still go after other little girls on Staten Island."

Passaretti shook his head vigorously. "No, this man would leave Staten Island as soon as he could walk again. Or else he'd find himself at the bottom of Raritan Bay with a cinder block chained to his neck. That's just a hypothetical." He grinned.

"But then he could assault girls someplace else," Gimble said.

"Hey, I can't be everywhere right?"

The detectives drove away not quite sure whether Passaretti had been toying with them. Did he actually break someone's legs and threaten his life, or was he simply putting on a macho front for their benefit? No way of knowing.

If their other interviews went like this one, they'd find themselves on a fast track to nowhere.

23.

Jackson had worried that Terrence Goodall might hide in his home after the first Gabriel murder made page one of the *Advance*. Yes, he wanted the guy to sweat, but not so much that killing him became more difficult. He needn't have worried. If Goodall was concerned, he didn't show it. Several times Jackson saw the guy in his front yard, either picking up his newspaper in the morning or tending shrubs his wife had planted long before she walked out of his life. Was he still hanging out on his back deck drinking beer now and then? Only time would tell.

Three weeks after the highly publicized Mayfield slaying Goodall looked away as he drove past the Jackson home one morning. Ancient history, he said to himself. Water over the dam and all that. He didn't know Jackson had joined the Army and wouldn't have cared if he did. None of "his boys" represented a threat, he had convinced himself, because they were too embarrassed to talk about what had taken place all those years ago. If they hadn't accused him then, they weren't going to dredge that stuff up now. Wouldn't happen. They steered clear of him, and he steered clear of them. Hell, he wouldn't even look at them.

This business about some convicted sex offender being murdered recently seemed to him totally disconnected from his own past. He had, after all, gotten away with everything. That other poor bastard, though? Most likely shot by the kid's father. This is the price you pay for being careless.

From his living room window Jackson watched Goodall's new Honda Accord roll by, and he saw the dirtbag look away. This was good. Goodall clearly felt safe about being outside his home, yet obviously he still thought about what he had done. Why else would he have looked away like that? What a shame it would be if Goodall didn't feel a twinge of guilt in that last fraction of a second before he left this world. But this was something Jackson couldn't control. All he could control was The Day.

Judgment Day.

Jackson had been patient. Painfully so. The desire to put a bullet in his abuser burned so hot that he sometimes felt nauseous. He was a junkie in desperate need of the only fix that could settle him down. And yet he had waited. First he had waited for rain, lots of it, because of his earlier visit to Goodall's yard. His scent was long gone by now, replaced by that of the kids who ran through the woods back there almost every day and the neighbors who walked their dogs.

He had also taken his time devising the perfect entry and exit plan. Killing someone in your own neighborhood, he knew, presented a large problem. You can't just walk over, shoot the guy, and stroll home. Well, you could, but then you'd spend the rest of your life in prison once those damn police dogs tracked you down. So he had considered and rejected several decent plans until the right one was ready to go. It was finally time to act.

Two nights later, just after dark, he drove from his home to a quiet side street near Historic Richmond Town, slightly more than two miles southeast of his front door. For this mission he carried only a light backpack whose chief contents were his rifle and a disposable cell phone. Travel would be slow -- an hour and a half or more each way, he figured -- since he'd be charting his own course through heavy woods and open fields as well as crossing a couple of roads where stealth would be extremely important. But by the time he was finished he would have left a trail that would lead the police nowhere.

He exercised extreme caution during the early part of the hike since there were nearby homes. But after 20 minutes he and his compass were utterly alone in the moonlit wilderness. The waterproof boots had been a wise choice since the recent rain had left the ponds and streams overflowing. This was a good thing, though, because it further reduced the likelihood of encountering other hikers. Who but a man on a mission would be out here at night in the middle of nowhere slogging through a swamp? Scout sniper Jackson was in his element.

When he finally sprinted north across Rockland Avenue an hour later he was on full combat alert. He was approaching the neighborhood, and he needed to follow a circuitous route that kept him as far from his own home as possible. For at least three weeks following tonight's mission he would not enter his own back yard or go near the woods in case the police were still out there with their dogs, searching for the killer's scent. No, the only trail they would pick up was the one that took them to Richmond Town and a dead end.

Ten minutes before reaching the perimeter of Goodall's property Jackson slipped into a thicket to eat a protein bar, sip some water, and assemble his rifle. Once the butt was attached he screwed on a bipod -- a lightweight two-legged stand to stabilize the rifle while firing -- because this would be the most important shot he had ever taken. On another day would come the opportunity to take out Archer Grande, the man who wanted to be America's Hitler, but that wasn't something he could afford to think about now. One mission at a time. Complete this one flawlessly, then plan the next.

Shortly after 9:30 p.m. Jackson took his position in the bushes behind Goodall's home. He lay flat on the soft earth, spread his legs behind him, and leaned into the rifle as it rested on the bipod. Man and rifle were now one. All he needed was the right target.

The kitchen at the back of the house was dark except for the unmistakable flicker of a TV filtering in from the living room. Through the rifle scope Jackson scanned back and forth between the small window over the sink and the sliding glass door that led to the deck. It was still early. He was certain his target would appear sooner or later.

Jackson relaxed even as his mind flooded with recollections of what Goodall had done to him, and where, and when, and how often. He remembered pleading with his mother to let him go to work with her instead of going over to Coach T's house. But she wouldn't give in, and he would never tell her what was going on.

His fault or hers? Shouldn't a mother have known? And years later, after Goodall had been arrested on child-porn charges, shouldn't she have suspected? Said something? Asked something?

Never happened. He was alone then, but he wasn't alone now. The rifle he held in these two hands was here to erase years of abuse, hatred, and shame. One squeeze of the trigger would close a long, humiliating chapter of his life and free him to tackle even greater challenges.

The kitchen light flashed on. Jackson took a deep breath and exhaled slowly, urging his senses to remain alert even as his heart rate slowed and his body grew still. He watched the shadow on the kitchen wall, then saw Goodall standing naked at the glass door with a can of beer in his left hand. Was the fat man hoping someone might see him? If so, this was his lucky night.

Goodall's right hand moved to the handle of the sliding door. He drew it aside slowly, almost as though he were taunting Jackson, who lay in the bushes with his finger over the trigger. Not yet, not yet. Exhale. Relax.

And then Goodall stepped onto the deck and sauntered to the railing. Stood there naked, silhouetted by the kitchen light, and sucked down his beer.

From a prone shooting position Jackson could have made the shot from 300 yards, especially when using a bipod to steady his weapon. But on this night he was firing from less than 30. As Goodall stared straight ahead into the black woods Jackson put the crosshairs on his abuser's nose and gently increased his finger's pressure on the trigger.

The bullet needed less than three hundredths of a second to reach the center of Goodall's face, which exploded in a crimson cloud. His body flew back from the railing and slammed onto the deck perfectly still. Game over.

As Jackson fled through the woods toward his car he found himself sobbing for the first time since he had been a victim all those years ago. The emotional release was both draining and empowering. The child was finally gone. A man had taken his place.

Thirty minutes into his hike Jackson removed the disposable cell phone from his backpack and sent a brief email to *Staten Island Advance* city editor Judith Mosely, who had shared a byline on the Francis Mayfield story.

Say goodbye to another bastard.   No more warnings.   They leave, or they die. Gabriel

24.

The first week of June brought glorious sunshine, clear skies, and fine poll numbers. Archer Grande felt positively invincible as he looked out over the East River from his top-floor penthouse. Things were good and were going to get vastly better. Come January he'd be sitting in the Oval Office barking out orders and changing the world. About goddamn time, he thought. Everything else he had accomplished in life was bush-league nonsense compared to being undisputed leader of the free world.

The elevator chime announced the arrival of Andrea Wilson, Pulitzer-winning reporter for the *New York Times,* who had been granted a private interview by campaign manager Vincent Chandler. Grande didn't like giving newspaper interviews. He much preferred a stage, where he could posture and rant for hundreds, or thousands, or, in the case of televised speeches, even millions of loving fans at once. Stand-up events put him in control, whereas one-on-one interviews tipped the balance of power in favor of the reporter. But this was, after all, the *Times*, and Wilson was, in fact, the paper's most admired talent, someone widely known for dealing in fact rather than opinion. So even though Grande was wary of her he grudgingly agreed to the session.

Wilson had seen opulence before during her years of meeting with the rich and famous, but she was still awed by Grande's full-floor, 9,000-square-foot space in one of Manhattan's most prestigious neighborhoods. Either of the living room couches, both French antiques dating to the mid-1600s, cost more than she earned in a year, and each of the Chinese vases nestled on priceless tables was worth well above $100,000. What most grabbed her attention, however, were the paintings she passed on the way to Grande's study. Originals by Turner, Monet, Cezanne, and Andrew Wyeth were as plentiful as the cheap prints that covered the walls of many lesser homes. If the apartment itself was worth $100 million -- a reasonable guess -- what was inside it was worth at least another $20 million.

"How long does it take to walk from one side of your apartment to the other," she wisecracked.

"I've never timed it," he smiled, "but I can if you'd like."

"No, that's fine. You have an absolutely gorgeous home, Mr. Grande. It's not quite as large as the Palace of Versailles, but it's definitely a keeper."

"My wife and I think so. And actually," he gushed, "the armoire in the corner over here is a Louis XIII piece that the experts tell me was made in 1839 and, believe it or not, once stood in the Palace of Versailles." It was a staggering claim, but Wilson had no reason to doubt it. Grande could afford the best, so a piece of furniture owned by a former king and now worth a million, give or take a few hundred thousand, was in keeping with his style. "A similar but later piece by the same craftsman is currently on display at the Louvre in Paris," he added.

For nearly an hour Grande and Wilson sat in the magnificent study trading questions and answers on the campaign and the candidate's key positions. When he finally glanced at his watch, she knew it was time to wrap up.

"A couple of final questions," she smiled.

"Shoot."

"Speaking of which, how do the shootings on Staten Island affect your plans for the big July 6th rally over there?" she asked.

He seemed not to understand the question at first. "Affect in what way?"

"Well, you have this madman who calls himself Gabriel killing people with a sniper rifle. Doesn't that bother you?"

He was unruffled. "He's killing child molesters. That doesn't bother me one bit. When I'm president I'll be pushing for a one-strike-you're-out law to get these perverts out of circulation for good."

"It doesn't bother you that a vigilante is acting as judge and jury?"

"I don't necessarily condone the method," he shrugged, "but obviously the courts aren't getting the job done. They give these child rapists wrist slaps and put them back on the street, where nearly 100% of them rape another kid. So maybe this guy is doing everyone a favor."

"A lot of voters might consider that a highly inflammatory position, Mr. Grande."

"Not the people who are voting for me," he grinned, "which is most of them. I could stroll naked down Fifth Avenue, and my supporters would still vote for me. In fact, I might pick up a few more voters. People love me. I say what the professional politicians are afraid to say. And as president I will do what those hacks are afraid to do."

"So you're not thinking about cancelling your big July 6th event on Staten Island?" she asked.

"*Events*, with an *s*," he corrected her. "We'll begin with a massive outdoor rally at the Staten Island Mall. After that we'll have a smaller outdoor rally at the country club for donors who weren't able to get tickets for the dinner. And then at the dinner we'll raise a few hundred thousand dollars for the campaign. So yes, it all goes on as planned. Americans who own guns don't worry me," he said, "because they know I'm on their side. In fact, I worry a lot more about the liberal sheep who *don't* own guns."

Andrea Wilson's exclusive *Times* interview occupied a full inside page two days later, and as usual she did a remarkable job of sticking to the facts. Whatever she thought about Grande -- and, for the record, she thought he was more than slightly demented -- was carefully omitted from her account, allowing the reader to weigh the candidate's views without editorial nudging. Response to the article was, as Grande had predicted, enormously positive. His supporters gave him high marks not only for agreeing to the interview in the first place -- the *Times,* after all, was certainly no big fan of his -- but also for his bold Wild West stance on the sensitive subject of dealing with sex offenders.

Stone Jackson read the story and was highly pleased on two counts. First, he appreciated Grande's undisguised support for the two killings. Hey, if a presidential candidate thinks you're doing the right thing, why stop? Second, and most important, he was glad to hear the July 6th events would not be cancelled.

It was time for Archer Grande to have himself measured for a fancy casket.

25.

Terrence Goodall's murder put the detectives back in the same hot seat they had occupied on numerous earlier occasions. The mayor expected them to wave a magic wand and capture the killer immediately, while community leaders and the press second-guessed everything they did or didn't do. But at least now Nazareth and Gimble had more urgent concerns than interviewing girls who had been sexually assaulted in recent months. They had just returned to the precinct from the third such meeting, and like the first two it had been a complete waste of their time.

Yes, the girl had been assaulted. No, the family didn't want police follow-up. In each of the three cases it looked as though the girl's father had decided to take care of business on his own. No one actually admitted taking revenge on a sex offender, but the detectives strongly suspected this is what had happened.

"Pete, you were born and raised on Staten Island," Gimble said. "What's with this place that everyone wants to settle scores on their own?"

"That's just how it is, Tara. Believe it or not, it's actually better than it used to be. I was born long after they built the Verrazano-Narrows Bridge," he explained, "but my parents tell me that before the bridge Staten Island was more like a separate country than part of New York City. People were intensely loyal to their own distinct neighborhoods and didn't like outsiders roaming around."

"Tribalism?"

"Is that one of your Stanford psych-major terms?" he laughed.

"Yeah, I guess. People feel a strong cultural or ethnic tie to their small tribe or village or neighborhood, whatever you want to call it."

"Okay, that fits. If you ask a local where he's from, he doesn't say Staten Island," Nazareth told her. "He says Graniteville or Mariner's Harbor or Tottenville or New Dorp. The other thing you've got going here is strong cultural identity, especially Italian, Irish, and maybe some German. Italian-Americans and Irish-Americans account for nearly half the borough's population, and historically both groups prefer to handle their own problems."

"In other words, we'll never get anywhere interviewing the girls and their families," she said.

"Pretty much, yeah. But now that we've got two Gabriel killings to look at I think we have a better way of approaching this anyway."

"And that would be?"

"We draw some circles."

"Circles?"

"Uh, huh. I'll show you."

He went to a large wall-mounted computer screen in the conference room and pulled up a map of Staten Island.

"This is a mapping website I discovered. Watch this. I mark the location of Francis Mayfield's murder, type in a radius of 1.25 miles, and click. Up pops a circle on the map."

"Why the 1.25-mile radius?" she asked.

"It's the distance between Mayfield's back yard and the spot where the killer parked his car."

"Okay, got it."

"Now the second point. I mark Terrence Goodall's house, put in the new radius of 1.75 miles, and click. Now I've got two circles."

"And they overlap."

"Correct. We don't know anything about the killer except a) where he killed his victims and b) where he parked his car. I have a hunch, and it's only a hunch," he emphasized, "that the killer lives within a mile of where the circles intersect."

"Now I'm lost."

"Let me back up a step. I've been thinking about this a lot, mostly at 2:00 a.m. when I'd rather be sleeping, and I believe the two killings are not at all random. In fact, I think it's highly likely the killer is a sex-crime victim who's seriously on the warpath."

"Why not just another nut?" she asked, clearly not convinced.

"All the crazies we've gone after before have had what they believed was a logical rationale for killing. In this case the most logical motivation would be revenge. This is just a wild guess," he nodded, "but I believe the killer was abused himself or is seeking revenge on behalf of a family member."

"Okay, that makes sense. But how do the circles on the map fit in?"

"Whoever killed Mayfield and Goodall knows the Greenbelt," he began, "as well as the neighborhoods surrounding it. He knew exactly where to park for both murders, and he planned comfortable hikes for himself -- far enough away from his vehicle that no one in that neighborhood would hear the rifle shot, but close enough that he could get back to the vehicle and drive away before the police followed him."

"So far so good."

"Furthermore, in both instances the path through the woods was optimal from a soldier's perspective. I've looked at topographical maps," he said, "and this guy took basically the same routes I would have followed if I had studied the area. I did this sort of thing quite a bit while I was in Afghanistan, and I'm convinced this guy really knows the terrain."

"So the path is carefully planned in advance?" she said.

"Right. In addition, after visiting both crime scenes he selected the absolute best location from which to fire. That doesn't just happen by chance," he reasoned. "It's the result of professional judgment based upon a lot of research. This is the behavior of a trained sniper."

"You think we're dealing with a trained sniper?"

"Either that or a very good lookalike. This guy knows what he's doing."

"Okay, Pete. Back to the circles. Why do you think he lives within a mile of where the two circles intersect?"

"Intuition, I suppose. It's not possible to know these woods as well as this guy does unless you've spent a lot of time in them," Nazareth reasoned. "So right now I wouldn't be at all surprised to learn he lives right alongside the Greenbelt. That would certainly match up with the level of planning involved. He uses the car, I assume, because he can't walk to the crime scenes from his home without leaving a scent that dogs could follow."

Gimble valued her partner's opinion, but she realized it was only that -- opinion, not fact.

"You're building assumptions on top of assumptions, Pete. What you're saying isn't crazy, but I have trouble connecting the same dots."

"So do I," he laughed. "But, hey, what else have we got? If we assume for the moment that he lives within a mile of where the two circles intersect, we can at least create a hypothetical third circle."

"As though he's planning another shooting?" she asked.

"Yes, and I think that's a foregone conclusion. I say that for two reasons, Tara. First, he's completely invisible right now and sees no threat to his operation. On that basis alone I believe he keeps on killing. But second, and this is simply more guesswork," he added, "it's possible he's trying to hide his real target in the midst of many targets."

"Explain, please."

"Let's suppose the killer was abused by someone and decides to kill that person. Maybe there's a police record that would link the two of them, right?"

"Right. Okay, so you think that by killing a few extra sex offenders," she continued, "he reduces the possibility of our identifying the real link."

"There you go. Right now we've got two victims, either of whom may have sexually assaulted this guy Gabriel, whoever he is. Pretty soon we could have three . . . or four . . . or five. Who knows? Let's say we end up with five murders," he offered, "and let's say each dead sex offender had molested 10 kids, which is probably on the low side. That means we'd have 50 sex-crime victims with a possible motive for killing."

"If you're on target, Pete, that means we've got to nail this guy soon if we're going to have any chance at all."

"Agreed. That's why we have to add another circle to our map. Let's assume he wants to use neighborhoods that are relatively distant from each other because he's too smart to use the same parking spots over again."

Gimble got on board Nazareth's guessing game. "And if we plot the addresses of registered sex offenders who live somewhere along the Greenbelt boundary . . ."

"Like the first two victims . . ."

"Then we may be able to spot Gabriel's next target before he does."

"Anything's possible, Tara, and anything is better than nothing. Let's look at some hypotheticals."

Using an online list of registered sex offenders they searched for any who had been arrested for assaulting children and, importantly, who also lived at the edge of the Greenbelt. Next they searched for addresses located at least one mile away from the two murder scenes. From the resulting list of five candidates they chose two that in their opinion best represented the kind of person Gabriel might be after.

The first hypothetical victim lived near the intersection of Arthur Kill Road and Richmond Road not far from Latourette Golf Course. The second lived to the north alongside 164-acre Willowbrook Park. When Nazareth superimposed circles on the two hypothetical victims, all four circles overlapped at a point in the woods near the heart of the Greenbelt.

"This certainly isn't hard science, Tara," Nazareth said, "but my gut tells me Gabriel lives within a mile of that point." He had no idea how right he was. Jackson's home was, in fact, six-tenths of a mile from the spot.

Gimble studied the map, deep in thought. "Unless he's living in the woods," she said, "which I strongly doubt, then he's in one of three neighborhoods at the edge of the circle: New Springville, Lighthouse Hill, and Manor Heights. Lots of homes, Pete."

"For sure. And that assumes these circles actually mean something."

"Which they may."

"Or may not."

"Well, as you've said, anything's better than nothing," she smiled. "So where do we go with this?"

He shook his head slightly. "On a wild goose chase, probably."

"When did that ever stop us?"

"Right, never."

"Okay, then. Let's figure this out."

26.

Jackson didn't mind driving nearly two hours each way to the firing range deep in the woods of northern New Jersey. The trip always gave him plenty of time to think, and thinking was something any self-respecting scout sniper valued. These days he was deciding which Staten Island sex offender would be next on his list. Lots of choices, of course, but only one would be the perfect fit for that moment. Timing is everything, he thought. Even if he were to kill 100 of them eventually, he needed to nail all the victims in the proper order so that the police never latched onto a predictable pattern. In his line of work predictability could easily lead to catastrophe.

He was also beginning to sketch out his plan for Archer Grande, since the campaign events set for July 6th on Staten Island were less than a month away. Did shooting Grande at the big Staten Island Mall rally make the most sense, or should he take the guy down at the smaller country club gathering? Either way, the mission date was cast in bronze because after July 6th he might never have another chance. Much research needed to be done before pulling the trigger on this one.

In the meantime, he squeezed off as many rounds as his limited income would allow, and he got better every time out. Almost too good, in fact. He had chosen the distant New Jersey firing range because it offered anonymity. But now when he showed up there were always one or two regulars who wanted to watch him in action, especially when he was working at 300 yards. At that distance he routinely grouped 25 shots in a tight two-inch circle on the target, a feat no one else at the range could come close to matching.

"God-DAMN! You're good," the guy behind him hooted after Jackson had finished his late-morning practice. "Have you done any club competitions?"

Jackson pretended not to hear him. The shooting earmuffs gave him a reasonable excuse for not responding, but he didn't much care whether the guy believed it or not. He was here to sharpen his skills, not make new buddies.

"Hey, great shooting," the guy said, louder than before. Eventually he figured out he wasn't wanted and strolled off muttering to himself, leaving Jackson to clean up the area, stow the rifle, and head home. Maybe it's time to find another range, he thought as he threw the car in gear -- a place where people aren't so chummy. Who the hell comes to a firing range looking for pals anyway? Open a Facebook account if you're desperate. Don't waste a busy man's time.

He would, in fact, be incredibly busy over the next few weeks. Tonight he wanted to finalize his choice for the next sex-offender mission. From a list of eight strong candidates he would select the best one according to his strict operational criteria. First, the target had to be among the worst of the worst, and that meant finding someone who had abused a young child. Second, the target needed to live as far as possible from each of the first two murder scenes. And third, the target should have money -- the more money the better. Jackson was disgusted to think about convicted child molesters living the good life, as both Mayfield and Goodall had done. Finding a rich target would really make his day.

As for Grande, well, he was a dead man walking. Jackson could easily take the guy out from 400 yards, so he didn't care whether he shot him at the mall or at the country club. Sometime in the coming week he would scout both locations looking for the perfect sniper position and the ideal escape route. The police and Secret Service would be out in heavy numbers on July 6th, of course, but none of them knew the Greenbelt the way he did. He was confident that by the time the big day arrived he would enjoy an overwhelming advantage.

So much to do for one man.

At 9:17 that night he sat at the kitchen table, alone except for a large topographic map of Staten Island and a bottle of high-protein drink. He was as combat-ready as a man could be and sorry he couldn't find more challenging terrain for his next mission. The tougher the terrain, after all, the harder life would be for his pursuers. Maybe one day he would take his Gabriel show on the road and eliminate some trash in Maine or Vermont or New Hampshire. But for now he had to settle.

The Lighthouse Hill neighborhood had three things going for it. To begin with its highest point was 145 feet above sea level. The climb was a laugher for someone at his elite fitness level, but he figured it would be a serious chore for police in street gear. In addition, it was a highly exclusive big-bucks community -- lots of self-satisfied rich folks, including his next target, enjoying life in their multi-million-dollar homes. And finally, the neighborhood was readily accessible from Forest Hill Road, a strategically important route that ran alongside the southwestern boundary of the Greenbelt for two miles or more. This meant Jackson could park right next to the woods, hike the mile and a half to the kill zone, and safely exit the area without attracting attention.

Lighthouse Hill also offered the advantage of being nearly two miles from the site of the second shooting. By scattering the victims geographically he could keep the cops searching for a pattern that didn't exist and groping for connections they would never find. The more sex offenders he killed, the lower the probability that the police would ever link him to Terrence Goodall, the only victim he had ever actually known.

At the moment the late Terrence Goodall remained a bit of an issue. Jackson knew the police would be visiting neighbors asking about anyone who might have had a motive for killing that useless waste of life. Although Goodall had never been arrested for molesting any children, surely someone must have suspected. What if someone remembered that Goodall had cared for Jackson in his home? Okay, so what? If the police visit and ask whether the guy molested you, you laugh at them, he told himself. Hell no, he never molested me. He was a great guy. Great coach. Great target.

The police would never know what Goodall had done. End of story. But if by some chance they were suspicious and found a way to search the house, Jackson thought, this whole thing comes crashing down. No way they can get their hands on the rifle. It's the only thing that could tie him to the murders.

He went down into the musty basement where old cans of fruit, vegetables, and chili lined the lopsided shelves he had built for his mother while still in elementary school. One day soon he would throw all that crap out, but tonight he was interested only in the sagging drop ceiling he had installed during his junior year of high school. He had planned to create a fancy weight room where he and his friends could train. The weight room never happened, but the ceiling turned out okay. And now it would prove highly useful.

Jackson gently lifted out one of the panels near the far corner of the basement, carefully inserted the rifle, and closed the ceiling again. His four boxes of ammo went first in a large plastic bag, then into the ancient freezer chest under a layer of 20-year-old Birds Eye vegetables and grim packages of supermarket hamburger.

Genius is in the details, and he was mastering all of them.

27.

Brigitte Evianna Artois, otherwise known as Mrs. Grande, jolted awake at 3:47 a.m. and abruptly sat up in their $2.1-million canopy bed. Her heart was pounding, and she was drenched with sweat. The disturbance roused husband Archer from a sound and pleasant sleep.

"Huh? What, what . . ."

"Oh, God, Archer. I just had the most awful nightmare." Tears streamed down her face. "But it was real. I've never had a dream like that. I was right there. It was actually happening."

"What was happening?" he asked, still fogbound.

"I was in some awful doctor's office," she told him, "and he said I was pregnant. I said that wasn't possible, but he insisted. And then suddenly you and I were here in bed, but there was a baby sleeping on the mattress between us. You wanted to talk about the election, but I kept telling you to be quiet or you'd wake up Baby Archer."

"Baby Archer?"

"Yes, our son. He looked just like you, only tiny. And he was so real I swear to you he was right here on the bed between us. I can't believe it was a dream."

"I'm no expert on dreams," he offered, "but between the campaign and the story about your being pregnant, I'm sure your subconscious just got a little carried away."

"Archer, this couldn't have been just a dream. I'm scared," she sobbed. "It was so real. What if I'm actually pregnant?"

"That's not possible," he said calmly.

"Not likely, Archer, but possible."

"You're on the pill, right? So how can you be pregnant? This is just a bad dream, Bridge."

"Listen, Archer. The theoretical effectiveness of the pill I take is 99%, which means there's a 1% chance I can still get pregnant.

But the typical effectiveness is only about 91%, which means there's a 9% chance."

"What the hell is *typical effectiveness?*" he snapped.

"Well, for instance, if you don't take the pill at precisely the same time every day then you're not using it perfectly."

"But you don't ever forget to take it, right?" She didn't answer. "You don't forget to take it, right, Bridge?"

"I don't think so."

"You don't think so? How the hell could you not be sure?"

"Do you take your goddamn precious vitamins every day?"

"We're not talking about vitamins! We're talking about having kids."

"You think I don't know that? And, yes, I think I've taken one every day. But on some of your campaign trips my schedule was so screwed up it's always possible I forgot."

"God almighty! You think you forgot?"

"No, I didn't say that," she whined. "All I said is it's always possible."

"Well that's just great. What I really need at 53 is a kid," he groaned. "A little baby to crawl around the Oval Office while Daddy runs the world."

They sat in uncomfortable silence for a minute or two. Brigitte worried about her modeling career while her husband thought about how a baby in the family would interfere with his routine. Neither wanted to give up anything.

"Okay, look," he said finally, "I'm sure this is all just a nightmare because of what's going on with the campaign, but tomorrow you can see the doc and find out for sure."

She took a deep breath and exhaled slowly. "Archer, I already know."

"How the hell can you know?"

"The dream was so incredibly real."

"Bridge, it was a dream! Not real. Fake. Brain cells playing tricks on you in the night. Go see the doc, and it'll all be okay."

"Fine, I'll see the doc," she murmured. "But I already know."

"You can't know. Go back to sleep. It'll be fine."

Late the next morning Brigitte returned from the doctor's office and found her husband at his desk savoring a cup of Hacienda La Esmeralda coffee -- a gift to himself at nearly $400 a pound -- while reviewing his schedule with campaign manager Vincent Chandler. She wore a cynical smile on her lips.

"Well?" Grande said brightly.

"Well," she answered, "the modeling agency tells me there are no opportunities for fat, pregnant cows."

She turned and left the room.

28.

"I keep seeing circles even when I'm not looking at the map," Gimble laughed. She and Nazareth had studied the circles on the Greenbelt map for nearly an hour, hoping to find something other than dumb luck that might drive their investigation into the Gabriel killings. But they had reached a dead end. The four circles -- two representing actual crime scenes and two marking hypothetical murders -- looked a lot more scientific than they actually were because they were based on a string of assumptions.

"I think we've gotten as far as we're going to with all the guesswork, Pete," she said, "so what do we do now about these two possible crime scenes?"

His right hand cradled his chin as he studied the map. The wheels continued to turn, but he knew they weren't meshing properly. Nazareth was frustrated that his almost legendary gift for knitting facts together was of no great use when all the key facts were missing. Guesswork and luck hadn't made him one of the NYPD's most valuable assets. Yet here he was with two names -- Thomas Bronfman and Douglas Ridley -- that had essentially been plucked from thin air.

"Well, it's a safe bet we're not going to put around-the-clock surveillance on the two guys," he reasoned. "Even if we knew they were actual targets, and we don't, we still have no idea when Gabriel might go after them. For all we know they could be numbers 25 and 26 on his list. There's no way I can make a case for manpower on something like this."

"Then what about surveillance cameras?" Gimble asked

"That's a possibility," he nodded. "If we use motion-detecting infrared cameras we'd certainly capture some footage, but I don't know whether the detail will be terribly clear. The real trick, though, is to videotape someone *before* he kills, not after."

"If motion triggers the camera it can also trigger a floodlight," she offered. "That would most likely stop him, right?"

"Yeah, I suppose so. But that means the light would come on every time something moves. And most often that's going to be a neighbor, or a deer, or maybe even trees blowing in the wind," he said. "It's one thing to use a motion-sensing light behind your own home and another to light up the woods 30 or 40 yards away. The one-two-two switchboard might take a lot of nasty phone calls over that."

"Then I vote to use the camera. That's our best chance to identify   Gabriel."

"Unfortunately, it'll be after he's killed a third victim."

"Then at least we'll prevent a fourth."

"Man, I hate flying blind like this," he said, obviously angry at not having any sense of control over events.

"We use the cameras," Gimble said, "but at the same time we put on a full-court press at the two murder scenes. We go door to door until we find something that points us in the right direction. That's all we can do."

Only one of the men they had identified as a possible Gabriel victim agreed to have a surveillance camera installed in his back yard. Douglas Ridley had been scared to death ever since the first Gabriel murder and jumped at the chance to gain anything in the way of police protection. Thomas Bronfman, on the other hand, angrily rejected the idea as an invasion of his privacy and even accused the detectives of trying to spy on him after he had "paid his debt to society."

"Now there's a man who needs to be watched," Gimble said as she and Nazareth walked away from Bronfman's front door.

"Damn right," he said. "I bet he's as dirty as they come and has something to hide. Maybe he's back to his old tricks."

"Wouldn't surprise me. In fact, it would surprise me if he weren't. He's worth mentioning at the precinct."

"Most definitely. But first let's head over to Terrence Goodall's place and see what some of the neighbors can tell us."

The neighbors didn't tell them much. Most of the people Nazareth and Gimble interviewed had moved to the neighborhood long after Goodall's arrest on child pornography charges. The first time some of them had learned of the guy's past, in fact, was from the *Advance* article about his murder. Meanwhile, several of the old-timers remembered Goodall as an outstanding coach and a genuinely likeable person despite his indiscretion. Had they known about the molestations, of course, they would have held a different opinion. But they didn't.

Only two of Goodall's secret victims still lived on the block: Jackson and his one-time friend Ed Linden. Both were at work when the detectives showed up, so they temporarily became footnotes to the investigation. The most productive conversation by far was with Sarah Carmody, the woman who had tended the Jackson home immediately following her friend Aggie's death. Carmody had spent her entire adult life in the neighborhood, knew almost everything about everyone, and loved to talk. Nazareth and Gimble gave her the opportunity.

"Everybody called him Coach T," she told them, "and the kids all loved him. He was one of the nicest men on the block. I have no idea how that business with child pornography ever happened, but I'll always believe it was the wife who framed him somehow. She was never any good."

"So you don't think he was interested in children?" Gimble asked gently.

"Not like that. God, no. He had two girls of his own, and I never heard any of the neighborhood kids say a bad word about him. As a matter of fact," she added, "the woman next door, Aggie Jackson, asked Coach T to take care of her son when she worked, and he did that for a couple of years. Never any problem."

"Does Mrs. Jackson still live there?"

"No, she died a few months ago. Her son lives alone now. Stone Jackson is his name."

"And you never heard her or the son complain about Mr. Goodall's behavior?" Nazareth asked.

"Not once, ever. Aggie certainly would have told me if there was anything wrong," she assured them. "We didn't have any secrets from each other. Aggie would never have been able to keep her job without Coach T's help, believe me. And as for Stone, he was just a boy who liked playing baseball and hanging around with the other kids. He's a fine young man now. Has a bank job."

"Do you remember what other neighbors thought," Nazareth said, "once the news about the child porn charges came out?"

"Everyone was shocked," she recalled, "but a few of us blamed the wife. I think she wanted the husband's money without the husband, so she set the whole thing up to get him arrested."

"What about the people who didn't blame the wife?" Gimble asked. "What did they think?"

"Some people have their minds in the gutter all the time, so a few people on the block suddenly said he was no good and wouldn't let their kids go near him."

"They thought he had a sexual interest in children, in other words?"

"Some people, yes," she sneered. "But they were wrong. If Coach T had been bothering any of the children, we would have known. Certainly Aggie Jackson would have known."

"I'm sure you've read all the newspaper accounts," Nazareth said, "so you know we don't have any firm suspects. Why do you think someone would have wanted to kill him?"

"Well, I know some crazy person who calls himself Gabriel claims he's going to kill child molesters," she said indignantly, "but if that's why he killed Terrence Goodall, he had his facts all wrong. I think the person you're after just likes killing and is using any excuse he can think of to justify murder."

"You may be right, Mrs. Carmody," said Gimble. "We certainly appreciate your time."

"I'm glad to help, detectives. If you have any other questions, I'm always here."

As they walked to the car Gimble said what they were both thinking. "She thinks Goodall's wife set him up?"

"Yeah, that's a little odd, isn't it? I can imagine a wife shooting her husband in the head, but not framing him for possession of child pornography."

"I agree. Child-porn charges would be embarrassing for her and the children, not just the husband. I can't see it."

"Neither can I. I didn't get the sense she was lying to us," he said, "but she obviously has a problem letting go of her opinions."

"So are we finished here, Pete?"

"I'd like to talk with the Jackson kid sometime, since he apparently has first-hand knowledge of Goodall's behavior. But I don't expect to get anything new. Sounds as though everyone loved old Coach T."

"Except for the guy who killed him."

"Well, yeah, except for him."

29.

Private chef Delphine Gaulier served another of her magnificent dinners to Archer and Brigitte Grande, who sat quietly at a candlelit table alongside the floor-to-ceiling window that looked north toward Central Park. Creating a different world-class meal five nights each week for a mega-rich, hard-to-please couple wasn't easy, but for $225,000 a year -- or roughly three times what she had earned as executive chef at one of Manhattan's top restaurants -- Gaulier was willing to challenge herself.

This evening's main dish was delicate sea bass in a light caviar sauce with steamed whole baby vegetables under an Asian glaze. Brigitte loved sea bass no matter how Gaulier prepared it, but she would have enjoyed a glass of wine as well. Tonight's selection was 2013 Araujo sauvignon blanc from Napa Valley, a $90-a-bottle treat that husband Archer would have to enjoy alone.

"You're not having wine?" he asked, unaware that he had tiptoed into a minefield.

"You're quite serious, Archer?" Her words dripped with sarcasm.

"What? You don't want sauvignon blanc? Or would you rather have something French?"

"I can't drink any kind of wine from any country on the entire goddamn planet while I'm pregnant," she snarled. "Do you remember I mentioned something about being pregnant earlier today, or did that get lost in all of your important campaign business?"

His eyes widened and his mouth hung open. "Of course I remember," he said innocently. "I just assumed this wasn't an issue."

Brigitte glared at him. "Oh, really. And why not?"

"Bridge, we agreed a long time ago that we didn't want kids, right? So what's the problem all of a sudden?"

153

"Well, oh wise one, I guess the problem is that *all of a sudden* I'm pregnant. This is not just some cheap campaign stunt you and your ass-kisser-in-chief Vincent Chandler dreamt up. I'm actually carrying a child, Archer. *Our* child. And that means in another eight months we'll need to widen all of our doors so that I can waddle through."

"Now wait a second," he said nervously, "all the things I like to do in this world work just fine without kids. I'm not interested in turning our lifestyle upside down just because you forgot to take a pill one morning."

Brigitte rose slowly and dropped her pink linen napkin into the sea bass with caviar sauce. She forced a half-smile to her lips. "The pill may not be 100% effective, Archer," she said as she walked away, "but abstinence most definitely is. Let's resume this conversation eight months from now, shall we?"

Grande finished his meal and half the bottle of wine before phoning Chandler, who three minutes earlier had been escorted by the maître d' to a prominent table at La Grenouille, one of Manhattan's fanciest French restaurants.

"I want to finish working on the New York City schedule," Grande snapped.

"Okay," Chandler offered meekly. "Tomorrow early?"

"Today now," Grande answered. "I'll be waiting."

For a flicker of a moment Chandler considered asking for a sharp knife to go, then remembered that Archer Grande was the ultimate meal ticket. He had grown to hate the guy, yes, of course, but there was no way out now. Chandler had built his entire future on the upcoming election. Getting his boss behind the big desk in the Oval Office was essential.

"Did you hitchhike here?" Grande asked derisively when Chandler arrived less than 15 minutes later.

"It's Manhattan, Arch."

"Gee, is it really? Damn, all day long I thought I was in St. Moritz," he taunted. "No wonder I couldn't find my skis."

Chandler desperately wanted to tell Grande where to put his skis but thought better of it.

"Good," said Grande. "So we're in Manhattan. Now let's wrap up the schedule for July. I already know I'll be jetting around the country for the second half of the month, but I want to know more about the big outdoor rally on Staten Island."

"July 6th at the Staten Island Mall."

"That's the one. Why a shopping mall parking lot, Vince? That's more appropriate for a carnival than an important campaign rally."

"People like shopping malls, Arch. And this one happens to have 7,000 parking spaces. If we do this right, we could have 20,000 people turn out for the afternoon rally."

"20,000?"

"Absolutely. That's a big number, and we'll get lots of aerial footage we can use once you're nominated at the convention. Great *man of the people* stuff."

Grande enjoyed being a man of the people as long as he didn't actually have to live among them. "All right. If you can get 20,000 people to attend, then it's worth doing. But what about the small event at the country club? Why the hell do I need to do that one?"

"It's invitation-only, Arch, and some of these people have maxed out their campaign contributions for you. We just don't have room for them at the private dinner. These are some of your strongest financial backers, and all you need to give them is 15 or 20 minutes."

"I have a better idea," Grande said. "Invite them to the giant rally at the mall, but give them special seating up front. That way they can all take a bow or something."

Chandler shook his head furiously. "No, no good. These people will abandon ship if you kiss them off. Some of them were very unhappy when they found out we didn't have enough room for them at the dinner. This special outdoor event is the least we can do, Arch."

"Fine, then. Just make sure they're all paying customers. I don't want any freeloaders in attendance. And make sure there are no protesters at either place. No asshole protesters."

"We'll have plenty of muscle at the mall, Arch. Any protesters will be escorted into the woods if necessary. And you won't have to worry about the country club event. Everyone there will be a huge fan of yours."

"Good. Change of subject. Brigitte says she's going to have the baby."

"You don't sound happy."

"I should be happy? My life isn't perfect as is? If I want to go skiing in Switzerland in the morning, I pack a suitcase and fly there in my private jet. If I feel like swimming in Hawaii, I go. If I want to sleep late some morning, I do. So tell me, Vince," he roared, "how does having a baby in the house make my life better?"

"This is much better for your numbers, that's how. Our plan was to announce Brigitte's phony miscarriage, and you would have gotten a sympathy bump in the polls. But when people see her climbing onto the stage in maternity clothes, they'll eat it up, believe me. SUPER MODEL TOSSES CAREER FOR MOTHERHOOD. Man, that's a great headline. Mr. & Mrs. Main Street will be ankle deep in saliva."

"You really think so?"

"No doubt whatsoever, Arch. This is fabulous stuff."

"A kid's going to be a real pain in the ass."

"Not for you," Chandler smirked. "That's Mommy's problem. And, by the way, Mommy and Baby will help guarantee you're reelected to a second term."

"Man-of-the-people stuff."

"Amen, brother."

They shared a joyous high-five.

30.

June 21st. Sunset: 8:31 p.m. Temperature: 87 degrees. Commence operation: 8:59 p.m. Target location: Lighthouse Hill. Primary objective: Michael Cascio.

Jackson stuffed the mission log into his lightweight hunting vest and walked out the back door. He had parked his car at the rear of the house to minimize the risk of snooping. The backpack in his right hand was light tonight -- rifle, ammo, basic emergency gear -- and he planned to be home in bed by midnight at the latest. As he backed down the driveway he congratulated himself once again for having spotted Michael Cascio amid the other sleazeballs on Staten Island's long and growing list of sex offenders. This guy made most of the others look like saints.

Eight years earlier Cascio, then 23, had been convicted of second-degree rape, a class D felony, in a case involving a 12-year-old girl. He was sentenced to 10 years in prison, served three, and returned to his coddled life on Lighthouse Hill, where Mommy and Daddy maintained their palatial home. Cascio's father pulled down $7.5 million a year as an attorney for a giant drug company, while his mother earned another $1.7 million as CEO of a private hospital. Both had dismissed their son's behavior as mere "biological indiscretion" following the trial. The father had even drawn some fire after telling a newspaper reporter that the girl looked more like 18 than 12, but the whole thing died a natural death once young Michael Cascio went off to serve his time.

The 10-year sentence, Jackson had learned online, might have been a life sentence if the judge had been able to consider Cascio's childhood sex offenses. But the records in those cases had first been sealed by the court while he was a minor and then mysteriously lost in the system by the time he was charged with the 12-year-old's assault. In the absence of formal evidence to the contrary, the judge had no choice but to view Cascio as a repentant first-time offender.

Injustice was more than just a word to Jackson. It had become a way of life. If he was the only man strong enough to right America's glaring wrongs, so be it. He'd work alone and hope that in time others would join him in eradicating cockroaches like Cascio.

Archer Grande, on the other hand, was a different type of threat altogether. He was one of the powerful few who could, if allowed to sit in the Oval Office, almost single-handedly destroy democracy and the American way of life. Grande was a coarse, mean-spirited monster whose speeches increasingly seemed modeled after Hitler's. And the man had to be stopped at all cost. If he withdrew from the race, perhaps he could be allowed to live. If not, he had to die.

Jackson parked his car on Forest Hill Road next to the deep woods. Almost any place along this particular stretch would have served his purpose since all the homes were across the street, but he was fortunate to find a space under a burned-out streetlight. To anyone looking out a window from the opposite side of the road he would be nothing more than a momentary shadow. He was cautious nevertheless, so he spent 10 minutes studying the windows of the nearest homes with his binoculars and watching for any movement in the yards. Nothing. Good to go.

After double checking to see that the car's interior lights were switched off, he grabbed his bag from the back seat and slid out the passenger side so that he could vanish quickly into the trees. The heat and high humidity seemed to have energized the mosquitoes, so he stopped and slathered on some 100% DEET repellent. No way he could line up a perfect shot later in the evening with bugs flitting in front of his face. And he wanted this to be a perfect shot. Two earlier scouting trips to Cascio's home had told him all he needed to know about this guy, and he wanted tonight's kill to be a masterpiece.

He had parked slightly north of Latourette Golf Course because he didn't want to risk crossing the fairways, even at night. No such thing as being overly cautious on a serious mission. By hiking southeast from this point he could remain deep within one of the Greenbelt's most heavily forested sections, far from prying eyes until the final steep ascent to the back of Cascio's home.

The hike was mostly uneventful. Except for a few boggy areas where standing water had produced swarms of flying insects, he had an easy time of it. The dark woods reminded him of the South Carolina wilderness where he had sharpened his skills earlier in the year. Much flatter than Sassafras Mountain, of course, but otherwise silent, forbidding, and remote. Drop a man here blindfolded, Jackson mused, and he'd probably assume he was hundreds of miles from civilization. The Greenbelt was truly an amazing place.

Every so often a spooked deer clambered out of a thicket, and twice Jackson heard the mournful hooting of great horned owls, bold night hunters whose prey included rabbits, raccoons, and even small pet dogs unfortunate enough to wander too far afield. As he approached a shallow stream he heard the loud splash of a one-pound bullfrog retreating to the water. He filed that away for future reference. One day soon he might camp out here and live off the land. A plump frog would make a fine meal.

Suddenly Jackson froze in mid-step. Voices. Talking and laughing. This wasn't good. He had reached the eastern boundary of the golf course, where two fairways stretched into the desolate woods. Whoever was out there was close enough to Lighthouse Hill to hear the shot when fired and, worse, could end up crossing his path as he exited the kill zone.

He crept closer to the voices, fingering the Buck knife on his belt. Killing bystanders wasn't part of his plan, and he would reluctantly abort the mission rather than risk blundering into an unfortunate confrontation. But he wanted to know what he was up against before retreating.

He peered out of the bushes at a guy and a girl, both in their late teens. Their voices were clear from where he knelt among the shrubs at the edge of the fairway, and in the moonlight he watched the couple pass a joint back and forth as they jabbered away about a movie they had watched. He would give this one shot, then bail out if it didn't work.

"NYPD!" he screamed. He began stomping up and down in the undergrowth, hoping he sounded like several police officers running toward the young couple.

A high-pitched "Holy shit!" was the only sound one of them made. Jackson couldn't tell whether it was the girl or the really scared guy. Either way, they took off down the fairway toward the clubhouse parking lot and were still running at top speed when they finally disappeared from view. He was certain both teens would keep their mouths shut about the incident and suspected they would soon find a different spot for their late-evening trysts.

With that momentary threat resolved, Jackson now prepared himself for what he had known all along would be the trickiest part of his mission. Only 300 yards remained between him and his target, but they were the most challenging 300 yards he had yet faced. The steep hill ahead of him would make finding a comfortable shooting position difficult. Even worse, the hill was dotted with grand homes whose owners enjoyed spectacular views from their back decks. Would people be sitting on those decks tonight enjoying the warm summer breeze? Would neighborhood dogs detect his presence and sound the alarm? He wouldn't know until he had committed himself to the final ascent. From that moment on he would let his instincts guide him.

He assembled his rifle, chambered the one round he had budgeted for this mission, and crept toward the cluster of four homes high above him. The Cascio place was second from the right, marked by an enormous deck that seemed to hover 20 feet in thin air. It was actually braced by massive steel beams that dug into the hillside below, an engineering feat that only the rich could finance. There was no way Jackson could approach the deck head-on because of the steep terrain. Instead he needed to angle himself roughly 75 yards to the left and would have to shoot across the gently curving hillside when Cascio appeared.

He hadn't left this critical part of the operation to chance. On his earlier intelligence-gathering visits Jackson had learned that young Michael Cascio enjoyed long late-night soaks in the hot tub that occupied one corner of the immense deck -- the corner closest to where Jackson now nestled against the hillside, rifle in hand. On his first scouting mission he had seen Cascio frolicking naked in the hot tub with a young friend at 10:15 p.m. The second time Cascio was alone in the hot tub at 11:00. This didn't necessarily mean the guy was there every night, but Jackson believed the odds were in his favor.

Time crawled by. Sweat dripped off his forehead on the sultry night, and swarms of mosquitoes buzzed around his face despite all the DEET he had applied. Nothing he could do about that now. He had become one with the hillside and would not move again until he either spotted his target or abandoned the mission. By 10:30 he had grown concerned that Cascio wouldn't show. Every now and then he heard car doors slamming in the distance, but he saw no one. In this fancy neighborhood, he figured, all the rich folks must go to bed early so they can get a jump on making more money the next day. Maybe that's all they did. Sleep, make money, sleep. And they call it living.

At 10:50, when Jackson was almost ready to pack his gear and leave, Cascio's deck lights came on. They were harshly bright at first but were quickly dialed down to a soft glow. Whoever worked the dimmer switch apparently wanted a bit of mood lighting. A few moments later the young man stepped out of the kitchen and onto the deck wearing only a blue towel around his waist. Through his scope Jackson checked to make sure it was the son, not the father. Yes, the son, without question. Taller, thinner, more hair.

Cascio dropped the towel, stepped naked into the hot tub, and slowly settled in for a long soak. The luxurious hot tub sat high above its surroundings. So high, in fact, that Cascio's head poked well above the deck's top railing, providing a small but inviting target. From this distance, slightly more than 80 yards, Jackson could normally put a couple dozen rounds in a target that size. But the conditions tonight were anything but normal. His shooting position was unnatural and somewhat unstable because of the uncomfortable slope, and he'd be firing at a spot roughly 30 feet above his eye level. After adding darkness to the equation he regretfully decided he would hold out for a larger target.

Once again he sat motionless on the hillside, waiting for the perfect moment, while all around him nature went noisily about its business. A lone owl called from an oak branch behind him. A chorus of tree frogs at a nearby pond trilled their eerie serenade. And somewhere far across Lighthouse Hill a dog barked in the night.

Fifteen minutes passed, then 20, then 25. That's when Cascio stretched, reached for his towel, and stood up in the hot tub. He slowly dried his chest while enjoying the soft caress of a warm summer breeze on his bare body. He was glad to be alive.

Jackson placed a single round squarely between Cascio's shoulder blades. The exit wound, according to the initial police report, was the size of a baseball. But it was nothing compared to what had taken place inside the chest cavity, where the medical examiner would eventually spend nearly an hour attempting to identify bits of shredded heart tissue.

Cascio was blown from the hot tub and landed face down on the $125,000 Brazilian walnut deck. His parents, asleep in their bedroom on the far side of the house, heard nothing but the soothing hum of the central air conditioner. At 7:15 the next morning his mother would step onto the deck to enjoy a cup of coffee before leaving for work, and her screaming would chase the crows that had settled on her son's body.

But for now Jackson had the night to himself. He stowed the rifle in his knapsack and calmly entered the woods for a leisurely hike back to his car. Along the way he sent a short text message to the *Advance* before dropping his burner phone in a stagnant pond. *They leave or they die. So be it. Gabriel*

At four minutes past midnight he was home, showered, and ready for bed.

31.

The motion-activated video camera the police had placed in Douglas Ridley's yard showed a great deal of activity, all of it worth nothing to Nazareth and Gimble. If anyone was targeting the convicted sex offender the evidence didn't appear in the 65 different clips captured over four days. Twenty of the short videos featured Ridley's retired neighbor who walked his pit bull five or six times each day without once ever cleaning up the mess. The remaining snippets starred kids tossing footballs or baseballs, a small herd of deer bounding through the undergrowth with their white tails held high, windblown tree limbs, and various other non-threatening and generally boring activities.

But the detectives voted to keep the camera rolling in the wake of Michael Cascio's murder.

"We had the right idea, Pete," Gimble said as they walked the latest crime scene, "but the wrong potential vic." They were part of a large NYPD contingent that had descended upon the Lighthouse Hill neighborhood that morning, desperate to find meaningful clues. But the guy they hunted had once again vanished without a trace.

Nazareth was more frustrated than angry. "What burns me is that Cascio was on our short list. If we had put cameras in five yards instead of just one," he fumed, "we would have had this son of a bitch. Now all we'll have is the usual dose of second-guessing from our favorite mayor."

"Let Chief Crawford deal with the mayor," she advised him. "You and I need to keep our heads in the game. We should expand the video operation."

"That's fine," he nodded. "We can get a few more homes under surveillance, but that's no better than roulette. All we're doing is gambling that the right number shows up. We need to be out there turning up leads."

"Okay, let's do it. We've gone door to door in only one of the three neighborhoods where we think the killer probably lives."

He thought for a moment. "New Springville and Lighthouse Hill are two of the three, which means there's a better-than-even chance Gabriel is willing to murder in his own neighborhood. That surprises me," he told her.

"If he's as good as we think he is, he probably wouldn't give it a second thought. He figures he's untouchable. Either way, all we can do is pound the pavement."

"Agreed. So let's go finish the first neighborhood. We missed a few people when we were there, and I'd like to circle back to them before we move on. There was one guy in particular, the one Terrence Goodall took care of so that the kid's mother could hold down her job."

"The neighbor we spoke with said there was never any hint of inappropriate behavior."

"Yeah, but according to her she knows everything," he laughed. "So I'd prefer to get the information directly from the source."

"Works for me."

An hour later they rang the bell at Jackson's place in New Springville and this time found him at home. His face was covered with sweat and the veins in his arms bulged when he came to the front door slightly out of breath.

"Mr. Jackson?" Nazareth said.

"That's me."

"Detectives Pete Nazareth and Tara Gimble, NYPD. We're investigating the murder of Terrence Goodall and speaking with some of his neighbors. Do you have a few minutes?" If Nazareth had seen what was happening inside Jackson's stomach at that moment, he would have immediately cuffed the guy and driven him to the precinct.

"Yeah, sure. Come on in," he said calmly despite a bad case of nerves. "Sorry I'm a little sweaty. I was just finishing my last set."

The small living room contained only one piece of furniture: a badly worn maroon fabric couch whose sides had been shredded by the family's cat decades earlier. Everything else was gym equipment. Nazareth noticed the eye-popping weight plates on the bench-press machine but didn't comment.

"This is the living room of your dreams, Pete," Gimble kidded.

"Pretty much," he laughed.

"You work out a lot, detective?" Jackson asked.

"I have a pretty good gym in my apartment, but I always wish I had more equipment. You have a great set-up here."

"I played football in high school and got used to being in shape," he said. "I'm alone here and don't really need a living room, so I figured a gym makes sense."

"You bet. In the long run it's a lot cheaper than joining a gym," Nazareth said.

"Amen to that. One of these days I may ditch the second bedroom and put some decent cardio gear in there."

"Sounds good. Hey, listen, can we ask you a few questions about Terrence Goodall, the man who was murdered a couple of weeks ago?"

"Sure. Very nice guy. Great baseball coach when I was a kid. He was always good friends with my mother and lots of other parents in the neighborhood. I can't believe someone shot him like that."

"The person who killed Mr. Goodall is calling himself Gabriel," Gimble offered. "And this Gabriel character claims he's out to kill sex offenders. But as far as we can tell Mr. Goodall was never charged with anything other than possession of child pornography. Are you aware of any other problems he had with the police?"

Jackson shook his head gently, careful not to overplay the role. "I never heard anything bad about him except that porn business. And some people in the neighborhood, including my mother, always thought his wife set him up for that."

"Yes, we've heard that," Gimble replied. "Let me ask you this. We were told Mr. Goodall used to take care of you while your mother worked. Is that right?"

"Absolutely. She couldn't have kept her job without him."

"And during the time he took care of you there was never any inappropriate behavior?" she asked.

Jackson looked offended. "You're asking whether he raped me or something?"

"Mr. Jackson, we have to cover every possible angle on this case, so we have no choice but to ask."

"No, he never did anything wrong. As I said, he was a really nice guy. And I never heard any of the other kids say anything bad about him."

"Do you know whether he had any run-ins with neighbors?" Nazareth asked.

"Not that I know of. Some people stopped talking to him after the porn stuff hit the papers," he told them, "but I'm not aware of any arguments or fights."

"Had you spent any time with him recently?" Gimble asked.

"No. We just waved to each other now and then after I got home. But that's pretty much how it is with all the older neighbors," he explained.

Nazareth picked up on a phrase Jackson wished he hadn't uttered. "Were you away?"

"What's that?"

"You said you and Mr. Goodall waved to each other after you got home. Had you been away?"

"Oh, yeah, I was in the Army for a few months, but I ended up getting a medical discharge."

"Ah, understood. I was Marines myself," Nazareth smiled. "Where were you stationed?"

Jackson detected something he didn't like behind Nazareth's smile but knew he couldn't avoid answering the question. "Fort Jackson in South Carolina. I took a lot of crap over that, naturally.

The drill sergeant wanted to know why they'd name a base after a private."

"I love it," Nazareth laughed. "Yeah, I can see how a drill sergeant could bust your chops over that. How long were you there?"

"Only about a month. Then they found a heart problem, and I was finished. After that I worked in South Carolina for a couple of months. I came back right after my mother died unexpectedly."

"I'm sorry to hear about that. I didn't know she had died recently."

"Oh, yeah, just a few months ago. Happened fast. No one knew she was sick," Jackson told them.

"So you're back for good now?" Gimble asked.

"I don't have any plans to move. Right now I'm working part-time as a bank teller and hoping that leads to a full-time job. I'd also like to get back to school and maybe get a two-year degree."

"Well, I hope it all works out for you," she said. "I think we're about finished. How about you, Pete?"

"Absolutely. We appreciate your time, Mr. Jackson. If you think of anything else that might help us with this investigation, please give us a call." Nazareth and Gimble handed over their business cards and walked back to the car.

Before sliding into the driver's side Nazareth stood at the door and looked down the block. Goodall's place was nine houses down, same side of the street.

"Something on your mind, Pete?" Gimble asked.

"Not really. Just thinking how easy it is to lose track of people in your own neighborhood. When you're a kid you don't really pay much attention to the grown-ups," he offered, "and then when you're finally an adult yourself you basically lose touch with that older generation. You all just wave to each other now and then."

"That's pretty much how it goes," she nodded. "Sounds normal to me."

Another thought hit Nazareth as they drove off. "Hey, did that neighbor, Mrs. Carmody, tell us Jackson had been away?"

"Not that I recall. Does it matter?"

"I'm not sure why it should matter, but the subject sort of got slipped into the conversation as an afterthought."

"That strikes you as odd?"

"A little bit. Most guys who've just left the military make a point of mentioning it, especially at a time when Americans in general are extremely supportive of those who serve."

"Maybe he's just embarrassed over the medical discharge, Pete."

"I guess. But I have to say Jackson doesn't look like someone who would qualify for a medical discharge. He had enough weight on his bench-press machine for two people."

"Not every heart problem affects exercise, right?"

"Right, but why would a heart problem not get picked up during the pre-induction physical? How does it turn up only after he's actually in basic training? That's odd."

"So there's something he's not telling us?"

"Certainly possible," he nodded, "but it should be easy enough to find out. I'll see what Fort Jackson can give us."

Two hours later Nazareth was only partially satisfied with the details he had gotten from the Army folks in South Carolina. Yes, they could share Jackson's medical records with the police, but only if the NYPD formally identified him in writing as a suspect in a murder investigation. And in that case it would take a week or more to locate the records and forward them to New York. The sergeant who spoke with Nazareth said the only thing he could confirm at the moment was what he saw on his computer screen: Jackson had been released from his service commitment under an entry level separation.

"And what exactly does that tell us, Pete?" Gimble asked.

"Not much, unfortunately. All it means is that his commanding officer felt Jackson hadn't been in the Army long enough to be assessed for a regular discharge. I'm not sure that's what they would do in the case of a heart problem," he said, "but I sort of doubt it. In any event we have to wait for his medical records to arrive."

"While we knock on some more doors?"

"No reason not to. But I also want to find out what we can about Jackson. He said he spent some time working in South Carolina after leaving the Army. Maybe we can find out exactly what he was doing down there."

"Please tell me we're not going to South Carolina, Pete."

"It's a really nice state, Tara. But I don't think we'll need to go there for this. Let's try working with the police down there first. Maybe they can help us fill in some blanks."

"Fine by me, but I have to say Jackson seemed pretty calm to me. Didn't seem at all rattled."

"That's partly what concerns me. Even innocent people are usually a little nervous when they're being interviewed by the police. But Jackson either didn't feel anything or disguised his emotions completely. I worked with a few Marines who were like that, and they were seriously bad dudes."

"Killers?"

"The best, yeah."

She read the concern in Nazareth's face. "You're thinking this guy's a little spooky?"

"Not thinking. Just feeling."

"Good enough for me. Let's get on the phone with some South Carolina police departments."

32.

The Great Grande War settled into an uneasy peace when husband Archer finally realized his young wife Brigitte intended to have the baby, even though motherhood had never been on her to-do list. He wasn't at all happy over what he continued to view as an unfortunate accident, though he couldn't complain about its impact on the poll numbers. As campaign manager Chandler had predicted, the folks on Main Street found it somewhat easier to relate to the Grandes now that the superstar couple had a baby on the way. But poll numbers, he reminded himself, wouldn't help him get a good night's sleep when there was a screaming kid in the White House.

While the candidate brooded over the inevitable lifestyle changes a baby would bring, mom-to-be Brigitte began boosting the local economy with purchases that only the mega-rich might consider normal. The first item on her shopping list was a $2-million contract with Ariana Sauveterre, one of the hottest young fashion designers in New York City. For that tidy sum Sauveterre would meet with her wealthy patron four times each month throughout the pregnancy to provide up-to-the-minute guidance on all matters relating to Brigitte's changing figure. The fee covered advice only, of course. Maternity wear would be extra.

For $500,000 architect Marco Burgos designed Baby Grande's nursery as well as a dream suite for some lucky live-in nanny who would enjoy her own kitchen, bath, living room, and bedroom. The construction estimate for creating the two new spaces from an existing guest bedroom and adjoining office was $3 million. Decorating and furnishing would run another $250,000.

In addition to these and similar up-front expenses Brigitte set the annual ongoing budget for motherhood services at a hefty $4.3 million. This included such necessities as the nanny's salary and benefits, thrice-weekly in-home spa treatments, weekly in-home photo/video shoots to document the Grande family story, educational toys and tutoring, fashion consulting and wardrobe outfitting for Baby Grande, an extra chauffeur for helping Brigitte and the new arrival with their doctor visits and shopping sprees, and a mouthwatering annual gift to the Hobley School for a guaranteed spot in the pre-K class two years hence. An admirable 97% of Hobley's graduates were admitted each year to Ivy League universities, and Brigitte intended to make sure her child was included in those ranks by the time he or she was 17.

Vincent Chandler, meanwhile, kept his eyes focused on the election prize. He wisely avoided all mention of the pregnancy when speaking with Grande and focused instead on the faux assassination that he was convinced would seal the deal and guarantee his boss the presidency.

"I want to show you something that will make you very happy, Arch," he said as he uploaded a video to the large flat-screen TV in Grande's office. "This will absolutely make your day."

"Anything not related to maternity clothes, nurseries, or baby formula will make my day, Vince. I'm sick of being a father and don't even have a kid yet."

"You're about to see your ticket to the White House. Ready?"

Grande sipped his coffee and sat back in the $18,000 leather massage recliner to enjoy the show. The video opened with a sweeping panorama of intense blue sky and the snowy peaks of the Wasatch Range in Utah.

"I shot this myself three days ago, Arch."

"Martin Scorsese has nothing on you," Grande muttered.

"Okay, here we go."

The lens came back to ground level and revealed a long, open field nestled in a lush valley where a man in military camouflage worked with his back to the camera. Tall, broad, and lean, he was loading ammo into a high-powered sniper rifle. It was a gun anyone could buy for the right price, but in his hands it became something truly special, like a favored brush in the hands of Michelangelo. Archer Grande would surely get his money's worth.

The camera moved unsteadily toward the rifleman.

"Were you riding a horse while you shot this video?" Grande complained. "I'm getting dizzy watching."

"The field was a little rough, Arch. Stay cool. From this point on I stood in one spot and let Mr. X do his thing."

"Mr. X? Sounds like a comic book character, Vince."

"You don't want to know anything about him, right? So from now on he's Mr. X. Can we just watch the video?" he whined.

At this point Grande heard Mr. X's gravelly voice for the first time.

"The first round will be from 400 yards exactly. We've got a golf ball on a tee sitting on top of a wooden box."

Mr. X took a prone position, leaned into the bipod to stabilize the barrel, put the crosshairs on the golf ball, and squeezed the trigger. A downrange camera showed the golf ball being reduced to dust, and Grande was obviously impressed. In the next sequence Mr. X propped up a fiberglass mannequin whose back was toward the firing position. He attached a red plastic thimble to the outside of the dummy's right thigh with a small piece of two-sided adhesive tape.

"This round will be from 200 yards," the sniper said. "The objective this time is to eliminate the thimble without grazing the thigh."

He took his position, sighted, fired, and blew the thimble off the mannequin.

"Okay, let's check it out." He walked to the target and examined his handiwork. The thimble was gone, but the adhesive tape was still stuck to the mannequin's leg. "As long as the target is still," he said, "I can shoot a fly off his leg at 200 yards. End of story."

The video closed with a sequence of 10 shots fired at a standard paper bullseye from 600 yards. The first three rounds were a half inch off target, but the next seven passed through the same spot, leaving a hole just slightly larger than a single round would have made.

"And he's always this good?" Grande asked.

"Any day, any time, Arch. This is what you get. That's why he's so expensive."

"And you're sure he can be trusted to keep his mouth shut?"

"This guy had top-secret clearance when he was on active duty, and the stuff he's been into since then is even more sensitive. So, yeah, he'll keep his mouth shut before the assassination attempt. Afterwards, you won't need to worry . . ."

"Hey, enough. I don't need to know."

"Know what?" Chandler smiled.

"There you go. So this guy knows where he'll be positioned at the country club while I'm talking?"

"Absolutely. He'll be a couple hundred yards behind you and slightly to your right. He has high-def satellite images, topographic maps, and all the rest. He'll walk the area two days before the shooting to make sure everything's perfect."

"And how does he get away?"

"You really want to know this?" Chandler asked.

"I don't need all the details, but I want to know there's an escape plan. This guy gets caught, and we're finished, Vince. You know that, right?"

"I do, Arch. Less than two minutes after he shoots you he'll be in a safe house I rented near the country club."

"How can you be sure he'll get there without being caught?"

"Because we'll be creating a diversion. There's going to be a confirmed sighting in the opposite direction, and I'll make sure the police and Secret Service are running away from Mr. X. We've got it all covered, Arch. By the time this is finished you'll be an American hero. The election is yours. Period."

Grande settled back in his recliner and smiled. The warm, rich leather felt good in his hands. He'd want something just like this on Air Force One.

33.

On June 19th, 1994, Jenkins Fortenberry of Lost Creek, West Virginia -- an eyeblink of a town about an hour south of the Pennsylvania border -- awoke from a frighteningly vivid dream and proclaimed himself the Rev. Moses Hope, founder of the Church of God's Everlasting Protection. For the remainder of his short life he would believe God wanted him to be a snake-handling preacher as a test of his faith. Precisely why God had done so was anyone's guess since Fortenberry had never once thought about touching a snake, venomous or otherwise. Neither had he thought about visiting Salem, New Hampshire, which is where God apparently had told him the church should be headquartered.

Nevertheless, two weeks later, having illegally acquired five timber rattlers from a local dealer, he packed his 1983 Ford Escort station wagon and headed north. Eight hours and four bad turns later he found himself on the right shoulder of the Staten Island Expressway with a blown four-cylinder engine, five poisonous snakes in a large cardboard box, and a violent headache. The air temperature was 95, but the pavement temperature was closer to 130. If hell was a busy highway, Fortenberry had found it, and he was gravely concerned for his snakes.

After 18 minutes of watching cars and trucks roar by menacingly, he looked toward the deep woods that stretched south of his position and did the only thing that made sense to him at that moment. He picked up the box, climbed over the guardrail, and scrambled down the embankment toward the trees. After less than 100 yards he stumbled across the Staten Island Greenbelt's 12-mile-long blue trail and followed it into the heart of Deere Park, 40 acres of wilderness surrounded mostly by heavily populated housing developments.

Eventually he pushed his way into the densest thicket he could find. There, completely hidden from view, he turned the cardboard box on its side to release the snakes so they had a fighting chance at survival. For reasons that perhaps a herpetologist might understand only one of Fortenberry's snakes slithered off into the underbrush. The other four immediately turned on him and sank their fangs into his arms and legs. His frantic attempt to escape the thicket only compounded his problems: three of the snakes bit him once again while the fourth, the largest of the group at five feet long and three pounds, struck him twice more. Fortenberry learned the hard way that he was severely allergic to rattlesnake venom.

He was never missed, and his body was never found. Remarkably, however, four of his five rattlesnakes survived -- two males and two females. Between 1994 and 2015 those original four multiplied to a total population of 387, all residing comfortably inside the Greenbelt, where they harvested frogs, lizards, mice, and almost anything else they chose in the absence of serious competition. Although some of the rattlers remained in the vicinity of Deere Park at the Greenbelt's northern end, most of them gradually expanded the territory in search of food. Some of the snakes worked their way east into the Todt Hill woods while others migrated south toward the Pouch Boy Scout Camp and High Rock Park.

Over the years a number of sightings were dismissed by scoutmasters and parents alike as the product of overactive imaginations, and one local college professor wrote a highly technical and well-referenced article for the *Advance* in which he debunked the notion of poisonous reptiles on the Island. "We have no poisonous snakes other than those in the Staten Island Zoo," he declared, "and the probability of one surviving if it were brought here is laughably small." Since the professor had never actually ventured into the field to investigate, he remained blissfully clueless while the rattler population grew exponentially.

One particularly large community of rattlesnakes had taken up residence in the woods immediately south of Stump Pond, where the manicured graves of Moravian Cemetery met the neatly clipped fairways of the Richmond County Country Club. Here the snakes had everything they needed: plentiful water, an unlimited supply of edible critters, and an abundance of comfortable dwellings. Fallen trees and dense shrubs provided excellent year-round cover, though some of the snakes seemed to prefer the area's numerous man-made shelters, old mausoleums and abandoned maintenance sheds among them.

In virtually every way the location was ideal for the snakes as long as they and their human neighbors stayed out of each other's way.

34.

Senior Chief Petty Officer Hunter M. Bloodworth, U.S. Navy (Retired), carried the nickname "Bloodsport" throughout his 20-year career as a Navy SEAL. He was known by his brothers-in-arms as a quiet, genial man who derived enormous satisfaction from killing America's enemies, something he did with legendary skill in Iraq, Afghanistan, Pakistan, and a few other countries the U.S. officially denied having entered.

His activities under the Omega Program, a clandestine CIA-SEAL joint effort, allowed him to bend, break, or ignore many of the traditional protocols of war, using instead the classic do-unto-others rule. If your enemy likes burying people alive, bury your enemy alive. If he likes setting people on fire, set him on fire. And if he likes beheading people, behead him. Bloodworth had done all that and more without regret, and he was capable of doing it again in the right situation for the right price.

For conspicuous achievement in helping rid the planet of its worst inhabitants he had won the Navy Cross, Silver Star, Bronze Star, and Meritorious Service Medal, among others. When he had retired at age 41 three years earlier, the CIA made him an offer he decided to refuse. He correctly believed that in the private sector his unique skill set could generate a lot more income than would ever be possible through continued government service. As a self-employed security consultant he had earned more than $500,000 per year since leaving the military, but getting hired to fake an assassination attempt on Archer Grande was the coup of a lifetime.

On July 6th he would not only earn an immense fee for firing one shot but would also align himself with a future president. What that could do for his earnings was anybody's guess. And yet he was concerned. Did he really trust Vincent Chandler? Answer: not one bit. The guy was a weasel who would sell out his own mother for a chance to get ahead. Did he consider that Chandler might want to eliminate him once the mission had been completed? Of course. Why would Chandler want a witness who could one day blackmail his boss in the Oval Office?

Hunter Bloodworth was nobody's fool. That's why he had insisted on half the $1 million fee up front. If he never got the other half he'd still be well off financially.

After weighing his options he decided to change the game entirely for the Staten Island mission. Instead of faking Grande's assassination he would put a bullet in Chandler. Everyone would naturally assume that Grande had been the target, so the candidate would still be viewed as something of a hero when he continued campaigning. And with Chandler out of the picture Bloodworth would be in an ideal position to negotiate a handsome deal with Grande. Presidents often require the services of discreet men -- men far outside the government chain of command -- who will do whatever it takes to defend America from all enemies, foreign or domestic. A former SEAL with world-class killing skills could be a tremendous asset to a man as devious as Grande, and Bloodworth relished the thought of becoming the president's go-to guy.

What choice would Grande really have? Only two people would know about the phony assassination attempt, and neither would ever breathe a word of it to anyone. One would become the most powerful man on the planet while the other became perhaps the wealthiest retired SEAL in history.

Chandler had told Bloodworth to arrive on Staten Island for the first time two days ahead of the mission in order to walk the Greenbelt and make his final plans. But an operation as sensitive as this one required considerable advance preparation, so Bloodworth flew in unannounced two weeks earlier and took a room at a grimy half-star motel on the Island's north shore looking out toward the Kill Van Kull. Keeping a low profile in this distinctly down-on-its-luck neighborhood would be easy since the few residents he saw seemed stoned all the time. No one would remember the loner from Utah or his wreck of a rental car.

Before heading out the door the next morning he made sure the bottoms of his tan field pants hung below the Schrade knife that was safely tucked into its sheath on his right boot. The only other tool he needed for the day's hike was his cell phone, whose high-resolution camera and tactical GPS app would allow him to map the location of key mission sites. Over the next two days he planned to take whatever steps were necessary to assure success on July 6th.

The first day was all about hiking. He parked his car on Manor Road not far from Susan Wagner High School and stepped into the adjoining woods. From there he marched east into the heart of the Todt Hill Woodlands, then south through the heaviest section of forest to Ohrbach Lake.

After walking the lake's perimeter he headed due east past Stump Pond to the boundary of the Richmond County Country Club golf course. Along the way he photographed several acceptable places from which he might be able to shoot as well as half a dozen likely escape routes. He was enormously pleased by what the terrain offered. There was plenty of natural cover to conceal his movements.

At 2:15 p.m., having thoroughly searched the area, he stood inside a dense thicket alongside one of the golf course's fairways and looked over to the parking lot where Grande would give his pre-dinner speech. He carefully studied the site plan Chandler had provided and knew he had found the perfect spot from which to fire. Grande would be at the podium roughly 300 yards away, and Chandler would be seated to his boss's right a few yards closer to Bloodworth's shooting position. At this distance he could put a dozen rounds in any target he chose down to the size of a field mouse. Placing a .308 round in Chandler's head would be laughably easy and immensely effective.

Next on the agenda: planning the perfect escape from the kill zone. He would have a generous head start on the police and Secret Service agents, all of whom would naturally be completely disoriented at first and would then have to sprint nearly 300 yards in their street shoes over uneven terrain. Assuming they ran in the right direction, something he seriously doubted, they would be at least two minutes behind him. In two minutes Bloodworth could cover more than 600 yards with a light backpack and rifle, though just to make sure he might consider wearing his Merrell trail shoes instead of his favorite field boots on the big day.

All he needed now was a hideout roughly 600 yards away from the shooting location, and after an hour of scouring the landscape he found it. Deep inside High Rock Park was a huge oak that had been uprooted during the past winter by a combination of heavy rain and high winds. The fallen tree's huge root mass stood nearly seven feet high, and the gaping hole it had left in the soil was almost three feet deep. Bloodworth photographed the site from every angle, but he already knew where he was going with this.

Shortly after sunrise the next morning he was back in the Greenbelt, this time wearing sweats and running shoes. His only plan was to jog for two hours, give or take a few minutes, both on and off marked trails. Part of this was his fanatical drive to stay in SEAL shape, but the rest was reconnaissance. He wanted to see how many people were in the woods in the early hours, whether neighborhood dogs were a problem, and to what extent his stride was affected by the rough ground. By the time he had finished he was extremely pleased with the results. The Greenbelt was an ideal location for a man of his talents, and he intended to make full use of its generous resources.

He spent an hour that afternoon at Home Depot buying a few pieces of lumber, then returned to the Greenbelt after dark to continue his preparations at the fallen oak. Strapped to his back were several pre-cut lengths of 2x3 studs, three sections of half-inch plywood, a folding shovel, and some basic carpentry tools. Finding the fallen oak wasn't a problem thanks to the GPS app on his phone, and the extra weight he carried was barely noticeable. But travel was difficult nevertheless. Tree roots, fallen branches, and swampy areas slowed him down much more than he had expected. His future was riding on this job, though, so he took his time. He couldn't risk twisting an ankle just prior to the most important day of his life.

Forty minutes later he dropped the lumber at his work site and began digging. In less than a half hour he had a ditch seven feet long, three feet wide, and three feet deep in the soft soil where the tree's roots had been torn from the earth. At the far end of the ditch, extending into a large clump of wild shrubs, he dug a channel just large enough to accommodate his 6-3, 215-pound frame. Finally he used the 2x3 studs and plywood to build a sturdy cover that he set firmly in the earth atop the ditch. After he had finished burying the cover with a foot of topsoil and dried leaves, he had a cozy and invisible safe room. He would hide underground after the shooting, then walk away during the night once the police and Secret Service agents had given up their search for the assassin.

Early the next morning Bloodworth was once again jogging through the Greenbelt, memorizing the location of every path, ditch, stream, and fallen log he might encounter on July 6th. He also passed the safe room several times from different directions, making sure everything looked natural and that the tunnel entrance was completely concealed by the heavy undergrowth. When he compared the present site to a pre-construction photo he had taken, he was delighted. Everything was identical right down to the angle of a fallen oak branch that rested on the ground.

Things had gone exceedingly well. Now it was time to go back to Utah for a few thousand rounds of target practice.

35.

Nazareth and Gimble were confused by the cryptic medical report the Army had sent them. Yes, Private Stone Jackson's discharge was related in some way to a medical diagnosis. But the diagnosis was not at all related to his heart. The summary referred twice to *psychodynamics*, three times to *chromosomal translocation*, and four times to *cytogenetics*. Whoever had written the report had failed utterly to explain Jackson's problem in anything resembling English. Whether this had been intentional or unintentional was anyone's guess. In any event there was no mention of Jackson's assault on the drill sergeant, so the document didn't raise any major red flags for the detectives.

"Tara, do you have any clue what all this crap means?" asked Nazareth, obviously annoyed by the med-speak. "You're the psych major here."

"Could be anything, Pete. On the one hand, the mention of psychodynamics suggests some sort of emotional issue," she explained, "but the business about chromosomal translocation seems to point toward a serious medical issue, possibly cancer."

"Why cancer?"

"One way cancer develops is through what I guess you'd call breakage within chromosomes. And there you have everything I know on the subject. If I had to guess, I'd say the doctors discovered some sort of genetic abnormality, and that led to emotional issues on Jackson's part. But," she emphasized, "I could be very wrong."

"But it does make sense. I can see one leading to the other, and I understand why Jackson would lie about the heart problem. He's probably embarrassed by the emotional issues and angry about the medical diagnosis, which could be pretty bad. At the same time," he said, "let's remember he doesn't look like someone who's terminally ill. Just the opposite, in fact. He wouldn't look out of place on the cover of *Men's Fitness*."

"So do you want to push this? We can always go to South Carolina and talk to people."

He thought for a moment, then slowly shook his head somewhat indecisively. "Something isn't quite right, but I don't feel strongly enough about him yet, especially since the police down there had absolutely nothing on him."

The two South Carolina police chiefs Gimble had touched base with were glad to help with the investigation, but after several days of calling around the state they had both come up empty. Jackson's landlord said he had been a perfect tenant in every way, and the McDonald's manager vowed he'd hire the guy back in a second since he had done the work of two people without ever once complaining. This was an unlikely portrait of a deranged serial killer.

The detectives agreed they should keep Jackson in mind as they continued interviewing other Staten Islanders. For the moment, though, they had no compelling reason to question him further or place him under surveillance. As it turned out both Nazareth and Gimble had to abandon the Gabriel case for two days anyway to appear before a Manhattan federal jury deciding the fate of terrorist bomber Rahman Aziz. The duo had captured Aziz a few months earlier, foiling a major attack outside One Police Plaza, and they were more than happy to help seal the psychopath's fate.

The chief judge of the U.S. District Court in Manhattan, Adele Shiffren, had gone out of her way to make sure the unrepentant Aziz got the speedy trial guaranteed him by the Constitution. She was aided, in fact, by Aziz himself, who had dismissed his attorney's attempts to delay the trial. Aziz wanted a public platform from which to lecture on his ISIS-based hatred of America, and as far as he was concerned sooner was better than later. But the judge slammed the door on his plan, literally, when she declared a closed trial on the grounds that a public trial might undermine Aziz's right to fair and impartial treatment. It was a lose-lose for the man who had already killed several New Yorkers, including the former mayor, and had hoped to kill hundreds if not thousands more.

The detectives were pleased to be in the courtroom when Aziz was found guilty on all counts, among them first-degree murder, use of a weapon of mass destruction resulting in death, and bombing of a place of public use resulting in death. What would happen next to Aziz was, of course, a foregone conclusion. The last thing the government wanted to do was create a martyr, so the prosecutors gave no thought whatsoever to the death penalty. Taking that option off the table was especially easy in a state that most likely would have fought it anyway. No, Aziz would be sentenced to a string of consecutive life sentences and would spend 23 hours a day in a prison cell until he died.

After the trial ended the detectives spent a few hours at One Police Plaza, then went back to Nazareth's apartment to pack some additional clothes for the return to Staten Island. By the time they began the 30-minute drive that always took an hour it was after 11:00 p.m., and they hadn't eaten dinner.

"Those two hot dogs I ate for lunch won't get me through the night, Pete," Gimble told him as they cruised over the Verrazano. "And I'm not sure we have much at the house."

"Tell you what, then. We'll hit the first decent place we come to on Hylan Boulevard. How's that?"

"Two thumbs up."

Fifteen minutes later they parked at Richie's Diner and went in for two midnight meals: eggs over easy and hash browns for Gimble, ham and cheese on whole wheat for Nazareth. Their yawning had nothing to do with the food, which was simple but good.

"We're getting old, Pete," she laughed. "Falling asleep over dinner is a geriatric thing, isn't it?"

"I don't know, Tara. Maybe we're just beat from lots of early mornings and late nights. I think we still have a few good miles left in us, but we both need to sleep now and then."

"If we have kids someday are you going to get up with me in the middle of the night to feed them?" she asked seriously.

"That would be highly inefficient," he said not at all seriously. "Why have two people awake when one will do?"

"You're right, I suppose. How about this: I can sleep while you're up."

"Nice try, kid. How about we just plan on taking turns? That would work."

"Would it really?" she smiled.

"Absolutely. And, for the record, I'd be very happy to have kids once we actually set a date and get married. But that's really your call."

"Why so?"

"Well, first, you're the one who needs to get pregnant. You knew that, right?"

"Maybe you should explain it."

"Not here. And, second, I don't get to decide what you do about your career. That's your decision, and I'll always support it."

She had always liked what she read in his face, but never more than right now. "Well, since we're going on the record tonight, let me say that raising a family is something I'd very much like to do. And I'm sure we could juggle things for a while so that I'm able to get 20 years in and then retire."

"You've thought about this, eh?"

"Quite a lot, but only in between hunting crazies with my future husband."

"How about this: after we put our friend Gabriel out of business we take some time away from the job and do some real planning? Dates, places, the whole thing."

"Sounds good to me." They shook on it just as the waitress brought their check for $17.48 plus tax. Nazareth handed her his

Amex and looked around. Not too many people at this hour, maybe 15 total. A group of five -- four young guys and a girl -- had walked out earlier, and only two customers had come in since then. He didn't know what kind of business diners usually did at night since he and Gimble rarely ate out late, and it was now 12:50. All he knew for sure was that he was tired and needed to hit the sack.

As soon as they walked out the front door Nazareth noticed that the parking lot light nearest to their car wasn't working. The light had definitely been on when they arrived, or else he would have parked someplace else. He was not someone who took unnecessary chances.

"Stay here for a minute," he said.

"No, I'll go with you," she told him emphatically. "The light's out, and there are four or five people standing by their car across from ours."

"Four guys in their mid-twenties, one girl late teens. They studied us pretty hard when they left the diner before. Two of the guys look as though they can handle themselves; one of the others is 40 pounds overweight and can't get out of his own way; and the last one is a skinny user who'll probably break in half if you hit him."

"What about the girl?"

"Large pocketbook."

"Possibly a large gun."

"Anything's possible."

As Nazareth and Gimble approached their vehicle all four guys walked toward them. The tallest and fittest of the group had a nasty edge to his voice.

"Tina sends her regards, asshole."

"And who might Tina be?" Nazareth answered.

"Tina might be the girl you had your hands all over at that bar the other night."

Before Nazareth could deny ever having met Tina or identify himself as a cop the guy lunged at him with a knife, his three friends close behind. Nazareth latched onto the punk's knife hand and with one quick circular motion snapped the wrist while turning the blade back on his attacker. He simultaneously planted the toe of his right shoe under the chin of the second tallest guy and flattened him.

The overweight member of the crew hesitated, then reached in his pocket. Before he could remove whatever was in there Gimble fractured his left knee with a side kick and sent him screaming to the pavement. She was no match for her fiance when it came to kicking, but she was definitely getting better. When the skinny guy came for her she grabbed his long hair with her left hand and jammed her right under his armpit, then used his forward momentum to fling him up and onto the parking lot's chain link fence where he dangled like a scarecrow from the sharp barbs.

Elapsed time: less than 9.7 seconds. Tina, meanwhile, ran like the wind out of the parking lot and down Hylan Boulevard. A patrol car picked her up four minutes later and confiscated the 12 ounces of cocaine she carried in her fake Prada purse.

"So, Peter Nazareth," Gimble grinned as they finally drove home after writing up their report at the precinct, "what bar do you and your friend Tina usually hang out in?"

"Just some bucket of blood in West Brighton. Nothing special, but she likes it."

"I bet. But you're not going to see her for at least 10 years while she's in prison for criminal possession."

"At least she'll have her four friends to keep her company," he said. "Tina sang like a bird tonight, didn't she?"

"A lovely song, Pete."

"A jailbird's tune."

"And in three hours the birds will be singing for real outside our window."

"Right. And we'll still be sleeping in, Tara We're reporting late today. Maybe Gabriel will take some time off."

"Here's hoping."

36.

With three flawlessly executed sex-offender kills now under his belt Jackson turned his full attention to Archer Grande, the man who could not, would not, be allowed to occupy the Oval Office. Grande was the top story in every newspaper, magazine, TV station, and online news outlet in America, possibly the world, and his rhetoric was becoming more outrageous each day. He appealed to the country's growing lunatic fringe, among them those who hated immigrants, non-Christians, non-whites, and most other countries. The guy was generating massive support among crazies who had never considered voting before, and that accounted for much of his edge in the polls. But he had also skillfully customized each of his messages to key audiences, frequently omitting a few of his more ill-considered or outright dangerous ideas -- like boarding up every mosque in America. In this way he helped people hear only what they wanted to hear and thus gained support even from apparently sane voters.

Grande was a gifted and devious orator. The main difference between him and Adolph Hitler was that Hitler never possessed a nuclear arsenal.

Jackson had finally ruled out killing Grande at the huge Staten Island Mall rally on July 6th. Thousands of people meant hundreds of police and Secret Service agents roaming the area, and even the 2,800-acre Greenbelt wasn't large enough when dealing with those kinds of numbers. But the candidate's outdoor talk at the country club later that same day would work just fine. He figured there would be many fewer security types on the ground, and they would most likely have their guard down, convinced that a small group of wealthy donors represented no threat whatsoever. Maybe they would have everyone pass through a metal detector just to make sure all the guests were unarmed, and they would certainly be scanning the edge of the woods with binoculars in case someone attempted to approach the country club parking lot while Grande was speaking.

But what they probably wouldn't expect was an invisible assassin who could hide among the trees and strike from 400 yards out. A torso shot from that distance was a gimme for Jackson. Even if it didn't kill Grande it would certainly knock him out of the presidential race. A shot from 300 yards or closer, on the other hand, would go straight to the target's heart. DOA time.

For his reconnaissance mission he chose a mild but drizzly morning, believing the weather would keep most other hikers away. After leaving his car in the public lot at High Rock Park he hiked a half mile east to the rear boundary of Moravian Cemetery, then walked north into the heavy woods alongside the country club golf course. The spot offered plenty of natural cover, and his laser rangefinder put the distance to target at an acceptable 387 yards. But there were too many trees on the fairway between him and the general area where Grande's podium would be positioned. Maybe he'd have a clear shot on July 6th, maybe not. And he couldn't gamble.

So he slowly wandered back to the cemetery, eyeing potential shooting positions of every description: fallen trees, stumps, thickets, natural depressions, and even large headstones. The shooting angles were fine, but every potential site was far too exposed to be usable. From this area he would be visible not only to Grande's security team but also to folks who might be visiting departed loved ones.

He had just begun heading north again when he stepped on a heavy iron manhole cover hidden among tall weeds at the edge of the woods. Since the cover measured roughly three feet across Jackson assumed he had stumbled across something that might fit his needs. A few minutes later his search of the cemetery had, in fact, led him to the exit point of what clearly was an extensive corrugated-metal storm drainage system. Today only a bit of water trickled from the huge opening, but he could easily imagine thousands of gallons of water thundering out of the drain into the grassy catch basin during a heavy storm. His rangefinder put the mouth of the storm drain 218 yards from the country club parking lot, and the view was perfectly clear all the way.

Jackson's heart rate ticked up a few notches as he followed a straight line back to the manhole cover and marked the distance at 133 yards. If the storm line beneath his feet was 36 inches high over its entire length, a reasonable bet, he should be able to travel underground from the opening back to the manhole cover in something less than a minute after shooting Grande. Then he could climb out of the tunnel unseen and disappear.

He returned to the storm drain's opening, made sure he was alone, and crawled inside. He was delighted to find the entire tunnel clear of debris. This would absolutely work, no doubt about it. He could slip into the manhole hours before the rally, set up at the mouth of the storm drain just before Grande began speaking, and easily vanish into the Greenbelt within a minute of the kill shot. The only extra equipment he'd need that day was a manhole cover hook that he could buy at Home Depot for less than $20. His escape plan was complete.

Next came the all-important evasion tactics. The police and Secret Service would certainly be on his trail within four or five minutes, so time was of the essence. This meant that running to a parked car in broad daylight would be impossible. No, for July 6th he needed a hiding place somewhere in the woods not far from the cemetery, a spot where he could wait for several hours. Once the police and Secret Service had left the woods he could quietly disappear in the dark. If they returned with tracking dogs the next day all they would find was the same trail to nowhere that Gabriel always left behind.

He kept an open mind as he scanned the woods, viewing every shrub, tree, and pond as a potential safe haven. But he was keenly aware that a daytime operation was far riskier than his night missions had been. If enough people were hunting for him -- and he took that to be a given -- he would never escape detection if he simply crouched in the shrubs or climbed a tree. Digging an underground bunker might make sense, but he had never tried something like that and didn't have time to experiment.

His deep concentration was broken by a young deer that had been standing perfectly still in a small clearing no more than 15 feet away. Only a momentary twitch of the animal's tail had revealed its position. Why, Jackson wondered, had he not spotted the animal sooner? Answer: it was hiding in plain sight, blending in perfectly with its natural surroundings. Message received.

Now as he strode through the dense woods he stayed alert for places where his presence would most likely be considered normal. Would dressing as a park ranger or scoutmaster enable him to withstand police or Secret Service scrutiny? Possibly. But with a phone call or two they might be able to unmask him. What if he changed quickly into his jogging gear and became just another exercise buff out for a long run? Sure, that could work.

Before long he found himself walking the shore of Ohrbach Lake, and he grinned when the idea hit him. For most of his life he had fished this lake for bass, pickerel, and catfish. What could be more natural and less out of the ordinary than a man with a fishing pole at the edge of a lake on a summer afternoon? He could easily hide his tackle at the water's edge the day before his mission and be there fishing within three minutes of assassinating Grande.

As for the rifle, he could wrap it in a black plastic bag, tie the bag to a tree with sturdy monofilament line, and toss the package into six or seven feet of water a few paces away from his fishing spot. No one would ever notice it. The police would find a man relaxing on a blanket and drinking a beer while waiting for the fish to bite. There might be other things he could do to set the stage properly, but he already had most of what he needed. Like the young deer, Jackson would hide in plain sight.

37.

U.S. Senator Porter Dunston Willoughby was an extremely influential Democratic leader and spokesman, author of three highly regarded texts on American politics, and a frequent guest on some of the country's most popular TV talk shows. One late-June evening, while appearing on the highest-rated show of all, he decided to trash Archer Grande in what the world soon learned had been a terminally dumb move.

Willoughby and Grande had exhibited an almost genetic dislike for each other while classmates at prep school and had kept their distance both then and since. But when he called Grande "a supremely unqualified candidate with the integrity of your average goat," Willoughby provoked a response that revealed something unsettling about the man who seemed destined to win the presidency.

Throughout his years in prep school, college, and business Archer Grande had quietly and systematically gathered intelligence on everyone who crossed him in any way. Porter Willoughby had made the short list. And the dirt Grande had found swept under the Willoughby family rug was something he had kept to himself for decades, sensing it might come in handy one day.

Forty-eight hours after Willoughby's scathing comments Grande appeared in a nationally televised Republican presidential debate, where moderator Julia Montfort unwittingly provided the opening he needed.

"Mr. Grande, a number of top Democrats, most recently Sen. Porter Willoughby, have attacked not only your political views but also your integrity. What do you think is behind this tactic?"

"Desperation," he shot back. "They're losing, they know it, and they'll say anything. But what's truly pathetic, Julia, is that they chose Porter Willoughby to deliver a message on ethics. This is the guy who during his senior year of prep school fathered a child with his wealthy family's young Nicaraguan maid, paid the woman off to keep her quiet, and sent her back to her hometown of Condega. The good Senator has never publicly acknowledged his 33-year-old son, Tomas, who works in a cement factory in Nicaragua, and in fact has blocked his own son's entry into the U.S. by having him placed on a terrorist watch list."

Julia Montfort was not the only person left speechless by Grande's revelation. Even his most rabid detractors -- people who believed Grande was capable of anything -- were shocked he was willing to drop that sort of bombshell, whether true or false, on live TV. But, not surprisingly, no politician dared to tackle the subject on the record. The uninformed had just learned that Archer Grande was playing for keeps. Even when Porter Willoughby hanged himself in his $8-million Kalorama Heights home in D.C. three days after Grande's appalling announcement, no one was willing to pull the lion's whiskers. His opponents had good reason to be frightened.

Reaction from the press was universally negative, and words like *viciousness, pettiness,* and *vindictiveness* abounded in both news articles and editorials. But Grande was undeterred, especially when his core supporters gave him a resounding thumbs-up for trashing Willoughby, who had been mentioned as either a running mate on the Democratic ticket or a safe bet for secretary of state. The senator's suicide was taken as evidence of his lack of moral fiber and a clear signal that all other Democratic party leaders had better check their closets for the presence of skeletons.

Stone Jackson was repulsed by what he saw as the latest evidence of Grande's unfitness for the nation's highest office. The man who occupied the White House needed to be tough, of course, but Jackson knew the difference between wrestling alligators and pulling the wings off butterflies. What Grande had done to Willoughby was a case of raw, unbridled, dangerous power, like using a stick of dynamite to fix a clogged bathtub drain. It had been a savage, premeditated attack launched in response to nothing more than an insult. What in God's name would happen if Grande had the U.S. military at his disposal?

Jackson would make sure that never happened if, in fact, Grande stuck to his plan for the July 6th rally. Both the NYPD and the Secret Service had already let it be known that the candidate might need to cancel his visit because of the recent murders on Staten Island, but that was mere wishful thinking on their part. When asked about the rumor, Grande scoffed at the notion of weak-kneed handlers stepping in the path of a rampaging bull elephant.

"When I say I'm doing something, I do it," he boasted on a popular morning talk show, "and it's up to the supporting cast to get on board. That's how it is now, and that's how it will be for four, or eight, or however many years I serve as president."

The show's host, Darren Hollis, immediately jumped on Grande's phrasing.

"I'm not sure what you mean when you say four, eight, or some other number of years? It can only be four or eight, right?"

"Probably, yeah."

"The U.S. Constitution doesn't say *probably*, Mr. Grande. It says with finality that a president can serve only two terms."

"Sure. That's what it says," he grinned as time was up.

Back at his home office following the TV appearance Grande strutted like a proud rooster over his performance while campaign manager Vincent Chandler broke out in stress hives.

"Arch, I'm not sure you should have gotten into that business about more than eight years in office. I thought we agreed to leave that subject alone for now."

"I don't like sticking to a script, all right? I like to say what's on my mind at the time. You know that. And besides," he said casually, "we both know that a strong president can ram home a simple constitutional amendment. You're not getting jittery on me, are you, Vince?"

"I'm not jittery, Arch, but I think it's a mistake to talk about this on national TV, especially before you've begun the first term."

"The start of the first term is a formality, as far as I'm concerned. And when I'm president, I'll make goddamn sure the state legislatures vote for anything I give them unless they want to preside over their states' bankruptcies. Federal funding accounts for 30% of state revenue, Vince. The power of the purse can work magic."

"I get it," Chandler sighed, "but I still think you should hold off on that talk until after the election."

"And I think you should focus on your sniper friend Mr. X who's going to shoot me. Have you made sure he's not drinking too much or smoking crack?"

"Arch, this guy is absolutely first-rate in every way. He doesn't drink or smoke or use drugs or anything that would affect his performance. I've seen him in action, and he's all-world good."

"And he'll know where to hide before and after he shoots me?"

"Yes, as I've told you before he's arriving a couple of days ahead of the Staten Island events to make sure everything's set. After he takes the shot he'll be running to the house I rented less than 200 yards from the country club."

"Doesn't renting the house raise a red flag?"

"Not at all. It's an event facility. Technically it's a place where you can rest or change clothes or make phone calls while you're on Staten Island."

"And this is where he'll hide before and after the shooting?"

"Yes, Arch. He'll have the key, and no one is going to be searching there."

"And you're positive he won't be talking about this?"

"He won't be talking about this or anything else, Arch. Do you want more details?"

"No. Just be sure it's taken care of."

"It will be. Can I change the topic?"

"It's a free country."

"Thank you. The giant rally at the Staten Island mall is raising a lot of concern. I know, I know," he added quickly when his boss frowned. "You're going to do it no matter what the police and Secret Service say. But maybe we need to restrict access somehow. Right now it's looking as though 30,000 people could show up, Arch. If that happens, we could have riots on our hands."

"No, the police will have riots on their hands. If the people want to see me, let them see me. That's a good thing. Since when does a campaign manager not want a popular candidate?"

Chandler shook his head in exasperation. "It's great that people want to see you. All I'm saying is it's not going to be great if we have pandemonium at the mall."

"Then tell the police and the Secret Service to bring in more troops, okay? It's their problem, not mine and not yours."

"And, for the record, Arch, they really do have a nut with a rifle running loose over there, and the guy seems to be good at what he does."

"Right, killing perverts. That's a bad thing?" he snorted. "Come on, Vince. This is the kind of guy I'd like on the team, and I'd bet my last buck he'll be voting for me in November. Shooting pedophiles is a lot more useful than shooting deer. He deserves a medal."

"You're not going to say anything like that in front of an audience, Arch."

"Is that a question?" he sneered. "That didn't sound like a question."

"Arch, please, meet me halfway. You can't say something like that in public. A president can't condone murder."

"Presidents have a long history of condoning murder, Vince."

"In war, yes. But not in vigilante killings."

"Not just in war, my friend. Also in clandestine operations that safeguard the country."

"Against foreign enemies, yes. But not against American citizens. Please tell me you get that."

"Come on, Vince, I'm yanking your chain. You really are getting jittery on me, aren't you? You've got to lighten up a little."

Grande walked over to his antique armoire and removed a $2,000 bottle of Pappy Van Winkle bourbon. "Have a sip for success."

"It's too early for me, Arch."

"Not today, Vince. *Your* nerves are getting on *my* nerves. You need a drink."

Chandler hated bourbon but loved the idea of being a power behind the throne if his boss got elected.

He had his first drink of the day and wondered how much more of Archer Grande he could survive.

38.

Nazareth and Gimble spent three long days ringing doorbells in neighborhoods where they thought Gabriel might live. The people they interviewed were generally pleasant and tried to be helpful, but no one could offer more than the typical, "You might want to take a look at so-and-so down the street because he's a little weird." Every neighborhood on the planet has its weirdos, few of whom are serial killers. So the detectives knew they were spinning their wheels even while Gabriel was most likely lining up his next victim.

"After all the people we've met," said Nazareth, "the only guy who stands out in my mind is Stone Jackson."

Gimble wasn't convinced. "I don't know, Pete. He seems to live a pretty normal life, and he didn't strike me as being at all edgy when we talked to him."

"Something about his story just doesn't fit. That's number one," he offered. "Number two is that physically Jackson is the type of person who'd be highly capable of handling himself under battlefield conditions. His mysterious medical problems certainly haven't affected his fitness level. That home gym of his is equipped for an elite athlete."

"Okay, look, I always trust your instincts. If he's on your radar screen, we need to go back at him."

Nazareth's cell phone interrupted their conversation. Chief Crawford was even more agitated than usual.

"Your friend and mine the mayor is nervous as hell about Grande's visit to Staten Island on July 6th," Crawford griped, "and he wants you and Tara to prepare a formal written assessment of whatever security arrangements are in place."

Nazareth fought hard to keep his temper in check. "Is he really this clueless?" he asked. "First he has us checking out Grande's death threats, then he yanks us off that to hunt down Gabriel, and now he wants to pull the plug on Gabriel and have us police the police and the Secret Service. Does he have any idea what we do for a living?"

"Pete, I promise you he doesn't care what we do for a living. His only ambition is to stay in office, which means covering his ass 24/7. Guys like him succeed by never taking blame for anything."

"How do people like him ever get elected?"

"By operating in back rooms where they kiss the right butts and stab their buddies between the shoulder blades," Crawford said coolly. "This is how it works. You're a doer, Pete, so you have trouble understanding how someone who does nothing can move ahead in this world. But that's politics. Not just here, either. We have the same problem in Washington. The best and brightest never get elected because they're too good to waste their time being politicians."

"And then along comes Archer Grande."

"Who is also not one of our best and brightest. He's a snake in every conceivable way. But people are drawn to him because he says whatever he feels like saying, which is usually what a lot of other people have been thinking. He's rich, he's outspoken, and he's exciting."

"He's also crazy, chief."

"I suspect you're right. But unfortunately that doesn't disqualify him from serving as president. In some ways it probably helps him."

"Okay, what do you want Tara and me to do now?" Nazareth shook his head and gave his partner the look of a man sinking in quicksand.

"Stop whatever you're doing, and meet with whoever's in charge of security for July 6th. That means NYPD as well as Secret Service. Take a hard look at their plans, look for holes, and write it all up for me so that I can hand it over to the mayor."

"Who will use it against us if anything goes wrong."

"Not necessarily. If, for instance, you say the Secret Service plans are deficient, then he'll go after them if something happens to Grande."

"So Tara and I should play the cover-your-ass game along with the mayor?"

"Sometimes you need to, Pete."

"And this is one of those times?"

"I'm afraid so."

When Nazareth relayed the chief's message to Gimble she shrugged. "So we write the stupid report and go back to what we should be doing. When do we have to submit it?"

"July 1st by 5:00 p.m."

"Fine. That gives us two days. So we spend the rest of today meeting with the right people, and tomorrow we walk the locations to see whether their plans hang together. If the mayor doesn't like what he sees in our report, let him pester someone else."

"All we're doing is passing the buck. And I hate passing the buck, especially when I know the local precinct and Secret Service are doing things as well as they possibly can."

She took his hand and looked in his eyes. "We either do the mayor's bidding and get back to business, or we resign. I'm with you either way."

"I'm a lousy politician, Tara."

"One more reason I love you."

"All right, so we'll do the stupid report. But as soon as we wrap that up I want to get back to Stone Jackson. I know damn well he's playing some sort of game."

"And we'll find out what it is."

"You bet."

39.

The 737-800 carrying Hunter Bloodworth touched down 14 minutes early at 10:37 a.m. on July 3rd. He had slept soundly throughout the flight from Salt Lake City to Newark Liberty despite heavy turbulence that had left many of the passengers trembling, vomiting, and crying. A man who has learned how to get a good night's sleep in a war zone isn't troubled by some bumpy air.

He met Vincent Chandler in the baggage claim area, where Bloodworth grabbed the large hard-sided case that contained everything he would need for the July 6th mission.

"Any problems carrying what you needed?" Chandler asked.

"None at all, Mr. Chandler. Carrying weapons and ammo in checked luggage is perfectly legal," Bloodworth told him. "All you have to do is follow the rules and smile at the TSA people."

"Great. Just the one bag?"

"This is it."

"Do you need something to eat before we leave?"

"I'm good, thanks. Let's go visit your Greenbelt and see what we've got."

An hour later Chandler stopped his car on Manor Road so that Bloodworth could jump out and slip into the woods.

"You have the maps I gave you?" Chandler asked.

Bloodworth pointed to his forehead. "All up here now. I'll see you back here in two hours."

"Right here?"

"Yes sir, this is the spot. Adios," he smiled as he disappeared into the dense roadside undergrowth. He carried only a small backpack containing a Canon super-zoom camera, a slender field guide to New York birds, a bottle of water, and a half pound of trail mix. In the highly unlikely event someone needed to know why he was in the woods taking pictures in advance of Archer Grande's Staten Island appearances, he would be just another birder working on his photo collection. The driver's license and credit cards in his wallet identified him as Scott McArdle of Hopkinton, Rhode Island.

Twelve minutes later Bloodworth stood alongside the fallen tree that marked the underground safe room he had built during his first clandestine visit to the Greenbelt. Nothing more to be done except take a quick peek in the shrubs to see that the entrance hadn't been disturbed. After that he found a quiet place to sit, rest, and enjoy his snack.

Today's visit was all show, a charade designed to keep Chandler in the dark about the earlier scouting trip. So he was free to put a stopwatch to each step of his meticulous July 6th mission plan. By the time he was finished he had essentially memorized the location of every twig, weed, and leaf within 200 yards of his firing position, and he had rehearsed every movement down to the second. He was highly confident that killing Chandler and then vanishing would be easier than virtually all the assignments he had tackled as a SEAL.

Precisely two hours later he stepped out of the woods and climbed into the front passenger seat of Chandler's car. "We're good to go, Mr. Chandler," he said. "Piece of cake, in fact."

"Everything works for you?"

"You bet. I'll have a clear line of fire to Mr. Grande's thigh, and I doubt it'll feel like much more than a mosquito bite to him."

"What about the house I rented?"

"Perfect location. Lots of cover between the back yard and my firing position. No one will see me. Couldn't be better."

"Okay, so walk me through it," Chandler said eagerly. "I want to know what to expect."

"Sure. Tonight and tomorrow night I stay at the hotel. Then the night before the assassination attempt . . ."

"The *fake* assassination attempt."

"Mr. Chandler, I can shoot a freckle off a flea from that distance. I guarantee you Mr. Grande will be absolutely safe."

"Great. Continue."

"The night before the *fake* assassination attempt," he grinned, "I'll sleep in the basement of the house you rented. I won't leave the house until you call my cell phone 20 minutes before Mr. Grande is ready to speak at the country club. At that point I'll go out the back door with a backpack containing all my photography gear and walk over to the shooting position."

Chandler looked concerned. "What about the rifle? You can't walk around in the woods carrying a rifle."

"It's a takedown, Mr. Chandler."

"What's that mean?"

"It comes apart. It'll be inside my backpack, nice and small. I'll assemble it just before I'm ready to shoot."

"Got it. So you shoot Grande in the thigh . . ."

"First things first. You've got to make sure Mr. Grande sticks to the script. A couple of minutes into his talk he'll say *Is this the America you want?* Then he'll hold both hands out in front of him, waiting for the audience to cheer, and stand perfectly still for a count of four. If he doesn't do that, I won't shoot."

"He'll do it just like that. That's the only part of his talk he won't change."

"Fine. I shoot, then leave the rifle in the bushes while I walk off to take some more bird pictures. And don't worry, I already have lots of bird pictures in the camera in case someone checks. When things settle down I'll stroll back to the house and hang out there until you tell me what's going on with the police and the Secret Service."

"What if they find the rifle with your fingerprints all over it?"

"Even if they find the rifle they won't find my fingerprints, Mr. Chandler. Latex gloves," he wiggled the fingers of both hands, "that I bury someplace else."

"Sounds as though you've thought of everything."

"That's what I get paid for," he smiled.

"And there's nothing about the plan that bothers you?"

"Not a single thing. The weather forecast for the 6th is excellent, and the terrain is perfect. The only conceivable problem is that the police or Secret Service decide to have troops walking around in the woods. If that happens, I could have trouble setting up."

"Leave that part to me," Chandler assured him. "I'll tell them Grande is nervous as hell and wants every available body right there in the country club parking lot with him. You'll be fine."

"There you go, then. We're all set, Mr. Chandler. All you need to do is transfer 50% of the fee to my bank, and I'll take care of the rest. Here's the account number."

"Is this a Utah bank?"

"Negative. Cayman Islands. The money will work its way back to the U.S. eventually, but it will never be traced back to you or Mr. Grande."

"Excellent. So I'll drop you off at the hotel?"

"No, sir. Drop me off a few blocks from the hotel. We don't need to be seen together."

"Of course. Good idea." Smart man, Chandler thought. Too bad we need to get rid of him.

40.

Stone Jackson devoted the morning of July 4th to the customary fanatical two-hour workout in his home gym. He was in the best shape of his life by far, a testament to months of heavy training, smart eating, and clean living. Since he rarely used alcohol and never touched cigarettes or drugs he had no unhealthy habits to quit. Put him in a fighting cage with five other men, and he'd be the one to walk out alive.

After downing a five-egg-white omelet with diced ham and a large protein shake, he loaded his backpack and fishing tackle into the trunk and drove to a spot not far from the scout camp. From there he walked to Ohrbach Lake, where he planned to hide in plain sight on the evening of July 6th. Today was a test run, one last opportunity to reduce every detail of the mission to an exact science. Right here is where he'd hide his fishing gear in the bushes. Over there is where he'd stuff the rifle in a plastic bag before tossing it in the water. And here's the spot where he'd be sitting, fishing pole in hand, when the police or Secret Service came by after the shooting. No detail was too small to consider: the height of weeds in the fields, the clarity of the lake's water, the sounds of resident birds, and the patterns created by sunlight in the woods.

Satisfied that he was all set at the water's edge, he hiked up the steep hill to his left and studied the landscape in all directions, making sure he had the woods to himself. Then he crouched in the bushes to set up the first of three small improvised explosive devices he had assembled in his basement using ping pong balls filled with gunpowder. To each IED he attached a wireless detonator that he could activate from his cell phone. One push of the button would ignite the three devices in precise sequence: one second between the first and second explosions, three seconds between the second and third. Each device was too small to do any damage, but from a distance the explosions would sound much like rifle fire.

He walked back to the lake, verified he was still alone, and tightly wrapped a small brown blanket around his fishing tackle. After hiding the bundle in a thick clump of bushes, he covered it with leaves and swept the ground with a pine bough until he was certain his stash was perfectly concealed. This part of his plan was now complete.

As he walked toward the cemetery where he'd take the big shot in another two days he caught the tantalizing smell of meat on an outdoor grill. Hamburgers? Hot dogs? Steak? All of the above, probably. No doubt the folks who lived in those fancy Todt Hill homes were celebrating another Fourth of July with family and friends. He was momentarily rocked by a powerful deja vu moment that carried him back to the happiest days of his childhood, long ago before his father died, when the Jackson family would fire up the grill on July 4th. Friends would come over, and the kids were allowed to wave sparklers around in the dark. Those were the best times, the safe times. Long before Coach T trashed a kid's childhood.

Jackson quickly shook off the nostalgia and refocused on the here and now. He was the patriot who would honor his country by removing the single greatest threat America had ever faced. No foreign country and no Middle Eastern terrorist was as dangerous as Archer Grande, and every cell in Jackson's body screamed for action. He was a man on a mission, and he would not fail.

He strolled casually among the cemetery's headstones as he reviewed his plan of attack. Things would begin to roll late the next night, when he hid his rifle in the cemetery's storm drain. Then in the early afternoon of July 6th he would slip into the heavy shrubs that surrounded the manhole, lower himself into the tunnel, and wait patiently for five hours or so until it was time to creep forward and set up for the shot. He could eat, sleep, meditate, maybe even do some push-ups. If the police patrolled the cemetery before Grande's speech they would never bother to crawl the entire length of the storm system looking for a sniper. No way in hell.

The plan was flawless. All he needed was a live target.

41.

Lieutenant Aaron Crosby of the NYPD's Counterterrorism Bureau had been put in charge of the department's massive show of force in support of Archer Grande's visit to Staten Island. Never before had the borough received this sort of attention from the police, but never before had it hosted a top presidential candidate amid a crowd of 30,000 people, one of whom might be a serial killer armed with a rifle. Crosby wasn't pleased about having his plans second-guessed, but he didn't blame Nazareth and Gimble for that.

"I hope I don't offend the two of you," he said from his temporary desk at the one-two-two precinct, "when I say that the mayor is a genuine horse's ass."

"No offense taken, lieutenant," Nazareth smiled. "My father likes to say that there are more horses' asses than horses in this world. You, Tara, and I are on the same page about this one."

"Good. Well, since you're a Marine combat vet you know better than I do there's no such thing as a perfect security plan. We're throwing everything we've got at this, but I don't care how many cops we put between Grande and the crowd, someone can still get to him."

"Are you concerned mainly about the crowd," Gimble asked, "or about a sniper in the woods alongside the mall?"

"Yes," he grinned.

"I hear you," she laughed.

"Look, if we get anything close to 30,000 people out there," he reasoned, "we stand almost no chance of spotting the one person with a gun. If someone in the crowd decides to take a shot, we need to hope that he misses. As for a sniper in the woods, we don't know how good this Gabriel screwball is. He's been killing people from 50 or 60 yards, but that doesn't mean he's not good from 300 yards, right?"

"Based on his results so far," Nazareth said, "I'm guessing he's good from almost any distance. Can he find a clear line of fire from the woods beyond, let's say, 200 yards? Doubtful. There are just too many trees in the way. But he'll still have plenty of room to work. No way you can cover every possible shooting position."

"I agree completely. The mayor wants flawless security, but the three of us know that's impossible," Crosby offered, "and you should tell him that in your report. Just say the only way to be absolutely sure Archer Grande isn't shot on Staten Island is to keep him off Staten Island."

"That's what you'd really like, I take it," Nazareth said.

"You bet. But it's not going to happen. Grande's people tell me he's finished talking about it, so we do what we do and hope for the best."

The conversation the detectives had later that day with special agent in charge Tanya Hildebrand of the Secret Service was considerably less cordial than their chat with Lieutenant Crosby. Hildebrand, who occupied temporary space at the Staten Island Mall, didn't like having anyone question her authority or her intelligence, least of all what she perceived to be two inconsequential minions of the buffoonish mayor. Her brown hair was neatly clipped and short, as were her answers.

"What worries you most about security for Grande's visit?" Gimble asked.

"Nothing worries me, detective," Hildebrand replied with a tight smile. "We do this all the time."

"A crowd of 30,000 people is pretty big, though."

"A presidential inauguration on the streets of Washington, D.C., is bigger, and we do those every four years."

"Will security be just as tight for Grande's speech at the country club?" Nazareth asked.

"For the record, we don't do *loose* security. We protect the candidate in exactly the same way wherever he goes."

Gimble wanted to lean across the conference room table and smack Hildebrand but wisely considered the impact doing so would have on her NYPD career. "Is there anything else you suggest we put in our report?"

"Well," she mused, "why not mention that the Secret Service reports to the director of homeland security, not to the mayor of New York City?"

With that the interview was over, and the detectives headed off to walk the perimeter of the parking lot where the stage and bleachers were being set up for Grande's rally.

"Pleasant woman, isn't she?" Nazareth said.

"A royal bitch is what she is. I understand she doesn't like having someone look over her shoulder, but at this point in her career she should understand that you and I were simply following orders."

"And at this point in her life we're not going to change her personality," he replied. "But in our report we should note that she didn't seem particularly interested in sharing ideas with us. I hate buck-passing, but I'll make an exception for Hildebrand."

"I'll write that section."

"It's all yours."

Nazareth identified himself to the burly guy in charge of the construction crew and stepped onto the empty stage. He stood where the candidate's podium would soon be placed and shook his head in disgust.

"Don't like it?" Gimble asked.

"If I look straight ahead past those stores on both sides and beyond Forest Hill Road all I see is trees. Seriously deep woods. It wouldn't be an easy shot," he said, "but I can name at least 10 guys who could make it on every try." He looked to his right and studied the trees that ran alongside Richmond Avenue. "If someone set up over there he'd have a much shorter distance, but there's really nowhere to hide. The area is too exposed."

"So you're thinking the shot would have to come from the woods across Forest Hill Road?"

"Not really. I think the biggest risk here at the mall is a shooter in the crowd."

"Someone who doesn't care about getting caught, you mean?"

"Right. It happens, and there's not much you can do about it. But for a nut with a rifle . . ."

"Like Gabriel."

"Like Gabriel," he nodded, "a much better place to target Grande would be the country club parking lot. That whole area is surrounded by woods."

"And may I assume that's where we're going right now?"

"You may," he smiled.

Twenty minutes later they pulled into a space at the Richmond County Country Club, and Nazareth could hardly believe what he was seeing. At the back edge of the parking lot, adjacent to a perfectly groomed fairway, was the raised platform from which Archer Grande would deliver his pre-dinner comments to a large group of invited guests two nights later. The candidate would be facing Todt Hill Road as he spoke, with his back exposed to the woods surrounding the golf course. A shooter working from directly behind Grande could readily conceal himself less than 400 yards from the stage. Nazareth imagined himself crouching in the bushes taking aim. For a sniper with only marginal talent a shot to the torso would be a layup.

It got worse. If someone chose to angle a shot from the cemetery grounds he could get the distance down to 250 yards or less. This meant a head shot was easily within reach no matter what type of rifle the shooter carried.

"If our friend Agent Hildebrand isn't worried about this layout," Nazareth said gravely as he surveyed the terrain, "she's never fired a rifle. From a shooter's perspective this is just about as good as it gets."

"I'm no pro, Pete, but I've recently destroyed paper targets at 300 yards with a .22 rifle."

"Anything from a .22 on up could be lethal at this distance," he nodded, "and our friend Gabriel sure as hell isn't using a .22. He's been firing 5.56 NATO rounds, which means he could work as far out as maybe 800 yards if he's really good at what he does."

"So basically there's no way to protect Grande from sniper fire?"

"Sure there is. All he has to do is cancel the speech," Nazareth declared. "And someone needs to make that happen."

"I doubt anyone can."

"I'm willing to bet the Secret Service could force him to cancel the outdoor talk here."

"Special agent in charge Hildebrand? Seriously? The woman who has everything perfectly under control? You can call her if you want, Pete."

"Yeah, forget that idea. What we'll do instead is write this all up as fast as we can and get it to Chief Crawford. Recommendation number one will be to have Grande cancel the outdoor appearance at the country club because his safety cannot possibly be assured."

"I agree that's the right thing," she said reluctantly, "but I guarantee you Grande isn't going to cancel."

"Then he doesn't cancel. And he also probably doesn't get shot, which is great. But if some nut is out to kill him on July 6th," he added, "it's going to happen. End of story."

42.

The ferocity of Archer Grande's reaction was unusual even for him. Vincent Chandler had just passed along word that the mayor wanted to cancel the outdoor speech at the country club, and for a few moments he thought his boss was having a stroke. Grande's face turned bright red, the veins on his neck popped out, and his mouth was so twisted with rage that he could only sputter when he tried to speak.

"Arch, calm down," Chandler urged, "it's only a suggestion. You can do the speech if you want to. The guy's just looking out for you."

"By making me look like a goddamn wimp?" he screamed. "That's looking out for me? Why not suggest I pull out of the race while he's at it? How about I build a concrete bunker and hide in it for the rest of my life?"

"Arch, fine, I'll let him know you're not changing the plans."

"No, here's what you tell that cowardly son of a bitch. You tell him I think the mayor of New York City needs to be at the country club to introduce me, okay? Tell him that if he's not on the stage with me that night, he can say goodbye to some fat-cat job in Washington. Can you do that, Vince?"

"Yes, Arch, I can do that. I'll make the call. But," he said hesitantly, "there's one more thing."

"And what the hell is that?"

"The mayor said if you refuse to cancel, he at least wants you to wear body armor during the talk."

Grande had already spent his fury and had nothing left but sarcasm. "On July 6th," he began, "when it's 90 degrees and humid, I should wear a 50-pound bulletproof vest?"

"They really don't weigh that much."

"They don't?"

"I don't think so, no."

"You don't think so. That means you've never worn one?"

"No, I've never worn one."

"Good. Then here are two things I want you to do right now. One, call the mayor and tell him to stick his bulletproof vest. Two, go buy yourself a bulletproof vest and wear it all day on July 6th. Then on July 7th tell me how it felt."

"You really want me to wear a bulletproof vest?" said the chastened campaign manager.

"Isn't that what I just said?"

"Yes, it is."

Grande gave him a casual salute. "Adios, Vince. Happy shopping."

Chandler's day got immeasurably worse when he phoned Mayor Dortmund and passed along Grande's summons. The mayor was sitting in a sand chair at Siasconset Beach on Nantucket when he took the call and screamed so loudly that his two tiny granddaughters began wailing. Yes, he would be there as ordered to introduce Grande at the country club even though it meant interrupting an extremely expensive family vacation. But he insisted that Chandler alert the Secret Service to the change and demand extra protection for the evening.

Agent Hildebrand was even less kind when Chandler dutifully called to say the mayor wanted extra protection.

"We're talking about the mayor of New York City?" she asked sarcastically.

"Yes, of course."

"Is he a presidential candidate?"

"No, he is not a candidate, as you well know," Chandler answered.

"But he does have nearly 35,000 police that he can order around as much as he'd like. Am I correct in that, Mr. Chandler?"

"You are correct in that. Look, all I'm doing is passing along a message."

"If you pass along a message concerning candidate Archer Grande, who is presently under Secret Service protection, you'll find me highly responsive. But if you call on behalf of the mayor, who is not and will not be under Secret Service protection, you'll find that I'm not terribly interested. If your mayor wants more protection, tell him to hire more cops. Is there anything else I can do for you?"

He hung up without answering. Note to self, he thought. Once Grande is president and I'm chief of staff, Tanya Hildebrand will occupy a one-person office on Little Diomede Island in the Bering Strait, halfway between Tin City, Alaska, and the easternmost wilderness of Russia. She had just joined a long list of people whose lives he planned to ruin once he began pulling strings in the White House.

Enough with the phone calls and daydreaming. Now he had to go shopping for body armor. Archer Grande was an easy man to hate, but the potential perks of being on his team sometimes seemed worth the suffering.

43.

By 11:00 a.m. on July 6th a faint blue haze had settled over the Greenbelt, and the place was more Central American jungle than urban parkland. The National Weather Service called for the temperature to reach 97 degrees, a record high for the date, but the relative humidity would produce a heat index of nearly 120. This, of course, was hardly the kind of day thousands of people should gather to meet Archer Grande at the Staten Island Mall. Grande's inflammatory rhetoric never needed the kind of emotional boost a ferociously hot day could provide.

The NYPD's man on the scene was torn between somehow forcing a cancellation and adding extra uniformed officers in case the huge rally exploded. Lieutenant Crosby, who stood to lose his career if things went south, made one last pitch for pulling the plug.

"This will be like baking a can of gasoline in the oven," he told his boss, Captain Kevin O'Shaughnessy, when they spoke by phone shortly after noon. "When Grande starts in on Hispanics, Muslims, gays -- basically any of the groups he usually antagonizes -- the place could blow."

The captain was unsympathetic, chiefly because he was in Manhattan, far from the scene of what could easily become an uncontrollable riot. "It's, what, four hours before Grande is scheduled to speak? How many people are already there, lieutenant?"

"A couple thousand, I guess. And we've already got major traffic tie-ups in every direction."

"So you're thinking we just hang a big CLOSED sign outside the mall? And then everyone drives home?"

"Well..."

"Let me be blunt, lieutenant. If you felt this strongly about the event you should have said something a week ago, because it's too damn late to cancel now," he yelled. "So I don't care if you have to use fire hoses on the crowd. Just keep things under control. The show goes on."

"Can I at least get additional officers?"

"Same answer. If you needed more cops, you should have mentioned that to someone a week ago. I can't invent them for you. I'm not Harry Houdini."

"I have a bad feeling about this."

"Next time have it sooner," O'Shaughnessy suggested.

Among the gathering crowd in the mall's sweltering parking lot were Detectives Nazareth and Gimble, both in casual summer clothes blending in with the early arrivers. They had no way of knowing yet which audience members were Grande supporters and which ones might be there to heckle. All they knew for sure is that the asphalt beneath their feet was 146 degrees. Not quite hot enough to fry an egg but certainly hot enough to make people uncomfortable. And uncomfortable people, they knew from long experience, sometimes had hair triggers. On a day like this almost anything -- a wrong word, a shove, a gunshot -- could spark all-out war.

The growing audience grew restless, hot, and edgy by 3:30. That's when Lieutenant Crosby launched what he later termed The Peace Plan. A refrigerated 18-wheeler parked 200 yards from the podium opened its door, and 50 smiling volunteers -- all of them employees of mall stores -- began loading shopping carts with frigid bottles of water donated by a local beverage distributor. Then they worked their way into the crowd, each of them accompanied by a uniformed officer who handed out the free bottles and traded high fives with the men, women, and children whose mood suddenly brightened. By the time Archer Grande was ready to speak the volunteers had gone through nearly 500 cases of water, and the NYPD had scored a major public relations coup.

Nazareth and Gimble stood by the speaker's platform and watched in amazement as the atmosphere grew increasingly festive.

"That was a brilliant move," Gimble said a few minutes into the process. "Talk about effective police action."

Nazareth wore an ear-to-ear grin. "I'm stunned, Tara. All day long I've been wondering how much force it would take to keep things under control here, and the right answer was none."

"See, you Neanderthals always think about breaking heads."

"Oh, now wait a second . . ."

"Teasing, Pete. Just teasing. I have to agree that I was thinking force might be necessary. But at this point I'd say the situation is under control."

Aside from a group of seven overly zealous anti-Grande protesters who had to be escorted from the premises, the crowd, which in the final analysis looked to be no larger than 9,000, was well behaved, loud, and frighteningly supportive of the candidate's key messages. Among these were a ban on mosques, a 40% tax on all imported goods, and the immediate deportation of all immigrants who had not yet attained citizenship.

Nazareth and Gimble had trouble understanding how Grande's "America for Americans Only" theme could be so well received in a borough where virtually 100% of the population was descended from immigrants. But all they could do about that was vote for someone who in their opinion wasn't certifiably insane. Today their only job was to help make sure the guy didn't get shot.

As soon as Grande left the stage the detectives jumped in their car and powered up the a/c.

"One down, one to go," Gimble said.

"Yeah, but it's the next one that scares me," he said gravely. "I ran combat ops in places exactly like the Greenbelt, and I promise you there's no way to defend Grande if someone in the woods is out to get him."

"We don't have to be there, Pete. We turned in our report, and now it's someone else's responsibility. Let's go back after Gabriel."

He looked at her and nodded. "Unfortunately I think that's what we'll be doing at the country club. But I hope to hell I'm wrong."

44.

While thousands of Staten Islanders were baking on the asphalt waiting for Archer Grande to speak at the mall, Stone Jackson parked his car at the edge of the Greenbelt and walked casually through the forest to Moravian Cemetery. He found the manhole cover, yanked it up with the puller he had bought a few days earlier, and tossed his light knapsack inside. After lowering himself into the drainpipe he replaced the cover and crawled toward the rifle he had planted there the night before.

The surroundings were reasonably accommodating, albeit a bit musty, for someone who had never been the slightest bit claustrophobic. The pipe's diameter was 36 inches, so he was able to sit back and enjoy a ham sandwich, peanuts, and bottled water by the light of a pale green glow stick. When he was finished eating he checked out the rifle one last time, made sure the bipod was securely attached, then settled in for a long wait. Through his wireless headset he listened to the mournful notes of Samuel Barber's *Adagio for Strings*, a piece he considered an anthem for the sad fate awaiting America if Archer Grande became president. Late that night, long after Grande had spent some time with the coroner, Jackson would celebrate with something livelier. Vivaldi, perhaps. Better still, Gershwin. Yes, Gershwin. This would be a night for American music.

Three hours after Jackson had crept into his shooter's lair the other would-be assassin, Hunter Bloodworth, left the rented safe house after receiving the go-ahead phone call from Vincent Chandler and moved cautiously toward his hideout at the edge of the golf course. Along the way he passed two boys of 10 or 11 who walked a docile golden retriever with a gray muzzle. They chattered about a tree house they planned to build when they got home and paid no attention whatsoever to the large man with the backpack. When questioned several days later neither of them would remember having seen a stranger in the woods on July 6th.

Bloodworth was utterly alone when he reached his sanctuary in the woods, a spot so thick with vegetation that he would remain invisible even to someone who walked within three feet of him. This, he told himself, was an ideal location from which to play the grand game. But on this day he would play by his rules, no one else's. The more he'd thought about it, the more convinced he had become that getting rid of Chandler was essential. To begin with he assumed Chandler would most likely try to have him fitted for cement shoes once the assignment was successfully completed. Like most campaign managers, Chandler was a sneak who cared only about money and power. This was not someone who would ever be comfortable sharing the planet with a witness to his crimes.

In addition, he believed he would be in a stronger position to negotiate a lucrative career with Grande once the conniving henchman was out of the picture. There was no way the candidate would be willing to get his hands dirty by putting a hit on him. No way. That's not something Grande could risk just prior to the election, and it certainly wasn't something he would dare consider once elected. No, the future president would definitely be willing to work something out.

He couldn't help but smile. Things were definitely looking up for Hunter Bloodworth.

45.

The country club parking lot resembled evening rush hour at Penn Station by the time Nazareth and Gimble arrived. A grounds crew was adding final touches -- flowers, a red carpet, American flags, and such -- to the speaker's platform while an NYPD sergeant went over assignments one last time with a squad of uniformed officers. Four Secret Service agents patrolled the parking lot's perimeter, occasionally asking reporters, workmen, or early-arriving guests for ID. And out on the most distant fairway special agent in charge Hildebrand and one of her men sped along the edge of the woods in a golf cart looking for potential threats but expecting none.

When Hildebrand returned to the parking lot 20 minutes later Nazareth immediately went over to speak with her.

"How's everything looking out there, Agent Hildebrand?" he asked calmly despite what his gut was telling him.

"Everything's quite under control, detective," she offered with the slightest hint of a smile, "just as I told you and your partner the other day."

"Tara and I would like to walk the woods before things get underway here. Do you have any objection?"

"I have a huge objection, yes," she said flatly. "I just finished checking the woods myself, detective, and I'm completely satisfied. In addition, Mr. Grande has specifically asked to have every available agent and police officer right here in the parking lot with him. He's not worried about people walking their dogs in the woods."

"Neither am I, actually. I'm worried about a sniper with a high-powered rifle."

"I checked the distance two weeks ago, detective, and I haven't lost any sleep over some nut named Gabriel hitting a target from 400 yards. Does your NYPD experience suggest people normally get shot from that distance?"

He shook his head slowly as he drilled her with his eyes. "In my NYPD experience no one has ever gotten shot from that distance," he told her. "But as a Marine in Afghanistan I saw 800-yard shots every day, 1,500-yard shots a few times each week, and seven verified 2,000-yard kills during my tour. So I suspect *some nut named Gabriel* could hit a man from 400 yards." He paused to let the words sink in. "But I guess your combat experience has taught you otherwise, Agent Hildebrand."

"My *Secret Service* experience trumps your Marine experience, detective," she smirked, "since I'm in charge here. You and your partner will not, I repeat, *will not* stroll through the woods today. I have two men with binoculars here in the parking lot, and they're both capable of seeing anything that goes on down there."

Totally disgusted by her attitude and poor judgment, Nazareth turned to walk away but not before delivering one final shot. "Tell them to be on the lookout for a puff of smoke," he warned her. "They'll see it about one second after the bullet hits Archer Grande."

By the time he rejoined Gimble his mood had blackened even further, but he realized he was powerless to change the situation. Fate had turned the op over to an agent whose self-confidence bordered on recklessness.

"Looks as though you and Miss Tanya had a lovely chat," Gimble said.

"Yeah, everything's just peachy here, Tara. She's got everything buttoned up, so you and I are free to sit on our hands and watch if we'd like."

"So we won't be checking the woods?"

"A resounding no to that. The woods are off limits according to commander in chief Hildebrand."

"Okay, so what's the plan?"

"Since we can't do anything here except watch, I vote we visit young Mr. Jackson. If he's home, I'll worry less about Grande getting shot tonight."

"Because your gut tells you Jackson is Gabriel."

"Not really, but he's the closest thing we've got to a suspect."

"And if he's not home?" she asked.

"If he's not home AND Grande gets shot," he said ruefully, "we'll know we blew it."

46.

Jackson sipped some water after finishing the last of his snack food -- a mix of dark chocolate, peanuts, and high-protein tablets -- then strapped on a pair of foam knee pads. He left everything but the rifle and bipod near the manhole and slowly crawled toward the mouth of the large drainpipe. The Republican gala was set to begin in 15 minutes, and Stone Jackson would be providing the fireworks.

Funny how life leads you by the nose, he thought. In the blink of an eye he had gone from being an abused kid to an Army private to a scout sniper to the country's foremost patriot. If eliminating child molesters was noble, then ridding the country of someone like Archer Grande was epic. The mission he was about to fulfill ranked alongside the signing of the Declaration of Independence. America would not tolerate tyranny, then or now. He would do what all reasonable countrymen knew should be done but didn't have the courage to undertake. He was a man among men whose time had come.

He stopped as he approached the end of the drainpipe and allowed his eyes to adjust to daylight. And he listened carefully for any sign that visitors might be strolling the cemetery's quiet paths. All he heard was the sound of birds calling to each other and the echo of "testing, testing" in the distance as someone made sure the podium mic was working.

While the crew in the parking lot made final preparations for Grande's glamorous invitation-only rally Jackson sat cross-legged at the mouth of the tunnel and adjusted the bipod to its proper height. Through the powerful scope he zeroed in on the spot where the candidate would stand in another few minutes. The sight line was perfect, and the distance was fine. He was warm but not uncomfortably so, sheltered from the blazing sun as he took deep, relaxing breaths. Except for the eight inches of rifle barrel that poked out from the drainpipe Jackson was invisible.

He was greatly amused by the police, Secret Service agents, and event organizers who scurried about the country club parking lot trying to look important and in control of things. Together they had successfully mastered the tiniest details of today's rally, but clearly they had missed the elephant in the room. How do you not plan for a shot from the woods? If he had been in charge of security he would have had cops and agents assigned to the entire perimeter of the Greenbelt within 500 yards of the speaker's platform. On a day like this with a man like Archer Grande in play there was no such thing as being too careful.

But Jackson wasn't complaining. A man with a peashooter wouldn't be able to get within 25 feet of the podium right now. A man with a high-powered rifle, on the other hand, would be able to squeeze off a shot heard around the world.

47.

After affixing his rifle to the tripod Hunter Bloodworth peered through the bushes and saw guests filling the bleachers in the distant parking lot. They furiously wiped sweat from their foreheads and attempted to cool their faces with cheap paper fans bearing the likeness of Archer Grande, but nothing helped. It would be hours before the sun set, and even then the only cure for the ferocious heat would be sitting directly in front of an air conditioner, assuming the massive strain on Staten Island's power grid didn't cause widespread brownouts.

The former SEAL had worked in hotter places as part of vastly more threatening operations, but the stakes had never been greater. He felt the pressure, no doubt about it, and the heat didn't help. When he studied the podium through his scope he immediately noticed the distortion of light waves caused by hot air rising from the parking lot's blazingly hot surface. He wasn't surprised, but he wasn't pleased either. When an entire mission rests on the success of one bullet, you hope for better conditions even though you've trained for whatever the battlefield might throw at you.

In a few minutes he would be stretched out in his safe room waiting for nightfall, and he could almost feel the cooling dampness of the underground shelter on his skin. Let the police and Secret Service agents traipse through the stifling woods for hours, he thought, battling the heat and mosquitoes while preparing themselves for the inevitable criticism that would follow their botched mission. How could so many professionals bungle a simple protection detail? Answer: they were no match for a man with his skill set and field experience.

Bloodworth was about to load the rifle when he heard a golf cart approaching quickly from his left. He froze as a man and woman in civilian clothes bumped along the fairway talking about the heat and passed within five feet of his position. His heart rate jumped momentarily as he considered how badly things might have gone if he had locked the bolt down a few seconds earlier. The sound could easily have given him away, and the entire mission would have disintegrated in seconds.

Way too close for comfort. He took a long, deep breath and forced himself to relax. This was no time to get rattled.

48.

From inside the air-conditioned clubhouse Grande watched his supporters crowd into the sunbaked bleachers. The day was still brutally hot, and he wasn't eager to endure the tropical weather again this soon after his appearance at the mall.

"Where the hell did everybody get those stupid fans with my picture on them?" he snapped at Chandler.

"One of your local donors thought it would be a cute idea, Arch. And people are glad to have them."

"Waving hot air on their faces makes them feel better? I really doubt that, Vince. Plus I don't like the picture. It makes me look as fat as you with your stupid bulletproof vest on." Chandler wished he could stuff the bulletproof vest down his boss's throat.

"Your donors don't care about the photo," Chandler said. "Right now all they care about is hearing a few words from the next president."

"And that's what they're going to get," he replied sarcastically. "A few words. I want to get this over with fast." Grande seemed edgier than usual.

"If you're nervous about the shot, Arch, don't be. This guy is the best."

"I'm not nervous about the shot," he lied. "I'm nervous about the heat. I can't stand hot weather. You know that."

"Arch, it'll all be over in a couple of minutes."

"Don't schedule two outdoor talks on the same day anymore."

"Okay, it won't happen again."

"Good. Because if you schedule two again, I won't do them."

"I get it, Arch." Chandler shook his head in disgust. "You know what you have to say, right?"

"Do I look brain dead?"

"No, I just want to make sure you've got the line right, because the guy isn't going to shoot unless he hears it."

"Is this the America you want?" he hissed. "Then I stand still for four seconds. Does that sound about right, Vince?"

"Yes. That's perfect. Thank you." His boss was often an easy man to hate, and at that moment Vincent Chandler was thinking how nice it might be if the shooter was off by a foot or so. Maybe a couple of weeks in a hospital bed would have a beneficial effect on Grande's attitude. But that wasn't part of the plan. No one would get hurt today.

At precisely six o'clock Chandler opened the clubhouse door and stepped aside as Archer Grande emerged to greet his adoring fans. The candidate smiled broadly, waved with both hands, and mounted the stage while his fans chanted AR-CHER, AR-CHER, AR-CHER. These were the second-tier rich, the ones whose campaign contributions were noteworthy but not large enough to earn them a seat at tonight's private dinner. So they cheered wildly instead, convincing themselves they mattered just as much as the mega-donors who would soon break bread with the next president.

Grande didn't care one way or the other. His impeccably tailored navy blue suit absorbed the sunlight that streamed onto his shoulders and back, making him feel like a man on fire. Each time he motioned for quiet the crowd screamed even louder. Under more tolerable conditions he would have welcomed the adulation, but not today. All he wanted was to get off the stage and out of the heat. But the yelling and chanting didn't stop until Mayor Elliot Dortmund shuffled to the podium, forced a thin smile, and said, "Ladies and gentlemen, it gives me great pleasure to introduce my friend and the next president of the United States, Archer Grande."

The introduction triggered another two full minutes of cheering, but finally the crowd settled in to hear Grande's message. After a few gentle words about traditional values and America's greatness he began pounding away at some of his favorite themes.

On Washington's professional politicians: "They're all parasites. We know that, right? A parasite is an organism that lives off other organisms. Have you ever heard a better definition of a professional politician? No, and you never will."

On international relations: "The problem with North Korea is that North Korea exists. If it didn't exist, we wouldn't have to listen to threats from whatever madman is currently running the place, right? We can fix this with the push of a button."

On Democrats: "Here's what the Democrats want, my friends. It's pretty simple. They want to reach into your pocket, grab all your money, and give it to someone who's too lazy to work. That's everything you need to know about Democrats."

But he saved most of his venom for what he termed "them."

"When I say *them* you know exactly who I'm talking about, right?" His supporters roared their approval. This is why most of them had come out to hear him on this hot, ugly day. The guy never pulled any punches, least of all when discussing terrorists, and his tirades were better than anything Hollywood could script.

"Listen, I'm not saying all Muslims are terrorists. Maybe they're not. All I'm saying is we can't tell the good ones from the bad ones. So here's what we do. It's simple, right? Am I right? We send *them* -- and I mean all of THEM -- over to the Middle East somewhere. All of them. Tomorrow! And then once they're able to prove to us they're not terrorists -- however many years that takes -- we allow them to come back one at a time." Everyone cheered, even those who thought that perhaps driving all Muslims out of the United States was, well, a bit un-American. If you didn't cheer at a Grande rally people noticed.

"I'm sure some Muslims believe you and I have a right to exist. But until I know for sure who they are, how do I defend against the next terrorist attack? Do I really want to lie awake every night waiting for the bombing to begin? Do you? Is that how you want your children and grandchildren to live? **Is that the kind of America you want?**" He reached toward the audience, palms up, demanding an answer. And he stood perfectly still. One, two, three . . .

49.

Stone Jackson had the candidate in the crosshairs, waiting for the guy to stop moving around. Because Grande customarily punctuated 98% of his words with dramatic gestures -- waving, flailing, shaking his fists -- he was hardly an ideal target. Several times Jackson's finger slipped over the trigger, only to retreat as Grande once again began pounding the podium or pointing to imaginary adversaries in the midst of his verbal assaults.

Jackson's lower back began to tighten as he sat cross-legged at the mouth of the drainpipe. He didn't know how long Grande's speech was supposed to last, and he suddenly grew concerned that he might not get a shot off before his prey was once again surrounded by police and Secret Service agents. But the mere thought of wasting all those months of fanatical training was unacceptable. What the hell was wrong with him anyway? Was he losing his nerve? He had realized, of course, that shooting Archer Grande would be somewhat different from shooting one of those child-molesting maggots, but had he underestimated the magnitude of the challenge? Had he failed to recognize his own limitations?

And then it happened. For the first time since Grande had ascended the speaker's platform the candidate grew perfectly still. He had just challenged his supporters with a question about the kind of America they wanted, and now he stood before them utterly motionless. One, two, three . . .

Less than 150 yards away from Jackson's position Hunter Bloodworth lined up the Chandler head shot. He could have squeezed off a round at any time but saw no reason to deviate from the original plan on this particular point. It amused him, actually, to think of the treacherous campaign manager sitting there, confident and smug, waiting for his boss to catch a bullet in the leg when in fact his own head was in play. Would there be a flash of recognition? In that thousandth of a second before he died would Chandler know that he had been double-crossed? Would he have any final regrets about a life devoted to manipulation and deceit?

Bloodworth didn't think deeply about such things. He was simply intrigued in the way a black widow spider is intrigued by a cricket caught in a web. Allowing contemplation to interfere with action wasn't one of his shortcomings. No, today's outcome had been a foregone conclusion for weeks.

And then over the distant loudspeaker he heard Grande utter the words that would precede four seconds of stillness: *Is that the kind of America you want?* One, two, three . . .

Jackson and Bloodworth squeezed their triggers within three-tenths of a second of each other -- so close together, in fact, that neither assassin heard the other's shot. Jackson's 5.56 round left the muzzle at nearly 3,000 feet per second, while Bloodworth's larger .308 round flew toward its target at roughly 2,700 feet per second. The speed difference didn't matter much since both bullets made contact in half a heartbeat. All that mattered was placement.

Jackson delivered his bullet slightly under Grande's right shoulder blade, angled toward the heart. The violent impact crater produced by the bullet as it passed through the candidate's chest proved instantly fatal, and Grande toppled sideways.

Bloodworth made the more masterful shot of the two. Shooting from a position several feet below his victim, he managed to place his round at dead center of the occipital bone on the back of Chandler's skull. The bullet tore through the campaign manager's brain and put him face down on the platform 100% DOA.

Bedlam followed. As screaming onlookers jumped or got shoved from the bleachers in a wild stampede, Secret Service agents rushed toward the two fallen victims. Most of the police, on the other hand, attempted to control the frenzied crowd, though a half dozen of them drew their weapons and set up a perimeter at the back of the clubhouse facing the distant trees.

They saw no one and heard nothing, but they were ready for whatever might come next.

Nearly seven minutes passed before NYPD Sergeant George Overstreet was able to send three teams of four officers into the woods to look for signs of the shooter. All they knew at this point was that someone had killed two people and might be looking to kill more, so they moved as cautiously as possible and stayed alert for any movement along the edge of the golf course or the adjoining cemetery. They were easy targets, and they knew it.

The officers systematically pushed their way through tangled shrubs and dense patches of waist-high weeds in a frantic but fruitless effort to locate the shooter. They questioned a startled husband and wife who were visiting a relative's grave in Moravian Cemetery, but the couple hadn't seen anyone during their visit. And they briefly detained a teenage jogger who had nearly gotten shot when he came barreling around a bend in the Greenbelt's Yellow Trail midway through a steamy three-mile run.

No fewer than five cops walked past the mouth of the large storm drain inside the cemetery grounds. Two even poked their heads inside, then moved on after finding no evidence of activity. One of the same officers later turned his ankle slightly when he stepped awkwardly on a manhole cover hidden in the undergrowth. At no point, though, did any of the police come across signs that a shooter had been there. Whoever had shot Grande and Chandler was gone without a trace.

Nazareth executed a furious U-turn on Hylan Boulevard and roared back toward the country club as soon as the shooting report came over the police radio. The flashers and siren helped speed them on their way, but they were already too late to do anything for the two victims.

"Your good friend Agent Hildebrand will be looking for work as a school crossing guard," Gimble said soberly.

"Yeah, but there's small comfort in that, Tara. I should have pushed her harder to defend against a shooter in the woods."

"We don't know what happened yet."

"I do. If two men are dead and there's no suspect," he said, "that means the shooter was in the woods a couple hundred yards away. This could have been prevented."

"I get it, but that's not on you. Hildebrand refused to listen, and it was her call. All you and I can do now is try to help find the killer."

"Easier said than done," he told her, thoroughly disgusted by the way things had gone. "A shooter in the trees would already have a three-minute head start on everyone else, and I'm guessing that turned into five or six minutes by the time someone went after him. He's probably on his way to New Jersey by now."

"Wherever he goes, we'll get him."

"Oh, we'll get him," he nodded. "But we could have gotten him before he killed two more people. Shame on us."

50.

Two minutes after murdering the top presidential candidate Stone Jackson was alongside Ohrbach Lake stuffing his rifle into the black plastic bag he had stashed there the day before. He knotted the top, attached the heavy fishing line, and tossed the bag 10 feet from shore, where it disappeared into the murky water. In a few days he would return at night to retrieve his weapon. Until then it was securely fastened to a sapling at the water's edge.

Thirty seconds later he was spreading out the blanket and fishing tackle he had hidden in the shrubs. He popped open a warm Bud Light for effect, stripped off his Army brown T-shirt, and cast a rubber worm into the lake. As soon as the lure sank to the bottom he reeled in the slack line, then gently pulled back on the slender rod to create a moving target that might tempt a fish. He had repeated the pulling motion five or six times when he heard the commotion behind him. Loud voices, police radios, heavy footsteps in the undergrowth. Jackson had bet his freedom on hiding in plain sight, and his bold plan was about to succeed or fail.

The odds of hooking a fish at that precise moment and after only one cast were absurdly low, but truth is, in fact, often stranger than fiction. The rubber worm attracted the interest of a hungry six-pound largemouth bass that fought wildly for 40 seconds as the police walked up and watched. As soon as Jackson had landed the big fish he turned and smiled at the cops -- four of them -- who were carefully studying him, his gear, and the surroundings.

Jackson did his best to look surprised. "What's up, guys?"

"How long have you been here, sir?" Patrolman Devon Gibson wore the no-nonsense look of a man who had seen it all and hadn't been impressed.

"Couple hours, I guess," he said. "Hey, is it okay if I release the fish?"

When Gibson and one other officer nodded he unhooked the bass and set it gently back in the water. He waited for it to splash away before standing up and facing everyone.

"Listen, I have a fishing license as well as a permit for this lake," Jackson said innocently. "I've got them in my tackle box if you'd like to see them."

"That would be good," Gibson said. "But please turn the box toward us as you open it."

Jackson slowly turned the gray tackle box toward the officers, all of whom kept their hands close to their weapons. He opened the top, gave them a good look at the contents -- lures, hooks, cell phone -- then lifted out the license and permit that he kept safely in a plastic sandwich bag. Gibson took the documents and studied both of them.

"Shane Matthews?"

"That's me." The $200 Jackson had spent on a phony driver's license earlier in the year continued to pay dividends. He now held a full set of fake ID and two credit cards in the name of Shane Matthews.

"Do you fish here often, Mr. Matthews?"

"Whenever I can," he said, "for at least 15 years."

"And you've been here fishing for two hours?" he asked.

"About that, yeah. I'm not wearing a watch."

Gibson eyed him carefully, but the other three officers scanned the terrain, obviously convinced they were wasting valuable time on the fisherman.

"Have you seen anyone come by here in the last few minutes?"

"I've seen a few people since I got here, but the most recent was a jogger."

"How long ago was that?"

"Ten minutes, maybe."

"What did he look like?" Gibson asked.

Jackson paused thoughtfully. "Guy about my height, in his thirties probably. Dressed in running clothes. He had a pack on his back."

"What kind of pack?"

"Just a small backpack. Maybe the kind that holds water? I really didn't pay much attention."

"And which way was he headed?"

He pointed to his left. "Along that trail over there and up the hill. Seems like a pretty dumb day to be running, but everybody's different, right?"

Gibson handed back the fishing license and permit, and Jackson bent over to replace them in the tackle box. Before closing the box he discreetly pushed the SEND button on his cell phone, triggering the small explosive charges he had rigged in the woods the day before. The three sharp cracks passed easily for gunfire, and the police immediately jumped into action.

"Down!" Gibson yelled as he shoved Jackson to the ground. The other three officers drew their weapons and scattered. One knelt behind a large oak while the other two took prone positions and trained their guns on the hillside.

"Is that shooting?" Jackson screamed.

"Hell, yes. Keep your head down," Gibson ordered. "We had two people killed a few minutes ago."

"Oh, God. Oh, God," Jackson whimpered. He trembled and looked as though he might start crying. It was a convincing display. But at the same time he was totally confused. The cop said two people had been killed. How could that be? He replayed the scene: target in the crosshairs, shot fired, Grande falls, and that's that. Although Jackson hadn't stuck around to watch what happened, he had heard only the one shot. And he sure as hell hadn't hit two people.

"Stay here and don't move," Gibson shouted to him. "Guys, up the hill on my count. Keep moving side to side, okay? Don't give him a target. Three, two, one, go."

All four cops zigzagged up the hillside, guns aimed low ahead of them, while Gibson yelled to whoever was up there. "NYPD. Drop your weapon, and come out with your hands up." Gibson had been on the job for nine years and had survived his share of bad situations, but a loud voice inside kept telling him that this was *the one.* Today was the day his wife would get *the call*, the one that so many other wives had gotten. Despite the bad vibes he ran hard and was the first man to reach the heavily wooded hilltop, an area so dense with shrubs that a dozen men could have been hiding up there.

"NYPD!" he yelled again. "You're surrounded. Drop your weapon and come out with your hands up."

After 15 minutes of searching the woods and finding no trace of the shooter, Gibson and his buddies went back to the lake, where Jackson was still lying face down on the blanket with his hands clasped over his head.

"It's all clear here," Gibson said, "but you should leave the area."

Jackson jumped to his feet and began pulling his shirt on. "You don't need to tell me twice. I'm out of here." He paused and looked around nervously. "Is it safe to go back to my car?"

"Where are you parked?"

Jackson motioned to the south. "In a development about a quarter of a mile from here."

"You should be fine," Gibson told him. "The guy we're after seems to be running in the opposite direction. Just go straight to your vehicle, and don't waste any time getting there."

"On my way. Good luck catching this guy."

"Yeah, thanks." Gibson grabbed a call on his radio and forgot about the fisherman who hustled down the trail like a scared rabbit.

51.

Hunter Bloodworth was thunderstruck. After scoring a direct hit on Vincent Chandler's skull he had held his shooting position for a count of two and in that moment caught the commotion to his target's left. He moved his scope just in time to watch Archer Grande collapse to the stage. How could that be? He had fired only one shot, and Chandler went down. There was absolutely no way his bullet could have struck both Chandler and Grande. Impossible.

But he had no time to figure this out now. He quickly set the rifle in the backpack, covered that with some topsoil and leaves, and bolted for his safe room. All he needed to do now was dive into the underground shelter and wait for nightfall. He would have hours to think about what he had just seen. Had Grande, in fact, been hit? Or had he simply collapsed after seeing Chandler get shot? Yeah, that was probably it.

Bloodworth covered the distance to his shelter in less than a minute and a half, even though he stopped several times to listen for sounds of approaching footsteps. He knew the police and Secret Service agents would need at least two minutes to get from the clubhouse to his shooting position, probably much more amid all the confusion. So he wasn't worried about them right now. But he had to make sure he didn't get spotted by some dumb jogger out in all this heat or some nosy kid walking a dog.

He located the clump of shrubs that concealed the entrance to his safe room and knelt alongside it, listening for voices or any other sounds of pursuit. Satisfied he was alone, he slipped quietly into the bushes. At that precise moment he was startled by the sharp crack of an errant golf ball on a large maple 20 feet away from him, and he dove headfirst into his underground shelter and scrambled out of sight in the dark.

Bloodworth did not know, and probably would not have cared, that a group of rattlesnakes is called a rhumba rather than a den, nest, or pit. But he immediately learned what it's like to bed down with 25 timber rattlers that have taken up residence in a dark, cozy place. The safe room was roughly twice his width, providing the frenzied snakes with ample room to slither around his entire body as they struck again and again. He couldn't see that he was face to face with at least 15 of them, but each time he tried to cover up several of them sank their fangs into his cheeks, neck, shoulders, or hands. When he tried to wiggle backwards out of the den they attacked his legs, pumping more venom into his thighs, calves, and ankles.

After more than 60 bites in less than a minute Bloodworth had been filled with enough venom to bring down a water buffalo. First came the intense pain, then tingling, then numbness. His pulse grew rapid and weak. He struggled for breath.

And then he no longer cared about anything. His brain simply shut down, and the snakes went back to sleep.

52.

The victims' bodies had been driven away by the time Nazareth and Gimble returned to the country club, but chaos still reigned. EMTs treated a number of guests who had collapsed from the combination of heat and emotion, and a half dozen cops tried to herd the remaining Grande supporters back to their cars and away from the NYPD crime scene experts who had taken over the investigation. Agent Hildebrand sat alone near the clubhouse with her cell phone to her ear as someone from Washington explained in crude terms why she should update her resume.

Nazareth and Gimble spent some time walking the area and helping the injured. Eventually they bumped into Sergeant Overstreet, the on-scene commander, and asked if they could assist him in some way.

"You could probably shoot me," Overstreet replied grimly. "That would beat being torn to shreds by all the second-guessers who'll be after my badge."

"There was nothing you could have done about this, sarge. I tried talking sense to Agent Hildebrand, but she was going to do this her way. She owns it."

"I hope you're right. This was supposed to be the safe rally today, and look at the goddamn mess."

"How many shooters did you have?" Nazareth asked.

Overstreet was baffled. "How many shooters? Just one. Two perfect shots." The sergeant shook his head disconsolately as he relived the episode. He had more than 20 years on the force and figured the time had probably come to retire.

"Sarge, do you know if any of your guys are recent combat vets?"

If Overstreet wondered why Nazareth wanted to know he didn't show it. He simply looked around the parking lot and pointed out a young dark-haired guy.

"Sal Ramirez, pretty sure. Been on the job about two years."

Nazareth walked over to Ramirez, who had just ordered a freelance photographer away from the crime scene investigators.

"Paparazzi son of a bitch," Ramirez muttered as the photographer stalked off complaining about a violation of his Constitutional rights.

"They're just like flies, Officer Ramirez," Nazareth said as he showed his shield and ID. "You can swat them away, but they can't resist the smell of death."

"You got that right, detective. That asshole wanted some pictures of blood stains. Can you imagine that? Two people are on their way to the morgue, and some guy tells me he has a right to take pictures of blood stains."

"Were you in the parking lot when the two men were shot?"

"Yeah, absolutely. I was standing at the far end of the clubhouse with my back to the golf course. My job was supposed to be crowd control, but the crowd was perfectly calm until the shooting started."

"The sergeant tells me you have military combat experience. Is that right?"

Ramirez nodded. "Army, Iraq."

"Since everyone here seems to have a different opinion, I'd like your thoughts on exactly what happened. How far apart were the two shots?" Nazareth asked.

"Really close. At first I thought the second one was just an echo, but when I ran to the stage I saw that two men were down."

"Do you think both shots were fired from the same position?"

"Absolutely. The shooter wouldn't have had time to move between the two shots."

"Would he have had time to reload?"

Ramirez thought about that, and for the first time his face showed a flicker of doubt. "No way he could have reloaded manually," he said, "because the shots were too close together. I assume he was using a semi."

"He had time to line up the second kill shot that quickly?"

Nazareth watched as the young guy rummaged through his memories of Middle East combat. Acquire the target, lock on, adjust, squeeze. Perfect shots didn't come easily.

"No way in hell, detective. There's no way someone could have lined up the second shot that quickly." Ramirez was stunned by the revelation. "Why hadn't that hit me before?"

"Because we all usually run with the most obvious explanation," Nazareth explained, "and in this case a lone shooter seemed to fit the facts."

"Not anymore. Damn, we're looking for two killers?"

"That's my guess. Why don't you fill in the sergeant while I catch up with my partner?"

He worked his way over to Gimble, who had just finished speaking with a man whose wife was being examined by an EMT. The couple had been sitting almost directly in front of Vincent Chandler at the moment his face exploded, and the wife had collapsed and gone into shock.

"The husband said Chandler was blown almost straight ahead, and that's what the blood from the exit wound seems to show. Of course," she added, "the whole scene was immediately trampled, so it's tough to say for sure."

"What did he say about Grande?"

"He was obviously focused on Chandler at that point, but his recollection is that Grande fell hard to his left after getting shot."

"Which wouldn't have happened if he had been shot directly from behind, as Chandler was."

"Too soon to tell," she offered, "but right now you and I are probably on the same page, Pete. I'm thinking two shooters."

"And if one of them isn't Stone Jackson, it's time for me to turn in my shield."

"We go pick him up?"

"If this guy is as good as I think he is," Nazareth reasoned, "picking him up won't do us much good. He showers, gets rid of the clothes, hides the gun. By the time we arrive he's watching TV and drinking a beer. He'll never confess, and we have zero evidence."

"So what's the alternative?"

He shook his head. "Can't think of one. For all we know he's already on his way out of town, right? So let's go to his house, make sure he's still here, and lean on him."

"Sounds like a plan."

But before they reached the car someone called from behind.

"Detective Nazareth?" Officer Devon Gibson jogged up to the two detectives, sweating heavily after scrambling through the Greenbelt in search of a phantom killer. "Glad I caught you."

Nazareth offered his hand. "Pete Nazareth. This is my partner, Tara Gimble."

"The two folk heroes," Gibson laughed. "Yeah, I've read all about you. Hey, the sarge said you're working this case."

"In a roundabout sort of way," Nazareth said, "I guess we are."

"Okay, well, three other guys and I got shot at over by the lake not long after the killings. It looks as though the guy was running northwest, probably out toward Manor Road."

"Did you get a look at him?"

"No, but we spoke with a guy who was fishing there," Gibson said, "and he told us he had seen someone who might have been the killer. If so, the guy we're after is over six feet and maybe in his thirties. He must be in pretty decent shape, too, because he was running with a knapsack on his back."

"You think maybe it was the weapon?"

"No telling. The witness just remembers a knapsack."

"Is the witness still here?" Nazareth asked.

"No, I had him clear the area because we were getting shot at. There was a lot going on," Gibson said somewhat sheepishly. "I really didn't pay a whole lot of attention to the fisherman once we started taking fire."

"Understood. What did the fisherman look like?"

"Scared, mainly. I thought he was going to pass out on us. A little over six feet, I guess. Early twenties probably. Looked in good shape."

Gimble grabbed her cell phone, sensing where this was headed. She pulled up the photo that had been included with Stone Jackson's Army medical report.

"Did the fisherman look anything like this guy?" she asked.

"Shane Matthews, yeah, that's him," Gibson nodded.

"Shane Matthews is the name he gave you?"

"Absolutely. He had ID."

"This guy's name is Stone Jackson," Nazareth told him, "and he's our top suspect in the Gabriel murders."

"Oh, man, don't tell me." Gibson looked as though he'd taken a hard punch to the gut.

"Hey, we've got nothing on him," Nazareth said quickly, "so this could be a false alarm. But the fact that he was using phony ID is interesting. Any chance you can take a ride with us?"

"Absolutely. Let me just tell the sarge what's up."

Two minutes later Nazareth, Gimble, and Gibson were flying along Richmond Road in the detectives' 365-horsepower unmarked, heading toward Jackson's New Springville home.

"All Jackson had with him was fishing tackle?" Gimble asked.

"Absolutely. He was actually reeling in a large bass when we found him," Gibson said.

"He would have hidden the gun already," Nazareth chimed in. "Either he left it right where he took the shot, or he dumped it before you got there."

"I really find it hard to believe he'd shoot someone and then just hang out by the lake fishing," Gibson replied. "That's a pretty high-risk move."

"Not really. As long as you can keep your emotions in check, hiding in plain sight is often a brilliant move. Hey, it worked, right?"

"Yeah, unfortunately. But what about the shots we heard while we were questioning him?"

"Not sure," Nazareth answered. "Could have been kids with firecrackers, or more likely it was something Jackson had rigged up himself. We'll find out eventually."

"Man, if he actually pulled all this off, he's one very slick dude."

Nazareth nodded. "He's also dangerous as hell."

53.

Jackson toweled off after a hot shower and marveled at how relaxed he was despite the day's pressures. He was ecstatic. A few months ago he was a boy nursing old wounds. Now he was a giant among men. When the right man meets the right moment, he told himself, greatness follows. And here he was, living proof.

He slipped into his favorite lounging outfit -- loose basketball shorts and old running shoes -- and opened the fridge. Two weeks earlier he had bought a six-ounce split of inexpensive champagne in anticipation of today's achievement. He normally didn't drink, but he felt a small celebration was in order. Whatever successes he might enjoy in the future, this one would always remain special. The world would never know precisely how much damage Grande might have done as president, but surely all reasonable people would rejoice over the guy's killing.

Jackson passed quietly through his home as he sipped the chilled champagne, making sure he had addressed even the smallest details. The clothes worn earlier in the day had already been stuffed in the basement ceiling. He had removed the fake ID from his tackle box and hidden it in the freezer. And he had dumped all the supplies used in making his three explosive devices. He half expected those two detectives to visit again within the next few days. But if they did, they would find nothing that could tie him to any of the murders.

Fifteen minutes later he stood in the back yard alongside the gas grill, tending a 12-ounce sirloin steak he had chosen for his celebratory meal. Something about the smell of sizzling fat invariably carried him back to his childhood and the good days, the innocent days. But perhaps years down the road the same smell would also carry him back to this day, July 6th, when man and moment had blossomed into a glorious act of patriotism.

He speared the steak with a 20-inch stainless-steel grill fork and flipped it just as a car rolled to a stop in front of his house.

The detectives already? If so, he was only moderately surprised since he had expected to see them again. But the timing was unfortunate. He had 46 grams of protein almost ready for the plate.

Nazareth left the vehicle first. He closed the driver's side door, looked toward the back yard, and waved casually. Then came Gimble from the front passenger seat. Very hot for a cop, Jackson noted. Hell, very hot for any woman. He'd enjoy being cuffed and interrogated by her. Definitely.

His mood changed abruptly when the rear passenger door opened and Officer Gibson stepped onto the sidewalk. Jackson recognized the guy immediately and knew that his world had just been turned upside down. His stomach churned, and he grew lightheaded. How in the hell had the detectives stumbled upon the one cop who could blow this thing wide open? More to the point, what could he do about it now?

The answer was sickeningly obvious. His rifle was hidden at Ohrbach Lake, less than a mile and a half from his back yard through the woods, and that weapon was the only thing that could prevent him from spending the rest of his life in prison. Since the Greenbelt was his second home, he knew he would have no trouble outrunning and outmaneuvering three lazy cops who spent all day every day sitting in cars or behind desks. Night would fall by the time he reached the lake and retrieved his weapon, and then he would vanish in the dark like a shadow.

54.

Jackson smiled at Nazareth and motioned for him to come to the back yard. Then he sidestepped nonchalantly to his left, apparently focused on the grill, until he was out of the detective's line of sight. He pivoted, hit top speed within five strides, and barreled into the woods with the grill fork still in his hand. He was 70 yards down one of his favorite trails before his visitors knew he was missing.

Gimble reached the back yard ahead of Nazareth and Gibson, and she immediately drew her weapon and spun toward the back door as soon as she realized Jackson was gone.

"He's not here," she yelled. "I've got the back door. Watch the windows."

Nazareth turned his attention to the windows on the side of the house while motioning for Gibson to cover the front door. At this point the surest bet was that Jackson had run into the house. Did he hope to bolt from the front door while the police huddled out back, or did he plan to stand his ground and go down fighting? Either way, they'd have their hands full tonight.

As Nazareth weighed the team's options he spotted a small white-haired man standing at the corner of his raised deck two houses over. The old man was waving furiously. As soon as he had the detective's attention, he pointed to the back edge of Jackson's yard. Nazareth saw the opening into the woods and took off.

"Damn it!" he yelled. "He's in the woods. Tara, get backup."

Gimble called to Gibson, who was warily edging toward the front door. "Devon, we think he's in the woods."

"You want me to go?" he called back.

"No, call for backup, and check the house just to make sure. I'm going after Pete." And she was on her way. Fortunately Gimble was no slave to fashion, especially when on the job, and she wore black leather Rockports that handled themselves capably in the field. She might not run a 5K in them, but for today's test they were fine. Besides, she knew that no matter how fast she ran she wouldn't be catching up to her partner. The best she could hope for was to arrive in time if Nazareth needed her help.

Forty seconds and nearly 300 yards ahead of her, Nazareth steadily gained ground on the younger Jackson. Nazareth was no longer a competitive runner and would never again run a sub-4:00 mile, as he had in college. But he could basically run forever and on a good day was still capable of breaking 50-flat over 400 meters, which was roughly 30% faster than the man he was chasing today. It was a question of when, not whether, he would catch up.

Jackson cruised comfortably toward Ohrbach Lake and laid plans for the rest of the night. Grab the gun. Head deep into the Pouch Camp section of the Greenbelt. Hide out until 2:00 or 3:00 a.m. Then creep over to Todt Hill and steal a car. By daylight he would be halfway to Maine, where he could survive in the woods indefinitely with minimal gear. No sweat.

When the trail straightened out for 40 yards Jackson looked over his shoulder, expecting to see nothing but trees and brush behind him. Instead, he saw Pete Nazareth pulling closer with every step. The adrenaline rush that kicked in at that moment was unlike anything Jackson had ever experienced. His senses grew profoundly alert, and he felt an energy surge that rocked his entire body. In that moment he had become invincible. His mind and body were suddenly operating on some awesome higher plane.

The trail veered sharply to the right, and Jackson disappeared from Nazareth's view. He knew instinctively that it was time to make his stand. He stopped short and turned, held the grill fork in his powerful outstretched hands, and braced for impact. In a matter of seconds Nazareth would fly around the bend at full speed and skewer himself on the sharp prongs. The wound might not kill him, but he'd sure as hell be finished running for the day.

As Nazareth raced toward the ambush a microscopic electrical impulse deep within his brain carried him back to a forest trail in Afghanistan. He and his men had been pursuing Taliban forces for three days, and they were closing in. But their point man, a young Wyoming guy named Lance Cody, triggered a powerful IED at a blind spot in the trail and was torn to pieces. It was the sort of thing a Marine buries inside himself but never forgets.

The detective would never know precisely why he decided to go airborne as he leaned into the turn in pursuit of Jackson, but that's what he did. He lowered his shoulder, pushed off hard on his left foot, and sprung high in the air ready to deliver a flying side kick.

The move caught Jackson completely by surprise. He was barely able to raise the grill fork above gut level by the time he caught the full impact of Nazareth's right heel on his upper chest. The powerful kick drove him to the ground, but he skillfully allowed his momentum to carry him into a backward roll. He sprang to his feet still holding the sharp grill fork.

Jackson lunged with his makeshift spear before the detective could remove his gun from its holster, but Nazareth countered with a spinning back kick that he drove deep into his opponent's midsection. Jackson doubled over and collapsed onto the upturned grill fork, which pierced his liver and came within an inch of his heart before getting hung up on a lower rib. By the time Gimble arrived less than a minute later Nazareth had cuffed Jackson's ankles together and was calling for an ambulance.

"Pretty much a perfect day for you, Pete," she smiled. "Running, sparring, and all that man stuff."

"Mostly sweating," he laughed. "I may need to burn these clothes later."

"So did Mr. Jackson here put up a good fight?"

Nazareth shrugged. "Better than most. But he's got a lot to learn."

"Well," she said knowingly, "he's got a whole lifetime ahead of him."

55.

Throughout the evening and late into the night Nazareth badgered the ME's office for autopsy results on Grande and Chandler. He needed to know whether the same gun had fired both deadly rounds earlier that day. After eight calls he finally succeeded in getting the City's chief medical examiner on the phone

"Why is this something that can't wait until tomorrow, detective?" Dr. Rita Leveson demanded. "You already know with 99% probability that the same person killed both victims."

"That's not the same as 100%, and that means we could still have another killer running loose."

"It's almost midnight."

"In that case you don't want me to call the mayor," Nazareth bluffed, "and that's who I call next. I hate to be a pain in the ass, doc, but this really can't wait."

Leveson finally caved and agreed to text him photos of the two bullets she was about to remove from the victims. Forty-five minutes later he put the images side by side on his laptop. Although Leveson would not comment on the two chunks of lead and refused to have them examined immediately by a forensics expert, Nazareth already knew what he was looking at. One bullet was significantly larger than the other, therefore could not have been fired from the same rifle. The smaller bullet -- most likely a 5.56 round from Jackson's rifle -- was the one that had killed Archer Grande.

Early the next morning Nazareth, Gimble, and a team led by Officer Gibson were back at Ohrbach Lake. Nazareth knew Jackson had hidden his weapon in the area after the shooting, and he didn't want it falling into someone else's hands.

"We start at the lake," he told the group, "and then work our way back toward the golf course. Check in the bushes, up in the trees, in shallow water, and anyplace else you can think of. The rifle has to be here."

Nearly an hour had passed before Gimble noticed the nearly invisible monofilament line running from the lake to the base of a small tree. When she tugged on it she knew she had hit the jackpot.

"I've got something here," she called to the others. She stopped pulling when whatever was attached to the line seemed to get stuck on the bottom of the lake. "Who's the fisherman in the group?"

Gibson pointed to Officer Julio Guerrero. "If it swims, my man Julio knows how to catch it."

Guerrero walked the line up and down the bank for several minutes before he worked it free. Then he gently and steadily hauled in the black plastic bag containing Jackson's weapon. After confirming that this was almost certainly the rifle used to kill Grande, Nazareth turned his attention to the remaining mystery.

"This wasn't the gun used to take out Grande's campaign manager," he told his colleagues, "which means there's another killer as well as another weapon. What we need to do now is walk every square inch of the golf course perimeter until we figure out where the two killers took their shots."

Gimble and two of the officers headed toward the cemetery while Nazareth and the others began searching near the center of the closest fairway. Within 40 minutes Gimble had crawled far into the drainage pipe and found evidence of Jackson's presence: used light sticks, snack wrappers, and three empty water bottles.

Nazareth's group, meanwhile, hit pay dirt when Gibson pushed his way into the thicket where Bloodworth had stashed his rifle before running to the underground shelter.

"Whoa, baby. Check this out, guys," he said when he opened the knapsack. "Serious weapon."

"A Nemesis Vanquish, to be precise," Nazareth said. "World-class sniper rifle that fires a .308 round. I'd bet my last nickel this is the one that blew Chandler's head apart."

"But why would a sniper leave his rifle behind?" one of the officers asked.

"Probably the same reason Jackson did: he plans to come back for it. On the other hand," Nazareth added, "if he was being paid enough for the job, he wouldn't really care about buying another $5,000 gun."

"You think he was a pro?" Gibson wondered.

"It's certainly the type of weapon I'd expect a pro to use, but why he would be hired to kill the campaign manager instead of the candidate is anyone's guess. We'll never know unless we catch him."

"Any ideas on how to do that?"

"Just one at the moment. I'll have a camera set up here and hope the shooter comes back for his rifle. You never know."

Hunter Bloodworth, of course, never returned for his rifle, and no one ever found his body. By late fall his underground shelter was completely covered by weeds and guarded by the rattlesnakes that had grown accustomed to his company.

56.

Nazareth and Gimble found leaving their temporary Staten Island home a distinctly bittersweet affair. Although they had both sometimes missed the frantic energy that seemed to crackle through the air in Manhattan all day every day, they had definitely grown fond of their gentler life. They enjoyed sitting on the deck in the early evening, sipping wine and listening to the bubbly call of wrens that had taken up residence in a tiny birdhouse on a sycamore branch. And they had gotten used to leisurely weekend walks along quiet streets where neighbors waved and said hello.

"So what do you think, Tara?" Nazareth asked as he backed the car out of the long driveway. "Is there a Staten Island home in our future?"

"I think I could get used to this," she nodded. "And if one day we have little Nazareths running around, I definitely don't want them running through Manhattan."

"I'm with you. Of course, we won't have any little Nazareths unless we actually get around to setting a date for the wedding."

"There is that detail," she laughed. "Seems like every time we think about the wedding we get pulled into another major case. At this pace we'll be starting a family when we're ready for retirement."

"Well, there *is* an alternative," he said slyly.

"And what might that be?"

"A good friend of the family is county clerk here on Staten Island. For $35 he'll issue a marriage license, and for another $25 he'll do the ceremony. Same day, no wait."

"And you know this because?" she grinned.

"I spoke with him an hour ago while you were taking a shower."

"Ah, I see. So you've got this all planned out, Detective Nazareth?"

"No plans, Detective Gimble. I'm just presenting an option. It's fine with me if you want to wait for a big wedding with thousands of guests."

"The big wedding that every girl dreams of?"

"I guess."

"Actually, I'd rather not wait until I'm old and gray, Pete. We could always have a do-over ceremony for the families, right?"

"We could, sure," he smiled.

"So how far is your friend's office from here?"

"Twenty minutes with traffic."

"Do you have the money?"

"I think I can come up with $60, yeah."

"Well, then?"

From the next book in the Detective Pete Nazareth series.

The Kirov Wolf

He had watched them like this before, carefully analyzed their every move from a safe distance. No detail had gone undocumented. He knew when they left their apartment each morning, when they arrived home, when they dined in, when they ordered takeout, when they closed the curtains at night and slipped into bed. It was all there in his laptop, a testament to the artistry of his craft.

But tonight was different. The long period of watching had finally ended. It was time to channel all that knowledge into action.

They walked hand-in-hand from a favorite restaurant three blocks north of their apartment building, oblivious to the jarring sounds and peculiar smells of a sultry summer evening in Midtown Manhattan. They were in love. This much was obvious. And love blinded them to the fearsome risks of wandering thoughtlessly in the night.

He checked his timepiece: 10:17 p.m. Later than usual for a midweek dinner. Why was that? Had they lingered over wine, gazing into each other's eyes? Had they spoken of love and dreams they shared? Or had they perhaps contemplated leaving New York City for a safer place? This could, after all, be a dangerous town.

Such things mattered enormously to him. He believed you could not do your job well -- no, perfectly -- unless you could float into another person's head like a wisp of smoke and see the world through his or her eyes. Achieving this level of intimacy is what separated masters like him from the many pretenders.

The couple paused, as always, just before reaching the door to their apartment building. They turned to each other, as always, and smiled. They kissed long and hard, as always, to the amusement of those who passed them on the sidewalk. It seemed a night for lovers.

He watched all this through a $13,000 Newcom Optik thermal scope from his rooftop perch across the street. He adjusted for the steep downward angle, took a deep breath, held it, and squeezed. The CheyTac M300 Intervention sniper rifle delivered its .408-caliber round, as always, precisely on target -- in this case the top of the man's disintegrating skull.

Things would most definitely get worse before they got better.

CPSIA information can be obtained
at www.ICGtesting.com
Printed in the USA
LVOW11s2324190117
521608LV00001B/102/P